NO TIME TO DIE

No Time To Die is a first book and an out-standing achievement. The author crystallizes in these pages the experience of a generation.

The character of Tony Allen can be taken as the prototype of all young men thrown suddenly and without foreknowledge into battle. The men who fight and die at his side become part of his life. He is in them all and with them all. Through them he attains to full maturity and penetrates at last to a world beyond fear.

The scene is magnificently set: the desert sky burning low with stars, the scorching sun by day, the frost by night. As the great tanks rumble into battle the dust rises in clouds to obscure them, and only the rattle of guns and the screams of mortally wounded men can be heard above the thunder of their advance.

Through the crucible of the author's imagination pass the horror, the brutality, the individual courage and the individual cowardice that go to make up total war. What emerges is a book of great sensitivity and even greater strength.

NO TIME TO DIE

Ronald Kemp

S T A P L E S   P R E S S

STAPLES PRESS LIMITED
Mandeville Place, London

STAPLES PRESS INCORPORATED
70 East 45th Street, New York

FIRST PUBLISHED OCTOBER 1954
SECOND IMPRESSION OCTOBER 1954

This Book is set in the Monotype Baskerville series

To

HELGA
MY WIFE

Made and printed in England by
STAPLES PRINTERS LIMITED
at their Rochester, Kent, establishment

I

The late morning sun beat mercilessly down upon the desert, drawing all moisture and energy from the weary troop. The cumbersome tank, flanked by the two 15-hundredweights, moved slowly over the uneven surface enveloped in a cloud of acrid, grey dust that filled the eyes and noses of the occupants.

Allen eased his bruised and aching body in the confined space of the turret, and raising his arm, he signalled the small party to halt. When the last engine was switched off he noticed how oppressive the sudden silence had become; he looked about him but except for his party there was nothing to be seen but sun, sky and desert, while behind the billowing dust slowly dispersed.

Williams, the bulky sergeant, climbed from his vehicle and approached the tank. He spoke without bothering to salute.

'Shall I tell the men they can brew up, sir?'

'Yes, Sergeant, we'll halt here for an hour,' replied the young officer.

Allen studied the map and estimated with the aid of a small ruler the distance they must have travelled since dawn. He glanced at his wireless watch and decided roughly where they were; but he was not very happy and he sensed that Williams had little confidence in his officer's navigation. After all, Allen had only joined the Regiment three weeks ago.

His period of training at the Base Depot in Cairo had twice been interrupted by sickness. Quite early he had gone down with an acute attack of enteritis, and then, shortly after starting a fresh course, he had been laid up with jaundice. When he had finished a second period of sick leave it was decided that rather than waste any more time at the Depot he should complete his training with his Regiment in the desert.

5

He had scarcely heard of a sun compass until the last fortnight, and now he had only that and the rudiments of desert navigation taught him in an hour or so by an impatient Intelligence Officer; and here he was, a hundred miles or so from his squadron and one hundred and fifty miles from Brigade Headquarters where he was due to deliver the tank. His task was to cross two hundred and fifty miles of untracked desert with scarcely a single feature by which he could identify his position, and what complicated matters for him was the fact that Brigade H.Q. was located only four miles from the enemy. If he missed it then it would probably mean an inglorious end to his effort. His mind was beset with these problems, and there was no one to whom he could turn for advice.

Howard, his driver, was unconcernedly making tea with Brown, the gunner, while Musgrove, the wireless operator, looked on.

It was then that Allen caught the first far-away sound of aircraft.

'Mount!' he shouted, but already the men were clambering aboard their vehicles, ready to move at the officer's command.

The noise of the aircraft increased. Far off, in the cloudless blue of the sky, the sun reflected on the three Savoias that, flying at a great height, were approaching on a course which would seem to bring them directly above the troop. Allen noticed one of the truck drivers with a rifle in his hand. The planes were flying at not less than ten thousand feet. Now they were overhead. Nothing happened: no bombs fell. The men watched the aircraft slowly disappear; then they returned to the business of brewing up.

Allen suddenly realized that he was very thirsty, and was glad of the hot tea that Brown handed to him a few minutes later. Drinking the warm strong brew his confidence returned. He saw himself as the bearded explorer of vast desert wastes, and he allowed his imaginative mind to run in fantasy on such adventure.

He was very young. He had celebrated his twenty-first birthday while still at O.C.T.U. only a few months back, and when he had passed out with one gilt star on each shoulder he had asked Mary if she would marry him. She was fair and very pretty and he felt extremely proud to show himself off in her company. He was also very much in love with her, but she had made him understand that their marriage would have to wait until the war was over, or at least until she had finished her studies at London University. She argued that they had only known each other for a few months and that the war might separate them for perhaps years and therefore, under the circumstances, it would be much wiser to wait until they were both absolutely certain about their feelings towards each other. He had then tried his best to persuade her to agree to their becoming engaged, but again she had gently but firmly refused.

On the last day of his embarkation leave Mary had gone with him to the station. On one of London's most crowded platforms he had taken her into his arms and, kissing her tear-stained face, he had promised to love her always. The guard blew his whistle and a few seconds later his train moved forward, and soon he had left her and England behind to join his unit in North Africa.

It was time to move on. Allen climbed back into the turret and ordered his driver to advance. The tank lurched forward, jerking Allen painfully against an ammunition box. He looked back to check that the two trucks were following, then, glancing at his watch, he leaned forward and adjusted the compass card. He wedged himself more firmly into the turret, and stared ahead watching the needle's shadow on the card. From time to time he gave directions to Howard over the inter-com.

Shortly after four o'clock they came upon the truck. Allen first noticed it as a vague shape distorted by the heat haze, but peering through his binoculars he saw that it was a stationary vehicle. He turned off his course to approach it, hoping that its crew would be able to pin-point their position, but when at last he reached it he saw that it had been burned out and abandoned. Lying on the ground were a number of spent rounds that had obviously been fired from its Bren gun, mounted as a protection from aircraft. The truck bore the scars of incendiary bullets. Close by were two shallow graves, unmarked. Allen walked over to the mounds and stood looking down at them, trying to imagine what lay beneath the few inches of sand. He realized that this was as close as he had yet come to the war. He had never seen a dead body and was not at all sure how he would react if ever he should be confronted with one.

When the sun went down he halted the troop for the night, and after he had shared with his crew a meal of bully beef and biscuits washed down with tea, he took his blankets from the tank, and spreading them on the ground covered himself without bothering to undress. He lay gazing up at a sky studded with millions of glittering stars. It was very peaceful here in this lonely spot only a few miles from war. He thought of Mary and wondered what she was doing at that moment, and whether she would feel proud of him if she could see him now. He listened to the voices of the men from the trucks and heard Howard his driver describing to Brown and Musgrove one of his more recent visits to the Berka.

'Black as the ace of spades she was, and to crown it all she goes and gives me a mucking dose, an' all for five mucking piastres!'

The following morning Allen waited patiently until the sun was climbing well into the sky before giving the order to move off, for he was anxious to travel only on his sun compass. Late in the afternoon they came upon a wide and well-worn track that eventually led them to Brigade H.Q.

That night he spent in a bivouac with George Amery, a captain seconded from his own regiment.

The bottle was half empty. Allen began to feel extremely pleased with himself. He had been given a task and he had accomplished it. The tank had been safely handed over, and now all that remained was to get the two trucks back to the Regiment. He felt entirely confident of his ability to navigate his party home.

'How's old Walters doing?' Amery asked.

'He's becoming worse and worse as the days go by. His stomach is killing him; he simply loathes the desert, and thinks and talks only of his wife and children. How they ever came to give him the squadron beats me. He's quite pathetically useless. God help us if he ever takes us into action!'

At that moment the noise of heavy guns could be heard in the distance.

'That's the Fort getting the wind up,' announced Amery. 'The Eyeties seem to get nervous at night, and then they poop off for all they're worth on the least excuse.'

The next day Allen woke up with a violent headache and a very dry mouth. He sent for Williams and ordered the trucks to be ready to start by ten o'clock. The hurried breakfast of sandy porridge and tinned bacon he could scarcely swallow; only the scalding tea was welcome. He rolled his blankets and loaded them on to his 15-hundredweight, and when all was ready he said good-bye to Amery and started off on the return journey to the Regiment – which he succeeded in reaching that same evening, no longer having the slow-moving tank to hinder the troop.

On arriving at Regimental H.Q. he sought out the C.O. and reported his return. The colonel seemed surprised to see him back so soon and inquired pleasantly about the trip. Afterwards Allen drove the two miles to the spot where his squadron was camped on the edge of the sea. He made arrangements for his men to be given a hot meal, and then, his duties temporarily at an end, he went off to find out if there were any letters waiting for him, but was disappointed to discover that no mail had reached the Regiment while he had been away. At last he took a towel and, walking across the beach to the rocks that overhung the deep pool, he undressed, and standing naked and flexed for a few seconds in the cool, short twilight he dived with scarcely a splash into the warm Mediterranean.

Major Walters stood beside his camp bed in his underpants, a glass of stomach powder in one hand, while with the other he slowly rubbed his distended abdomen in a circular movement. His mouth hung open in anticipation of the belch that would come to ease his discomfort.

A solicitor in civilian life and a none-too-successful one at that, he had made up a little for the disappointment of being unable to make the army his profession by obtaining a commission in the territorials. For a number of years he had attended his drill hall and annual camp with the rank of lieutenant, then, just before the outbreak of war he had been promoted captain, and almost before he had recovered from the shock of this elevation his Regiment was mobilized and he had been given a majority. Shortly afterwards he was transferred from his Regiment in England to find himself in command of a squadron of tanks in the Western Desert.

He was a conscientious and loyal officer, but out of his depth in the field – a fact of which even he was becoming increasingly aware. He knew all that there was to be known about drill, the keeping of accounts, the filling-in of all those innumerable forms with which the army seemed plagued, and the organizing of games, but when it came down to handling a squadron of tanks he was completely lost and no one under his command had any faith in his ability. Few seriously thought that when the time came to go into action he would still be in command of the squadron. His responsibilities lay heavily upon him. He worried about his wife and two young sons in far-away England; he wondered when, if ever, he would see them again.

Major Walters was tired out after an awkward, and for him humiliating, episode that had occurred the previous night. He was very upset and tried to imagine what the squadron must now be thinking of its commander. On that evening the colonel had driven over from his R.H.Q. to tell him about a warning that had just been received that the Italians might attempt to land agents along the coast from submarines. Walters was to make himself responsible for his squadron's area and ensure that a proper guard was mounted throughout the hours of darkness. When at length the colonel had driven away, the major sent for his five officers and, having explained the situation, he detailed each in turn to patrol the camp for an hour before calling his relief. At 11 p.m. Skeffington was due to finish his tour of duty and report to Walters. At 11.10 he still had not turned up, and Walters, who was still awake, became anxious and thoughtlessly went off to search for his lieutenant without even bothering to inform anyone of his intention.

The night was very dark, and by 11.25 he was completely lost. He thought of calling out but became afraid that some nervous sentry might shoot him before he could identify himself. He stumbled over sand dunes and barked his shins on the sharp rocks. Once he wept in his rage and frustration, but it was not until morning that he was at last able to make out the squadron, scarcely a quarter of a mile distant. Before bathing and shaving he had learned that Skeffington, discovering his absence, had assumed that his squadron leader had commenced his patrol, and so had gone off to his bed without giving the matter another thought. The other officers had slept the night through since there had been no one to wake them.

Walters belched fiercely and allowed his hate to work up for Skeffington. He intended to have the man's scalp for his thoughtlessness. Skeffington had already convinced most people of his uselessness, and now here at last was something concrete to hang on him. He finished dressing and went off in search of the target of his wrath; he never thought of sending someone to fetch him.

Second-Lieutenant Desmond Skeffington squeezed his lean, round-shouldered, six feet four into his squadron leader's station wagon and drove off in the direction of Regimental H.Q. He took it for granted that since Walters had been up all night he would now be sleeping and, therefore, had not bothered to ask if he might take the car. The fact was, he just had to tell someone about last night's fiasco. The rest of the officers of his squadron did not seem to appreciate the enormous humour of the situation, and when he had begun to discuss it with Tony Allen he had been rudely ordered to shut up.

He parked the Humber near the mess, and looked around for a worthy recipient of his stupendous news. He was a little disappointed to discover that most of his cronies appeared to be at work; then the colonel saw him.

'Skeffington!' he shouted from the flap of his tent.

The lanky officer quickly broke into a lope, and halted and saluted, somewhat out of breath, in front of his commanding officer.

'Why the devil are you hanging around over here? Hasn't Major Walters got anything useful to keep you occupied? Unless you have a job of work to do at my headquarters, get back to your squadron, and next time you honour us with a visit come on your own flat feet, you lazy young blighter, and don't waste your squadron's petrol. Now beat it, and report to your squadron leader and tell him to find you something to keep you busy in future.'

The colonel watched Skeffington get back into the Humber and drive away. What a useless piece of goods he was, he thought. B Squadron certainly had its share of duds, and the trouble was that with the restrictions on the use of petrol and ammunition, there was little opportunity for improving them. He would have to do something about the squadron before it could be allowed to go into action. Old Walters was as keen as they came but that didn't make him an efficient squadron leader.

Skeffington left the Humber in the squadron lines feeling that the whole world was against him that morning; then he saw Major Walters bearing down upon him, his mouth open and an angry look upon his countenance.

'Here, where the hell have you been?' he roared at a range of fifty yards. Skeffington was annoyed to notice that several of the men were listening and obviously enjoying the scene. The major did not wait for a reply. Closing the range and still shouting at the top of his voice he yelled:

'And where did you get to last night?'

'I was only doing my rounds, sir,' replied Skeffington a little hurt.

'Why the hell didn't you call me at eleven?'

'I thought it didn't matter, sir, if I was a few minutes late; it would only mean that you had so much less to do.'

'Since when have you started worrying about doing someone else's job?'

The major was almost hysterical with rage; he looked ridiculous and undignified. Skeffington sensed with relief that the men were no longer laughing at him but at their squadron leader.

'Well, sir,' he began, but at that moment the sound of the hand-operated siren from the squadron encamped two miles down the coast reached them.

Major Walters suddenly turned away from Skeffington and ran off to find his steel helmet and respirator. Captain Harvey's voice could be heard ordering the men to the Bren guns that were the squadron's only protection against aircraft. Those men who had no other duties he ordered to the slit trenches. By the time Walters had regained his self-control, of which the sudden significance of the siren had robbed him, the men were already running in an orderly manner to their posts.

Harvey, Allen and Skeffington stood close to the small trench which they themselves had dug when the squadron had set up camp. Now, faintly at first, could be heard the sound of the planes; the noise of their engines increased.

'See them?' pointed Harvey.

'How many can you see?' asked Allen, as he endeavoured to count the silver specks in the cloudless sky.

'About a dozen I think, and not an anti-aircraft gun in the whole bloody desert so far as I know.'

Smoke and rubble leapt darkly into the morning sunlight near the village a few miles to the north.

'It looks as if the poor Wogs are getting it this time. Perhaps they haven't spotted us yet,' suggested Harvey.

The planes were flying at a considerable height, and now they appeared to the men on the ground to be almost overhead. The sudden noise of the violent explosions from the direction of the village momentarily startled the little group of officers and made the earth tremble beneath their feet. Skeffington, who had not spoken since the planes were first heard, dived headlong into the shallow trench and cowered, face down, in the sand. Both Allen and Harvey were almost betrayed by his panic, but the latter quickly straightened himself to gaze up at the planes, still clearly visible. The roar of their engines was at its loudest when Harvey, reaching down, picked up a small pebble. He grinned broadly at Allen, whistled shrilly in imitation of a falling bomb, shouted hoarsely 'For Christ's sake look out!' and gently dropped the pebble on to the top of Skeffington's steel helmet. A strangled sob came from the bottom of the trench as the frightened officer's body tensed, and then with a sigh relaxed again. Even before the bombers were out of sight Skeffington climbed awkwardly from his refuge and hurried away to change his shorts. No one laughed as they watched him go, for this display of terror had turned the joke sour on the two officers who stood looking at each other in embarrassed silence.

In the late afternoon of the squadron's first experience of an air raid, Allen lay on the beach near his favourite pool. He was thinking of Mary, and the warm sun turned his thoughts into pleasantly sensual channels.

His day-dreams were interrupted by the noise of hob-nailed boots grating on the jagged rocks. He turned his head and saw his friend Peter Harvey making his way cautiously towards him. Harvey carefully lowered himself from the last rock on to the sand and came over and sat down beside Allen. He began to remove his boots. At last he lay nude, smoking a cigarette. His body was lean and wiry but, unlike the dark mahogany of his companion, his skin was red and peeling.

Allen broke the silence.

'That was a bad thing about Skeffington this morning. He's not going to be much use to the squadron if we ever get into a serious war. I've not seen the man since before lunch; as a matter of fact, Pete, I shall have the greatest difficulty in looking him in the eye again, I feel so ashamed for him.'

'You needn't worry any more on Master Skeffington's account. He's made a remarkably quick recovery. This afternoon he was happily supervising the stencilling of the Skeffington family crest on the side of his tank. It's all forgotten. The men will continue to talk about it for a few days until something else happens to take their minds off it, and no one will ever do anything seriously about getting rid of the bloody man.'

'Old Walters ought to make a move.'

'Don't be silly, he wouldn't harm a fly – besides, he'd never have the nerve to mention it to the colonel. He only goes near the C.O. when he's sent for to collect a rocket; he's got such a guilty conscience. He's terrified of being given something important to carry out. God, if we ever have to go into action with him!'

The distant siren sounded again. The two men lying on the beach could hear the planes, but they waited for each other's reaction, and neither moved. They listened to the sound of bombs exploding in the direction of the village.

'Those poor devils are getting it again,' said Harvey.

'Probably they've all cleared off by now.'

They heard the low whistle of the bomb become an ugly shriek and, instinctively rolling on to their stomachs, they

16

clawed the earth in a frenzied hope that the sands would protect them. The bomb exploded fifty yards down the beach covering the two officers with shingle that felt like the cold touch of death as it rained upon their naked, shrinking bodies. Then all became silent again, and they knew they were unhurt.

'Christ, they've dropped a bomb on us!' spluttered Allen, his mouth still gritty with the sand.

'What the hell did you think it was, a bloody leaflet?' Harvey answered as he grinned at his companion.

Some of the men were hurrying towards them but, when they saw that they were unharmed, they ceased to run except for one figure who soon identified himself as the squadron leader.

Walters's mind was in a turmoil. When the bomb had burst on the beach he was quite certain that it had fallen right on top of Harvey and Allen, for he knew the exact spot where they invariably spent all their leisure hours. The thought of their death affected him as if they were his own sons; he felt entirely responsible for them. Then he saw them standing naked and unscathed with the bomb-crater gaping only a short distance away. He was filled with joy and relief; he could have embraced them and wept. He shouted, still many yards away, and within ear-shot of the troops who were watching in expectation of a row developing between the squadron leader and his two officers.

'Where the hell have you been? If I catch you two down here on this bloody beach again I'll have you both court-martialled. If you have nothing better to do, then you should be with your men. You're too bloody lazy for words. I'll report this to the colonel, he won't stand for this sort of bloody nonsense. You might easily have both been killed. Get your clothes on. This is not a bloody nudist colony; there's a war on, and it's about time you realized it!'

He was quite close to them, and breathing heavily from the exertion of the shouting and running.

He raised his hand and Harvey ducked quickly away, believing that he was about to be struck, but Walters only laid his arm affectionately across the officer's shoulder.

'Are you quite sure you're all right, Pete?'

'Perfectly all right, sir.'

'And you, Tony?'

'Yes, sir.'

'God, you both frightened the very life out of me!'

He would have helped them into their clothes if they had not moved away from him. Together they walked across the sands in the direction of the squadron. On the way Walters bent down and picked up a jagged splinter of the bomb, but he quickly dropped it again, for it was still too hot to hold.

The major gradually regained control of himself. He had already forgotten his abusive outburst on the beach. He was both happy and grateful that nothing more serious had occurred.

Harvey and Allen were the two people that he trusted; the former, cool and experienced with the one desire in his mind to get the war finished as quickly as possible so that he could return to his job; the latter, younger and more energetic, might well in time develop into quite a useful leader. Of the three remaining officers, Skeffington was a dud, and Hargreaves and Turner were still very young and untried, and could not yet be relied upon to any great extent.

That evening Skeffington went out to the beach to select a suitable bomb splinter. When at last he had found one to his liking he sought out the fitter and persuaded the man to spend the next hour or so in turning it into a crucifix which he then proceeded to fix to the outside of his tank.

The mail orderly was distributing letters that had been delayed since leaving England. The men were complaining and grumbling about this, their only link with home. Several had received cablegrams which had taken as long to reach the desert as the letters. Everything was coming by sea via the Cape now that Italy had entered the war, and it angered the troops to know that the Italians were most probably receiving their letters a day or so after they had been posted in Italy.

Allen found one from his parents. There was one from Harvey's mother; he could expect none from his wife, for she had left him some months before the war had started.

'Nothing from Mary?' inquired Harvey sympathetically.

'No, not this time, damn it.'

'Don't let it worry you, you'll get a bloody great stack of them one day.'

'I hope so.'

'Never mind, my lad, just you wait until we get some leave in Cairo; you'll soon find a little bit of skirt to help you forget Mary for a while. Do you good. Make a new man of you. The very first thing I'm going to have when I go on leave is a woman.'

The khamsin put an end to all training. The wind blew fiercely about the camp, tearing down tents and whipping up the sand until the sun was obscured, and the day turned into night. The wind's breath was foul and hot, the sand seared the eyeballs and filled nose and mouth. The men took shelter where they could; some lay beneath their tanks protecting their faces with blankets, some wore their respirators, others climbed inside their vehicles, closing the hatches against the misery of the sandstorm, and there were those who sought refuge in the sea. The flies, beaten and dazed by the wind, clung desperately to the faces of the men. The moaning of the wind and the flapping of canvas drowned all other sounds. Seventy-two hours passed before the storm drove on leaving the men weary and beaten. There had been nothing hot to eat; few had tasted any food, for the sand ruined everything and quickly coated drinks with a thick scum of salty grit through which even the flies found it difficult to penetrate in their frenzied efforts to commit suicide.

Once more the blazing sun shone from a cloudless blue sky, and with its reappearance the squadron broke into activity. Guns were cleaned, for even the small calibre weapons protected by contraceptives were choked with the fine sand. Food was prepared and the men quickly forgot their recent ordeal. When the last tent had been re-erected and the men dismissed, the adjutant drove over from H.Q. with a message from the colonel, ordering Walters to strike camp. The Regiment was shortly moving up, and Walters's squadron must be ready to start in a few hours.

All the time the adjutant was speaking Walters stood with drooping shoulders and mouth agape. He fought against the panic that was overpowering him. The Regiment was getting nearer and nearer to the war. Soon it would be his squadron's turn. He would have to lead it, and make decisions, and the men would rely on him. This was his crucifixion; if only he possessed the courage to ask to be relieved of his command. His mind was dead, he no longer heard what the adjutant was saying. He thought only of the dreaded journey that was inevitably drawing them all to their destiny.

The adjutant repeated his last sentence.

'I say, sir, can you tell me where I can find Tony Allen?'

'Eh?'

'Where can I find Tony?'

'He's down on the beach, I suppose. What do you want him for?'

'The colonel wants him to navigate the regiment.'

'Christ, I can't spare him. He can't have him.'

'Then you had better come with me and tell him so, sir.'

'Oh, God! He and Harvey are the only ones I've got that are any good. Who'll help me if they take all my best chaps away?'

Allen sat in the back of the Humber. The colonel, who was driving, spoke to the adjutant sitting at his side.

'How far have we come?'

The adjutant checked the mileage.

'Thirty miles, sir.'

'Good, we'll stop here and see exactly where we are.'

The three officers studied their maps, and after a short discussion agreed on their approximate position.

'Can you bring the Regiment up here tonight do you think?' the colonel asked Allen.

'Yes, sir,' he answered without hesitation, but the confidence that rang in his reply did not echo in his mind. Navigation was still sufficient of a mystery to him in daytime; at night this would be a nightmare task. He knew very little of the movement of stars, he would be denied the use of his sun compass, and those mounted in the vehicles were always affected by the engines. It would mean he would have to stop and dismount at frequent intervals to take bearings with his pocket compass. What made it worse was the fact that there were so few objects on which he could take a bearing – the desert was almost featureless.

The driver of the 15-hundredweight that had followed behind the station wagon was filling up the tank with petrol from a two-gallon can. When the man had finished the colonel touched the empty container with his toe and said to his officers:

'We'll leave this here, it will mark the spot.'

Allen was quite sure they would never see it again. He pored over his map all the way back to camp.

The Regiment had formed up over a two mile front, and was ready to move. Allen's squadron was to lead. He climbed into the open 15-hundredweight which much to his annoyance Major Walters had insisted upon driving.

The squadron leader looked at his watch.

'Come on, Tony, it's nearly time, we ought to be moving or the colonel will be over, and we don't want any trouble.'

Allen was quite ready to start; he had taken a bearing and instructed the major to steer towards a small mound which could still be seen some distance away in the fading light. He was only waiting now for the exact minute to move. The march had been ordered to commence at six; it was still short of that by two minutes, and Allen was determined to wait for the precise moment, for he intended giving everyone a chance to start together. Walters, however, robbed him of the pleasure of signalling the regiment forward, for as Allen stood up in the truck and looked back at his command, Walters, his impatience overcoming him, suddenly let in the clutch and started off with a jerk that threw Allen into the rear of the vehicle.

The Regiment was on the move, and Allen watched the dust as it began to rise in a cloud behind him, then he concentrated on his navigation. They were travelling at eight miles per hour, which was a fair speed for the tanks. Allen frequently requested the squadron leader to stop so that he could jump down and take a bearing. Soon the short twilight had given way to night with a sky of twinkling stars. It was now too dark to take bearings on objects at a distance, and so he was forced to get Walters to drive on a star, and then after a short while had passed he would stop and check with his compass. It was very difficult pointing out the stars to Walters, and at last he asked if he could drive the truck himself. Walters replied in an unpleasant tone:

'I should have thought that there was quite enough to occupy yourself with without wanting to drive.'

'I shall find it considerably easier than having to direct you all the time, sir.'

Walters stopped the truck, and they changed seats. Allen could no longer see the Regiment he was supposed to be leading but the rattling and squeaking of the tanks assured him of its close proximity. No lights were permitted; each driver had to keep his eyes fixed on the vehicle directly in front of him. Occasionally flashes from the exhausts momentarily illuminated an area of the convoy and anxious drivers and commanders could once again assure themselves of their position. Several tanks had broken down with engine defects, two had thrown a track; these casualties remained where they had halted until the fitters' truck could get around to them.

They drove on through the night, wearily, their eyes smarting from the dust and lack of sleep. In the tanks the crews took their duties in turn and when a man handed over to his relief, he lay down on the floor of the rattling, vibrating, and dust-filled vehicle, and slept as soundly as if he was in his own bed.

Walters was beginning to worry. He knew little of navigation and, at the same time, he was aware of Allen's inexperience. He commenced to wonder if they really were on the correct course. His stomach was complaining and he could keep silent no longer.

'Do you know where we are?'

'Roughly.'

'Christ! Roughly is no bloody good. You should be able to tell us exactly where we are.'

Allen felt extremely angry. He knew that he was allowing Walters to sap his confidence, and if he lost that then he had also lost the Regiment. He made up his mind, then spoke to his companion.

'I'm doing my best, sir, but perhaps you had better take over.'

'Me? Christ, no! The colonel wants you to do it.'

'Then you must please keep silent. I can't give my mind to it if you worry me with your doubts.'

The major said nothing while he thought. Suddenly he realized the effect that his behaviour was having on Allen, and he began to panic.

'I say, old man, I didn't mean to upset you. Shall we try and find the colonel and tell him you can't manage in this darkness? He'll understand; someone else could easily take over.'

'It's all right, sir, we'll make it, or thereabouts.'

'Would you be happier if I left you on your own? I could travel in a tank.'

Allen did not bother to reply. He just thought to himself: what a man to have for a squadron leader!

The Regiment lumbered on through the night, leaving mechanical casualties in its wake. The colonel shared his tank with the adjutant and they both leaned on the turret gazing into the dusty blackness. The colonel was speaking.

'According to my calculations we should be there in another three minutes. Young Allen hasn't done so badly; at least he's kept on the right course.'

Before the adjutant could think of anything more than the usual 'Yes, sir', their driver had stopped the tank on the tail of the one he had been following. Voices could be heard shouting to the men to switch off their engines. The colonel turned to his adjutant and spoke again.

'Anyhow, that's near enough for me! This night driving is not my idea of fun.'

'I quite agree with you, sir. I for one shall be damn glad when this war is over and we can get down to some proper soldiering once again,' replied the adjutant.

The colonel laughed, then he climbed stiffly out of his tank and stood waiting for the squadron leaders to report to him; some of the crews were already spreading their bedding on the ground.

It seemed to Allen that he had only just stretched himself in his blankets when he was awakened by one of the men who told him that the C.O. wanted him. He staggered to his feet rubbing sand and sleep from his inflamed eyes. Dawn was about to break; the morning was fresh and beautiful, and the dew lay moist and cool on the scattered camel-thorn bushes. The flies were still sleeping. He found the colonel and saluted.

' 'Morning, Allen, go and get your maps, we're moving again. Going to take the Regiment sixty miles today, and we're off to reconnoitre the route and find a camp for tonight. Be ready in ten minutes.'

It was early afternoon when the colonel's Humber, followed by the 15-hundredweight, returned. Allen navigated throughout the one hundred and twenty scorching, dusty, and uncomfortable miles, eating from a communal tin of bully beef and sharing a packet of dry biscuits. Water was strictly rationed and the little he was permitted to swallow was hot and tasted stale. As soon as the party returned to the Regiment Allen made arrangements for the night's journey. His confidence in his ability to navigate had increased with his experience, and also by the very fact that the colonel expected him to continue in his role of regimental navigator. When at last he had completed his preparations, he lay down beneath his 15-hundredweight, which sheltered him from the fierce sun, and protecting his face from the flies with a handkerchief he immediately fell asleep, and did not stir until he was awakened for the evening meal of bully beef stew and tea. Soon it was time to move off again, and on this occasion he insisted upon travelling in his own tank; he had no intention of spending the coming eight hours sitting next to Major Walters.

The Regiment continued moving westwards until it eventually reached a position some few miles from the Italian front line. There it halted and set up camp to the extent of erecting a few tents for essential purposes. The vehicles that had broken down on the three days' journey were rounded up by the fitters until the last one had been repaired and brought in. Each tank was carefully overhauled, guns were cleaned and ammunition issued. The Regiment was now ready to go into action.

So far the fighting had been desultory. There had been no major engagement and scarcely any casualties. Each side was weighing up the other's capabilities, and at the same time bringing up re-inforcements and hoping that the lull would continue. Various unconfirmed reports reaching the Regiment stated that the enemy was far superior both in numbers and equipment; but this information failed to have a depressing effect on anyone as far as could be seen, and most of the men were only too anxious to get to grips with the Italians, of whom they had little fear. They referred to them in terms of amused contempt, seldom with hate or bitter animosity.

The camp was spread over a mile of featureless desert. Water had to be brought up in carriers from a distant well. Rations were scarce, and no fresh food or fruit ever reached the Regiment as nothing would keep in the intense heat. The diet consisted of bully beef and biscuits. Shortage of cigarettes was the men's chief complaint, for owing to the limited transport and resultant lack of space few seemed to reach the forward areas. Beer and spirits were non-existent. When off duty the men lay under their tanks, sheltering themselves from the blazing sun; covering their faces to keep off the multitudes of persistent flies, they tried to find forgetfulness in sleep.

One afternoon the brigadier drove over from his headquarters to inspect the Regiment, and after he had gone the colonel sent for the squadron leaders. When eventually Walters returned to the squadron his officers were standing in a group anxiously waiting to hear what news he had for them.

'This is it, chaps!' he said, and his tone and general air gave the impression that the entire squadron had been condemned to death. He continued with sagging shoulders and spiritless voice: 'Each squadron is going to take it in turn to patrol the wire for five days at a time, then it will come back here for a rest while the next one takes over. Major Wallis moves his squadron up tonight and after that it's our turn. Got that?'

There was a chorus of 'Yes, sirs'. He showed them on his map the area they would have to patrol, and told Allen he was to be responsible for the navigation. When the last question had been answered he left them and walked slowly away towards his tank, and sitting down with his back against a bogey, he gave himself up to his reflections. He thought of his wife, and wondered what would become of her. He was certain he would be killed, and in his nervous, depressed state he could see little future for the rest of his squadron. He made a mental note to tell his officers to make sure the men were prepared for the worst; that those wishing to make wills had been shown how to do so; that all wore their identity discs, and that each tank had its supply of morphia. He wrote to his wife; a loving letter with many terms of endearment but no mention of the squadron's activities. He even wept a little as he thought of her, and later that night when he lay in his blankets beneath the myriad stars he prayed that he would be given the courage to play the man. He even remembered to pray for his squadron's safety and success.

Skeffington made his way across the desert with long strides and slightly bent shoulders. He came to the M.O.'s tent and peeped inside. The doctor looked up from the returns he was endeavouring to complete to the satisfaction of some nosey-parker back in Cairo.

'Come in, Skeffington, old man, help yourself to a glass of champagne. Can you beat it? This form requires me to list the number of cases I have treated for chilblains in the last month; it'll be frost-bite next. Anyhow, what's the matter with you; or is this a social call?'

'Oh, it's nothing much, Doc, only my desert sore. We're going up to the wire in a few days, as I expect you know, and I don't want to be a hindrance to the squadron then.'

'Let's have a look at it.'

Skeffington removed the bandage from his knee and revealed the angry, pus-filled sore he had been encouraging with filth ever since Walters had told them about the coming patrol.

'H'm,' murmured the M.O. 'I don't think we'll have to

amputate at the moment. Get the orderly to bathe it and dig out the muck. He can do that every day until you go up to the wire. Then, when you come back, come and see me again, that is, of course, if you're still alive.'

Skeffington was both disappointed and hurt by the harassed doctor's callous manner, and he quickly left the tent to look for the medical orderly. This man was sympathetic but not particularly gentle: he had been a Tyneside riveter before being drafted to the Regiment.

Each day a water truck and a stores vehicle visited the squadron down on the wire. When these returned at night the men would wait for the drivers so that they could inquire what was happening at the front. The drivers, proud of their exploits in taking their soft vehicles so close to the enemy, invented the most hair-raising and heroic stories about the squadron's activities. These stories were only discounted when it was discovered that the squadron in its three days of patrolling had not required one visit from the ammunition lorry. The tanks still possessed every round they had started out with.

That evening Major Walters was moving his squadron up to take over from Major Wallis. In the late afternoon the sound of gunfire echoed about the camp. Heavy artillery, which must have belonged to the enemy, could be heard mingling with the machine-guns and two-pounders of the tanks. Everyone wondered what was happening. Was the squadron all right? Were there any casualties? But no one brought back any news, and they had to wait patiently until the evening, when Major Walters's squadron took over, and Major Wallis's squadron came back for its period of rest.

Walters was soaked with perspiration. His nerves were

at breaking point, and his stomach sent waves of nausea over him. He had received his final orders from the colonel, and was now standing in the turret of his tank summoning up the mental energy necessary to give the signal for the squadron to start. His thoughts wandered to his wife and what would become of her now that he was dead. He spoke hoarsely into his microphone.

'Go on, get a bloody move on,' and his driver correctly assumed he was meant to start. With a final noisy revving-up of the powerful engine the tank lurched forward. The rest of the squadron, believing the major was manoeuvring into position and not having received any signal from him to move, remained where it was. The troop leaders were expecting Allen to move to the head of the squadron since he was the navigator, but he was still well over on the right flank. The major's tank had travelled a hundred yards before Walters's mind registered the fact that he was moving in solitude. He shouted at his driver to halt then climbed from the tank and ran all the way back to the foremost troop. He stopped at the first tank and resting his hands on its nose, he paused to regain his breath. After a few seconds' silence he screamed into the startled driver's ear:

'For Christ's sake get a move on, you bloody fool; can't you see you're holding up the whole bloody squadron?'

Hargreaves, the troop officer, peered down at Walters, embarrassed by this outburst, and the major, recognizing him, shouted up:

'Don't suppose you brought any mail back from Headquarters for me, old man, did you?'

'No, sir, I'm afraid not.'

'Well, get a move on. We don't want to hang about here all night like a lot of chattering old women, do we?'

Now the entire squadron was moving forward. The

major began to run back towards his tank, but before he reached it the leading troops had passed him and were following the tracks left by Major Wallis's squadron. These were so clearly defined that no navigator was necessary, and the whole squadron knew its destination. Walters climbed breathlessly into his tank and ordered his driver to start, but the engine refused. He shouted threats and insults at the wretched man, but it was not until the last vehicle had disappeared behind its cloud of dust that the engine again burst into life and the distraught major was able to hasten after his erring charges.

They came upon Major Wallis's squadron at the beginning of the short twilight. The men were counting the tanks. Not a single one was missing; there had been no casualties. All of the men looked fit and most of them were wearing beards since there was not sufficient water for washing and shaving.

Major Wallis shook hands with Walters, and after a short conversation he directed his second-in-command to lead the squadron back to the Regiment while he went off in the station wagon with Walters to explain to him the situation and point out certain physical features. Walters went away with him without troubling to give any directions to Captain Harvey. He never even gave the order to dismount. After he had been gone for thirty minutes or so Harvey ordered the men from their vehicles and walked across to Allen's tank.

'I wonder how long they're going to be.'

'God knows! It will be quite dark in a few minutes. Let's hope he doesn't intend to move us again tonight.'

Skeffington and the other subalterns had joined the two officers. It was now completely dark. The group waited, and at length they heard the station wagon approaching. Walters stepped out and Major Wallis drove rapidly away to rejoin his squadron which by now had almost reached headquarters.

Walters was suffering under a great nervous strain. He saw the group of officers.

'What the hell are you doing gossiping like a bunch of old washerwomen? Why aren't you in your tanks with your men? We're in action now, let's have no more of this nonsense or I'll report the whole damn lot of you to the colonel. Go on, get back to your tanks, we're moving!'

The group dispersed, Walters climbed into his tank and started off leaving the others to follow. He gave neither orders nor signals; he told no one where he was leading the squadron. His mind no longer grappled with these things; all he was concerned with was to get the tanks to the area which Wallis had pointed out to him. This was a large hollow in the desert some miles from the enemy-held fort. The squadron had just over a mile to travel to reach the spot.

It was Allen who first discovered that the squadron was moving in a large circle. He had noticed earlier how brightly the Ursa Major constellation was appearing on his right; when he looked again it was on his left, and even as he stared wonderingly at it the Pole Star swung behind him and back again to the right. He ordered his driver to speed up until he was alongside Walters's tank. He signalled the major to stop, and shouted across to him, 'I say, sir!' but Walters roared back cutting him short: 'For Christ's sake don't shout, you bloody fool, or they'll hear you!'

Allen transferred himself to Walters's tank.

'Did you know that we have been moving in a circle, sir?'

'Christ, where the hell are we then?'

'I don't know, sir.'

'Why the hell don't you know? You're supposed to be the navigator. What do you think you're here for? It's high time you got it out of your mind that this is a boy scouts' picnic party. If you can't pull your weight I'll have you transferred, by Christ I will!'

'You didn't say where you intended to lead us when we started off, sir, you just ordered us to follow. I know I'm supposed to be the squadron navigator, but if you'd only let me know what you want to do it would make things a great deal easier.'

The truth of this gradually dawned upon Walters, and while he was trying to make a decision Harvey approached and climbed on to the tank.

'Where the hell are we, Pete?'

'I'm afraid I don't know, sir.'

'What had we better do now?'

'I should suggest we stop here until it gets light and we can identify our position. There's not much point in chasing about here if we don't know where we are.'

'Very well. Go and tell the men not to talk, and make quite certain that there is a man on watch in every tank.'

The squadron leader remained awake throughout the rest of the night. He had no idea of his position, and was haunted by the fear that he might easily have led his squadron straight into the enemy's lines. In the darkness he alternately wept and prayed. Shortly before dawn he visited each tank and ordered the crew to their action stations. It never entered his head to detail a subordinate to carry out this task.

When at last the light returned it revealed the fort a good two miles away to the north-west. Allen took a bearing with his compass and was soon able to work out their exact position. He fetched his map, and climbing on to Walters's tank he pointed with his pencil and said:

'This is where we are at the moment.'

Walters led the squadron in line ahead towards the hollow. Soon he was able to recognize it from his visit with Major Wallis on the previous evening, but instead of moving into the depression from which they would be invisible to the watchers at the fort he led the squadron on to its ridge, thus clearly silhouetting each vehicle against the skyline with a rising sun behind it. This was too much for Harvey who quickly ordered his tank alongside Walters's. Both tanks had now stopped with the rest of the squadron drawn up and halted. Harvey was arguing bitterly with the squadron leader who was screaming back abuse at him, but eventually Harvey had his way and they moved into the hollow apparently before anyone at the fort had discovered their presence.

Later that morning, at a conference of the officers, it had been decided to send out two patrols each consisting of a troop of three tanks. The duty of each troop was to watch an area between the fort and the nearest town, some twelve miles distant, and report back by wireless any enemy activity. Skeffington and Harvey took out the first patrols, and were to return to the hollow at dusk. When the six tanks had left, the rest of the squadron relaxed by their tanks ready to go into action should they be required. One man remained on duty in each turret, while the remainder of the crew sheltered themselves from the sun beneath the bellies of the vehicles.

The days passed; the troops went out on their patrols, the squadron area became infested with millions of flies, and those men who were not actively occupied soon became bored and restive and spent the hours grumbling about the monotonous rations, the lack of cigarettes and infrequent mail. They lay beneath their tanks and planned their first leave in Cairo, and invariably a woman featured prominently in their programme.

Trooper Albert Maxwell propped himself up against the track of his tank and allowed his thoughts to wander back to the little Herefordshire village and the farm on which he had been employed until he was called up. He disliked the army with its dull routine and the loud-mouthed N.C.O.s who seemed to enjoy bullying and punishing him on the slightest pretext. The truth was that poor Maxwell was not one of the best of soldiers. He was a willing and hard worker but not over gifted with brains. He was probably an excellent man on a farm, but the army had drawn him into its machine and turned him into a tank-driver. He had scarcely scraped through the course, and certainly would not have done so had the need for drivers not been so urgent at the time. Maxwell was feeling extremely sorry for himself. He hated the persistent flies and the intense heat and longed for the cool, shady interior of his village pub, and the secluded lanes where he had walked on many a summer's evening with one of the farm girls. He felt he could tell some of these city dwellers in the squadron what a roll in the hay really meant. He glanced at Trooper Davis sitting beside him in the sand with a pad on his knee – writing to his sweetheart in Manchester. What did he know of the country? Probably the only place he had ever made love was in some darkened shop doorway, and anyhow it always rained up North, or so he had been told. He moved his position to make himself more comfortable against the hard track that bit into his shoulders, but the pistol at his side dug into his hip so he loosened his webbing belt. His revolver was wrapped in rags to protect its mechanism from the sand. Trooper Maxwell withdrew the weapon from its holster and commenced unwinding the cloth from about the barrel with the intention of cleaning it, but the raucous voice of the S.S.M. shouting his name interrupted him in his task.

'Coming, Sergeant-Major!' he yelled, and getting hurriedly to his feet began to stuff the weapon back into its webbing holster, but the cloth that was wound around the chamber was too loose to allow the pistol to rest correctly in the holster. Trooper Maxwell, expecting the S.S.M.'s voice to break forth in abuse at any moment, gave an extra push on the weapon's butt; the rags that were caught in the trigger tightened, the hammer came back and forward in one movement, and the gun exploded, propelling the heavy bullet the few feet into the top of Trooper Davis's skull and out through the back of his neck. Davis's head and shoulders dropped forward on to his knees, and he rolled gently over on his side, the pencil still between his fingers. He was quite dead, the blood streaming from the large hole in his neck mingling in the sand with the brain that oozed slimily from his punctured skull. Men came running from their tanks while Maxwell stood staring down at Davis's lifeless body, the pistol now hanging loosely from his paralysed hand. A corporal quickly reached from behind him and gently removed it from his grasp.

'It was an accident, it was all an accident,' mumbled Trooper Maxwell.

The squadron leader pushed his way through the crowd.

'Get back to your tanks!' he shouted but no one moved.

'Christ!' he said when he saw Davis's body. 'How did this happen?'

'It was all an accident, sir,' murmured Maxwell.

'Did you do it?' asked Walters.

36

'Yes, sir, but it was an accident.'

'Put him under close arrest, Sergeant-Major, he'll have to go back to the Regiment. I'll signal for an escort. I suppose he's quite dead?' he inquired looking at Davis again.

One of the men sniggered.

'Christ!' screamed Walters. 'If any of you think this is a time for laughing I'll have the swine before the colonel before he knows where he is. I don't want any hard-boiled thugs in this squadron. We're still human beings, and by God you'll behave like 'em while I'm in charge. Now, Sergeant-Major, we'll have to bury Davis straight away. Get a blanket and wrap him in it and take him over there.' The major pointed to a spot about two hundred yards outside the squadron area. He went on:

'Take six of the men, and get these others back to their tanks. The war's not over yet, and I'm afraid we're going to see a lot more of this sort of thing before any of us get home.'

Six men volunteered for the burial party. Maxwell begged to be allowed to take part, but the squadron leader refused, ordering him to remain beside his tank until transport came from the Regiment to take him away.

They took Davis's blanket and gently laid him on it, straightened his limbs and covered his bloodstained face. It only required two men to carry him, for he was not a very heavy man. The rest of the party took shovels and picks from the tanks. They put the body down while they dug a shallow grave; the sand was only a foot or so deep and underneath was solid rock. The squadron leader stood bareheaded while the men passed the body down to those already standing in the grave. He did not know the burial service, nor had he been able to find a prayer book. When the men straightened up looking down at the slight figure in the blanket, Walters said:

'Almighty God, take into Thy care Thy servant, Trooper Davis. Amen.'

The men were still standing silently about the grave.

'Well, go on, chaps, for Christ's sake. Fill it in!' And he walked back to the squadron, leaving the men to their task.

It was the last day of the squadron's tour of duty before being relieved. Harvey and Skeffington were out on patrol watching the area between the fort and the town, the distance separating the troops being about a quarter of a mile. They had been out several hours and the sun was blazing down, sucking the moisture from the men and turning the tanks into ovens. Skeffington had halted his troop and, ordering his sergeant to keep a lookout, had climbed underneath his tank and fallen asleep. The crews of his remaining two tanks quickly followed their officer's example. An hour passed; the men slept, and the heat haze distorted objects so that it was almost a waste of time staring with aching eyes across the silent desert.

It was Skeffington's sergeant who saw the flash from the fort, but before he could make up his mind whether or not he should disturb his officer, the heavy shell burst with a vicious crack a few yards in front of his tank. The sergeant, who had been sitting on top of the turret, was blown three yards clear of the tank, and landed heavily on his back, where, fortunately for him, the yielding sand broke the full force of his fall. Those sleeping beneath the vehicle were galvanized into activity. Skeffington and the driver were inside the tank within seconds, and the sergeant, who was miraculously unscathed, joined them a close third. A second shell had already landed twenty yards behind the vehicle before the driver had got it moving. Skeffington, realizing that the enemy were rapidly getting their range, ordered the driver to turn hard right, but the man in his enthusiasm to obey the order, jerked back his stick with such force that the sudden pull of the tank against the soft sand snapped a pin, causing the track to fall serpent-like to the ground. In the meantime the third shell had arrived sufficiently close to rattle several of its splinters against the helpless vehicle's armoured side. Skeffington's other two tanks were already hastening away from the un-healthy area, when Harvey, seeing what had happened, ordered the rest of his troop to keep out of the way while he hastened towards the stricken tank as quickly as his own could travel, with the intention of towing Skeffington out of trouble. Once alongside the broken-down tank he leaped out regardless of the shells that were bursting about it at regular intervals of about fifteen seconds. He yelled at the tank's occupants, but no one heard him for they had shut all the hatches. He jumped on to the hull and hammered on the turret hatch with the butt of his pistol, shouting to the men to open up. At last they heard him, and the hatch was thrown back revealing Skeffington's terrified face beneath his steel helmet.

'Wake up and give me a hand with your tow rope or we'll all have had it,' ordered Harvey.

'Sergeant, help Captain Harvey with our towing chain,' said Skeffington, who had no intention of leaving the protection of his tank if he could help it.

'No, you, you windy bastard!' shouted Harvey, despis-ing the man so much he no longer bothered to use any restraint in his remarks to Skeffington before the men, but the willing sergeant was already unshackling the heavy chain and making it fast to Harvey's tank, which had by now placed itself in position to receive the tow. In less than two minutes they were moving slowly out of danger. Harvey found it difficult to believe that not one of the dozen or more shells that had fallen so near to the tanks had succeeded in causing a single casualty. The firing from the fort had ceased, and Harvey ordered his troop sergeant to have a shot at picking up the broken track, but not to waste time over it if the firing opened up again.

When they had all reached the safety of the squadron Skeffington came across to Harvey, who was watching the tow-line being unhooked.

'Thanks, Pete, old man,' he began. 'You saved my life that time.'

'Muck off,' growled Harvey, and turning his back on the subaltern he pretended to occupy himself with a nut that had suddenly come loose.

In the evening the squadron formed up, and waited for the relieving tanks to appear. Soon the rumble and squeaking of the approaching vehicles could be heard, and shortly afterwards Major Walters led his men back to the Regiment, leaving behind only Trooper Davis in his lonely grave.

The squadron had returned to the Regiment, and the men were quite content to relax and talk about their experiences of the last few days, for although they had seen little of the battle, nevertheless the conditions had been fairly exacting for the comparatively inexperienced soldiers. Most of them were considerably shocked by Trooper Davis's death, yet at the same time they could not help feeling a great deal of sympathy for Trooper Maxwell, who was now awaiting an escort to take him back to Cairo. A court of enquiry had already been held on the circumstances of the accident, and a summary of evidence taken. The men were convinced that once this evidence had been digested no further disciplinary action would be taken. Those who spoke to Maxwell did their best to comfort the unhappy man by telling him he was almost certain to be given a comfortable job when he reached Cairo or perhaps, better still, they would send him back to England.

Allen was leaning against his tank and endeavouring to sort into chronological order the several unopened letters he had just received from Mary; the latest was already two months old. He began to read, and was filled with excitement at the sight of the familiar handwriting and the mild terms of endearment which she regularly used. She wrote:

My dearest Tony,
   Mummy has just gone out to play bridge so I am sitting here alone in the lounge and writing to you, darling. It seems such a long time since you went away, and I can only hope the coming months will pass quickly so that I can have you back once again. Sometimes I wish we had married after all. At night in bed I think so much of you, and wish you were at my side . . .

Allen was smiling with happiness at the intimacy of her writing. He had stopped reading for a moment to allow his thoughts to wander along the tender lines suggested by Mary's letter, when he heard the sound of boots crunching across the shale, and looking up saw Skeffington bearing down upon him. He cursed as he felt the glow of happiness give place to anger and frustration. Skeffington spoke in his earnest and most aggravating manner.

'You know, Tony, this mail is absolutely infuriating. My letters are months old, it's quite ridiculous. They really ought to do better than this for the troops. I shall do my best to persuade my father to write to *The Times* about it. It ought to be brought to the notice of the people at home.'

'Yes, I know. My mail is just as old.'

'I wrote to my gunsmith ages ago,' went on Skeffington, quite oblivious of the cold look on Allen's face and the shortness of his reply, 'but I've never had an answer. I asked them to send me out a catalogue. My sixteen-bore is not quite good enough now. My grandfather gave it to me when I was fourteen, but I really need something heavier, don't you think?'

'Yes, I suppose you do.'

'Did you ever use a sixteen-bore?'

Allen's good manners were beginning to wear very thin. He was thinking of Mary's letter, and her exciting wish, and all the time Skeffington's monotonous voice beat into his brain with his dull and stupid conversation. Allen pulled himself together.

'Got to go and see the quartermaster. See you later on,' he lied, and hurried away from the complaining Skeffington, wishing that he possessed sufficient courage to tell the man exactly what he thought of him instead of having to make up some feeble excuse to escape from the fellow's empty chatter.

Later that day Allen was telling Peter Harvey about Skeffington's annoying behaviour. Harvey interrupted him:

'He can't help it, and it's up to us to set him an example he can try to follow.'

'Don't be pontifical, Pete. Who the hell do you think you're fooling? The man's quite useless in the squadron, and Walters ought to get rid of him. Apart from his uselessness he's also a complete bore. He fixes you with his glassy stare and goes on and on and on. For Christ's sake, can't they do something about him? The flies are bad enough, but now I'm beginning to believe our Skeffington is even more trying than they are.'

'Walters told me only the other evening he would like

to do just that, but apparently our Desmond's father is a big noise in the City and so Walters thinks for the sake of the old man he should be given a chance.'

'And what about us?'

'We'll have to put up with it. He's young; I expect he'll learn in time, and after all's said and done he's probably a damn-sight better than a lot of those bastards who are sitting at home letting chaps like him fight the war for them while they rake in the money and get the best jobs.'

The days passed quickly until once again it was the turn of the squadron to go out on patrol, and this time the men were about to experience a little more of the bitter realities of a struggle that had scarcely yet begun in this theatre of the war.

Allen had been watching the fort throughout the day. His eyes were weary of the sun's glare, and the haze made it difficult to distinguish objects at more than a mile or so, but at last his long vigil was rewarded. Something was happening a few hundred yards outside the white fort. He peered long and carefully through his glasses trying to make out what it was that was going on. Eventually he put down the binoculars and called up the squadron on his radio.

'Hullo Bolo, Bolo 3 calling, message for you. Over.' He repeated the call until the reply came back.

'Hullo Bolo 3, Bolo answering. Pass your message. Over.'

'Hullo Bolo, Bolo 3 calling. Twenty enemy outside fort with several guns dug in. Over.'

Walters received the message and told Allen to take no further action for the moment. He ordered the rest of the squadron not already on patrol to join Allen's troop. Soon eight tanks lumbered out of the depression down towards the gap in the wire where Allen was waiting. Walters led his tank towards the narrow gap, ordering the squadron to follow behind him in single file. The guns from the fort began firing as soon as the major's tank was through the narrow opening that had been torn in the fence, but so far they had not succeeded in finding the range and the small anti-tank shells were bursting a hundred yards or more from the vehicles. Once inside the wire, Walters ordered the squadron to turn right, still in line ahead, so that the tanks could traverse their turrets and fire broadside at the enemy. The squadron opened fire, but at the distance of nearly a mile it was quite impossible in the haze to see what effect it was having; also, the enemy had by now found the range, and shell splinters were beginning to whistle through the air, discouraging the tank commanders from leaning out of their turrets with their binoculars.

Peter Harvey, who was following immediately behind Walters, noticed that the tanks were keeping much too close behind each other and so making an extremely good target for the enemy. He was on the point of ordering them to increase their distances when his whole attention was occupied by Walters's latest move. The squadron leader had now turned sharply to the left, and even as Harvey watched him, he turned left again, and started off in the opposite direction to the rest of the squadron. He was putting himself immediately between the enemy and the following tanks, and so bunched together was the squadron that within a few moments it had formed a complete oval, moving round and round, so that the tanks on the outside were in far more danger from the guns of those on the inside than they were from the Italian artillery. The tanks close to the wire had to shoot at the enemy, then cease firing as one of their own tanks came into view a few yards away. Chaos reigned, and it was a miracle that there were no casualties. Walters had by now perceived the confusion his tactics had wrought, but so worried was he about what might happen next that he was incapable of giving the orders that would correct his mistake.

'Cease fire!' ordered Harvey over the squadron network, 'and form up on me.' He moved out of the circle and stood up in his turret, utterly unperturbed by the bursting shells, and signalled with his arms to the rest of the squadron, which was at last slowly conforming to his order. Walters moved outside the wire and halted, quite content to allow someone else to take over. Harvey was now leading the squadron, well spread out on either side of him, at full speed towards the enemy who was still firing but failing to stop the oncoming tanks. Harvey could plainly see the Italians at their guns, which were well dug in, but revealing themselves by their muzzle flashes. Then he saw that a large circular tank ditch separated the tanks from the guns, a ditch that it would be impossible to cross without equipment that the squadron did not possess. He spoke over the radio:

'Enemy guns two hundred yards, twelve o'clock. Fire!'

In a few seconds every tank was pouring accurate fire into a surprised and unhappy enemy. Italians could be seen straightening up and falling over their weapons while the survivors hurriedly took shelter in the deep trenches, deserting their guns, which had all ceased firing. Harvey, rezlizing that he could do no more at this stage without the help of infantry, ordered the rest of the tanks to withdraw to the wire while he remained halted with his troop to ensure that the Italians did not return to their guns and shoot at the retiring squadron.

Outside the wire they re-formed, and Walters took over again. For a long time the men watched the spot from which the Italians had fired, and when the sun began to sink and the haze disappeared a party of soldiers wearing red crosses on their arms came running out of the fort towards the guns. One of the tanks commenced firing but Walters ordered it to stop, and the Italians, who had thrown themselves on the ground at the first burst, got to their feet again and ran, climbing down into the tank ditch and up the other side. As the short twilight gave way to darkness the Italians returned to the fort carrying several of their comrades on stretchers. The squadron had inflicted its first casualties without the loss of a single man or vehicle. Four of the tanks had been hit, but fortunately for those inside, the armour was sufficiently thick to protect both crew and engine.

That night, when the squadron had settled down in the hollow, the men circulated from tank to tank, elated by their success and the excitement of their first real action. Trooper Dykes was showing his steel helmet to several of his cronies. There was a jagged hole in the side of it which had been caused by a shell splinter when it was hanging on the outside of his tank.

'Thought I was a goner when this one hit me,' lied Dykes.

'Don't be bloody daft, thou weren't wearing battle bowler. T'were 'anging on thee tank,' contradicted Trooper Entwhistle.

'An' even if old Dykes 'ad been wearing his bloody 'at the bloody splinter wouldn't have gone bloody through; 'is 'ead's too bloody thick,' announced Corporal Jenkins.

'Ah, shut thee mucking trap!' said Dykes amidst laughter.

Harvey and Allen were sitting with their backs resting against the wheels of Allen's tank. During the silence Allen's thoughts returned to the afternoon's engagement. He remembered it all very vividly. He had seen the danger

46

of Walters's move and had thought of taking over the squadron several seconds before he had heard Harvey's voice ordering the tanks to form up on him. He realized then that he did not possess Harvey's courage – or perhaps it was more sense of duty than courage. It had been much easier to keep away from the Italian guns, but Harvey, who he knew disliked being shot at as much as anyone, had forced himself to make the right decision. Allen felt ashamed of himself, and he comprehended that this feeling of shame was far worse than fear. He made up his mind it should not deaden his senses again.

'It's high time they got rid of Walters,' said Allen, and, hearing his own words, realized that he had just uttered the expression which almost everyone in the squadron had been using for several weeks now.

'Oh, he's not so bad,' Harvey replied in his mild way. 'He'll learn in time. We all have to, only some are quicker at it than others.'

'You're too charitably disposed towards him, that's your trouble, Pete. They ought to give you the squadron after this afternoon's effort. I thought for a moment the bloody fool was going to start his own civil war. How some of us didn't shoot each other up beats me.'

'I've got a little plan,' announced Harvey after a pause in the conversation. 'I'm sure they must send lots of stuff up to the fort, and as we never see anything, it obviously must come up from the town during the night. Now, my idea is to take a troop out just after dark and wait by the sand dunes near the track half-way between the fort and the town. We might have a bit of fun. I'll have a word with Walters and see what he's got to say about a midnight party.'

'I'll come with you, and you can leave your troop sergeant behind,' suggested Allen.

47

'I'd like to have you with me but I think I'll suggest taking young Skeffington.'

'Christ! Whatever for? I don't feel very flattered.'

'Don't be silly. It will do him good. It's time he got used to a spot of danger; besides, his family crest will help keep out the bullets and things.'

'Well, if that doesn't, the crucifix will.'

Harvey chuckled. He said, 'He hasn't grown up yet, poor chap. Perhaps he's still too much in love with his right hand. Someone should have explained to him the facts of life. That lad was badly brought up, I've always thought so.'

Allen fell asleep wrapped in his blankets and thinking of Mary. He longed for her; he had so much to tell her. He felt he had become a man in the few short months since he had left her. Surely she must feel proud of him; what a homecoming it was going to be. He hoped it would be soon.

The following evening, as soon as it became dark, Harvey led the three tanks out of the depression and down towards the gap in the wire. It was a very dark night, for the moon had not yet risen, and the tanks followed closely behind each other, moving slowly to make as little noise as possible. It took the troop nearly two hours to reach the dunes that flanked both sides of the well-worn track, and when at last Harvey sighted them he stopped, and getting out, guided each tank into a position from which it could cover the track without being observed. When he was satisfied with his arrangements he spoke a few words to Skeffington, then he climbed back into his tank to wait.

The night was absolutely silent except for the mush that came from the wireless headphones, and the hum of the dynamo. The dim blue light inside the tank lit up the faces of the gunner and the wireless operator.

Harvey felt extremely pleased with life. He was in charge of the party, and provided the enemy turned up he was in a position to give him something to think about. He grinned and stared into the night trying to pierce the darkness while he strained his ears for the slightest sound, but all was silent and still.

Skeffington, stationed fifty yards from the other two tanks, wished to relieve himself. For nearly an hour he had been trying to summon up sufficient courage to climb out of the tank, but he was sure something would happen as soon as he did. At last his need was so desperate that he had to risk it. His mouth felt dry, and as he hurried into the tank once more he wished that they were safely back with the squadron. Harvey was mad, he thought, to suggest this sort of thing. Why could he not have kept quiet? Walters would never have attempted such a danger- ous mission off his own bat, he was far too windy. He realized it was indeed much better to have a nervous squadron leader – at least he kept the tanks out of danger. And now here was Harvey trying to show off and collect himself a medal. He was obviously too stupid to feel afraid. Skeffington prayed that nothing would appear along the track. He wished he had never joined the Army; the uni- form was smart enough and he enjoyed wearing it at home in England; it was most satisfying to be in the company of a pretty girl and be saluted by the men in uniform. He used to spend many pleasant hours of his leave just walking up and down the main thoroughfare of his home town collecting and smartly returning salutes. And woe betide any rash fellow who pretended to be looking the other way. 'I say, you,' he would call out for the passer-by to hear, 'don't they teach you in your unit to recognize an officer?' and the embarrassed man would quickly salute and hurry away, shamed and red-faced.

The long night wore on and nothing happened. The men were beginning to feel tired, for the strain and excitement, long sustained, were at last having their effect. Harvey was disappointed and hoped that something would soon appear. He had waited so long; he would wait just a little longer.

Skeffington sensed the coming dawn; very shortly they would have to go and with any luck nothing would turn up now. His spirits commenced to rise as it rapidly became lighter. He was able to make out the shape of Harvey's tank halted by the neighbouring sand dune, and all the time it was getting lighter. The dawn had come at last, and soon they surely must leave, reasoned Skeffington. It was almost light; now he could see Harvey's tank quite clearly but the turret was empty. For a moment fear enveloped him. He looked for the third tank, but it was hidden by the dunes. He fought back his terror and then it surged over him again, forcing him to contract his stomach muscles, for there on the edge of the track, not sixty yards away, lay Harvey prone on his side in his greatcoat. Skeffington could hardly bear to look. He was incapable of either speech or movement. He wanted to tell the rest of his crew what he had just seen, but he was so frightened the words would not come. Then, even as he stared, Harvey moved and got quickly to his feet. He noticed Skeffington and grinning at him called across in a hoarse whisper: 'They're coming. Don't start firing till I give the signal; so watch my hand. I'll wave it like this.' He waved his hand in a downward movement; then giving Skeffington the thumbs-up sign he climbed quickly back into his tank. Skeffington could have wept as he realized there was no escape for him this time. He cursed Harvey for lying there like a boy scout with his ear to the ground.

In the distance could be heard the noise of engines revving up and slowing down as the vehicles negotiated the
treacherous sand. Harvey, recognizing the sound of heavy
lorries, was overcome by excitement. He grinned at
Skeffington and the other tank commander, and signalled
them to be ready. The lorries were rapidly approaching,
and then in the half-light Harvey saw them – two large
Diesel Lancias, the open backs full of Italians. The lorries
were scarcely fifty yards apart, and the leading one was
already about to pass the troop sergeant's tank. Now it
was almost in front of Harvey's tank while the second
Lancia drew level with the troop sergeant. Harvey
straightened himself up in his turret, and grinning happily
screamed 'Bastardo!' which he imagined meant something
rude in Italian, and waving his hand, gave the signal to
open fire. The three machine-guns spoke simultaneously,
and above their chatter and during the intervals between
the short bursts could be heard the dreadful screams of the
Italians. Both Lancias had stopped, the drivers either dead
or wounded. Those troops in the back of the lorries still
unscathed amidst that withering hail of fire were diving
headlong into the sand that gave no protection from the
guns. Thirty seconds had scarcely passed before Harvey
shouted at the troop to cease fire, then he ordered his
driver alongside the nearest Lancia. All his earlier enthusiasm had forsaken him, and he was sickened at the sight
of the carnage. From his turret he looked down into the
back of the Lancia, that had now become one vast pool
of blood that dripped through the floorboards on to the
sand beneath. Men were crying out, some groaning, some
stilled for ever, all ashen in the growing light. Skeffington's
tank came up, and when he saw at close quarters the
results of their handiwork he retched and vomited down
the side of his tank, fouling the crest he had painted such

a short time ago. Harvey climbed across from his tank into the Lancia and signalled the rest of the Italians to do what they could to help the wounded. He ordered Skeffington to stand guard while the crews of the remaining two tanks assisted with the wounded, but of sixty-four men only twenty-one were uninjured. Many were already dead. The Italians, silent and shocked, worked swiftly to succour the wounded. They helped side by side with the troop, and some still had weapons strapped to their belts, but now all thoughts were for the suffering. The little skirmish was over and for the moment English and Italians were only concerned with caring for the wounded. There was no hatred, no bitterness.

Harvey rapidly summed up the situation. If he signalled for medical help it would take hours to arrive, and it might be several days before the wounded reached hospital. Many would die from the shock of the journey across the hundreds of miles of uneven desert. He quickly made up his mind.

'Jenkins,' he called to his driver, 'see if you can start these lorries.' And while the man went off to wrestle with the Diesels, he inquired of the Italians if there was a man among them who spoke English.

'Yes, I can,' replied a sergeant, who had been bending over one of the wounded.

'Hurry, then, take the shovels and picks from our tanks and bury those that are dead, but first make quite sure they are dead. You'll only have time to dig one big grave, I'm afraid.'

The Italians went to work and lifted out the bodies and laid them in a limp untidy row on the side of the track. There were nineteen blood-soaked corpses gazing pale and staring-eyed up at the blue sky into which the sun was already climbing.

'The Lancias are okay, sir,' said Jenkins. 'They'll get us back to the squadron all right.'

'Good,' said Harvey and called to the Italian sergeant: 'Get all the wounded into this truck as soon as you can.'

As the Italians carried the injured men from the other truck Harvey leaned down and gently helped to receive them and lay them down on the bare wooden boards. He ordered the troop to bring their precious water bottles and dole it out sparingly to the wounded, who were already beginning to murmur '*Aqua, aqua*', in an increasingly plaintive chorus.

Within an hour the shallow communal grave had been filled in and Harvey spoke to the Italian sergeant.

'Get your best driver and four of your men and drive back to your lines with the wounded as quickly as possible. Order the rest of the men into the second Lancia with a driver. They will have to return with me. Now hurry, there isn't much time.'

The sergeant spoke to an officer, and the orders were issued. The officer shook hands with the sergeant and climbed into the lorry with the unwounded men. Then the sergeant formed up his party of five beside Harvey's tank and calling them to attention he saluted the British officer. Afterwards they climbed quickly into the Lancia with the wounded and made off in the direction of the town, while Harvey, after watching it for a few moments, signalled the rest of his troop and the lorry with the prisoners to begin the journey back to the squadron.

Later that day, after the prisoners had been searched and fed and then sent on in the Lancia under escort to the Regiment, Harvey sat in the shade of Allen's tank while they played chess. The game had only been in progress for a little while when Allen moved his knight, and breaking the silence, said:

'Check.'

There was a pause while his opponent studied the board.

'That's it, I'm afraid,' announced Harvey. 'Can't seem to concentrate any more. I just keep thinking about this morning's do.'

'Well, you certainly did a pretty good job by all accounts. You're almost sure to get a gong for this. They've been trying like hell to get prisoners for interrogation for some time, and you go along and do it for them.'

'Don't be silly. I'm not thinking about that. What's upsetting me is the fact that I think I could have brought in the whole damn lot of them without firing a single shot, and yet I had to go and murder and maim half the poor wretches. Then that bloody fool Walters had the nerve to tell me I should have brought back the wounded as well. I wonder what he'd have done if he'd been there.'

'Most probably he'd have succeeded somehow in getting himself captured, and a bloody good thing too!' answered Allen as he put away the chess men.

Skeffington was talking to Turner in a voice that was intended to carry to the men within earshot.

'We mowed the blighters down like ninepins. We had them fairly screaming for mercy. That'll teach 'em to go to war with us. They should stick to women and opera. They haven't the guts for real fighting. Why, they never even fired a single shot at us; they haven't the stomach for war.'

And over on Skeffington's tank, Andrews, his driver, was talking to the gunner who was at that moment engaged in rubbing off with handfuls of sand the dried vomit of his troop leader.

'Never knew he had so much guts,' announced the gunner, spitting upon the crest that his efforts had once again revealed.

That night Allen lay awake thinking about the incident that Harvey had so vividly described to him. He pictured the vast grave at the side of the track and thought of the parents and relatives in Italy who would not yet have been informed of the loss of their loved ones. What bitter grief and sorrow that lonely grave was about to cause – months, even years of heartache caused by a few seconds skilful pressure on a sensitive trigger.

Allen was down on the wire with the rest of his troop. The sun blazed, distorting any object more than a few hundred yards away. He felt weary and longed to climb out of his stifling tank and crawl into the shade beneath it and sleep, but he was supposed to be on watch and so he thought he had better make a show of carrying out his duties, although he was certain that nothing was going to happen. He looked into the distance, occasionally peering through the glasses hung around his neck. All was quiet at the white, sun-baked fort; there was no sign of any movement along the track. Allen's thoughts drifted across the miles that separated him from Mary. He wished she could see him now in his tank, bronzed and keen-eyed, probably at that moment nearer to the enemy than anyone else in the whole army. Surely her heart would melt for him and she would sink into his embrace with a sigh of surrender. Then his face broke into a smile as the foolishness of his thoughts dawned upon him and he realized that love's fulfilment was for him about as remote as the moon and would remain so for some long time to come. Suddenly he saw the dust rising up from a point inside the wire about two miles to the west. He stared long and earnestly through the glasses, but the haze robbed the distance of any shape. The noise of engines came to his ears; the crews of the other two tanks of his troop were now alert and looking from their turrets trying to distinguish what was coming towards them. Then he saw the motor cycles moving slowly and approaching along the inside of the wire. There were two of them, and as he looked he noticed that each one carried a pillion rider. He began to wonder what they could possibly be doing. He thought they must surely have seen his troop by now for there was no shelter for the tanks; the ground here was completely flat and in the open they must have stood out miles away. Even if it was impossible to tell what they were, the enemy should have known that they were something to be regarded with suspicion. But the motor cyclists came on, and now the staccato reports from the machines' exhausts could be clearly heard. Allen called softly to his troop sergeant.

'You take the second bike, but don't fire until I do.'

'Right, sir.'

The rusty barbed wire was about five feet high and coiled backwards and forwards over the ground to a depth of another five feet. The cyclists were close to the wire, so perhaps the combination of haze and fencing had obscured the tanks from their view; at any rate, the leading cyclist was now only a hundred yards from Allen and getting nearer with every second. The cyclists drew level, but Allen could not order his gunner to fire. The two on the bike were so utterly defenceless. Yesterday he would have fired without a thought and perhaps regretted it afterwards, but listening to what Harvey had said about his feelings when the Lancias had been taken, Allen was not going to shoot unless it was absolutely necessary. Instead he leaned from his turret and yelled at the top of his voice:

'Hi, you, where the hell do you think you're going?'

Although the Italian did not understand English, the

suddenness of the shout and the foreign tongue and his first sight of the enemy tank so shocked him that he braked suddenly, causing the machine to skid in the soft sand. In a second the driver and his pillion passenger were lying on their backs with the motor cycle, the engine still running, on top of them. The driver of the second machine, taking in the situation at a glance, turned sharply to his right, away from the wire and made straight for the fort as fast as his cycle could carry them. The troop sergeant waited for Allen's signal then ordered his gunner to open fire. The machine-gun burst into action, the tracer bullets leaping alongside the fleeing cycle and passing it, but still it did not stop. The gunner aimed more carefully and fired another burst, and the figures crouching low over the speeding machine straightened up. The cycle wobbled and skidded, and fell over, two figures lying prone behind it about two hundred yards from the wire. The riders of the first cycle got to their feet with hands raised high above their heads when the gun ceased chattering, and Allen waved them towards their comrades lying silent in the sand. Allen's next problem was to get through the wire, for there was no gap in it for well over a mile or so in either direction. He called to the Italians already running towards the prostrate men. He signalled one to return to the wire, and waved the other on to help the injured couple. When the Italian had reached the wire Allen and the sergeant already had the heavy chain tow rope untied. Quickly they backed the tank right up to the fence and having made fast the tow, Allen and the sergeant climbed on to the top of the turret; then, holding the heavy hook in their hands they swung it backwards and forwards, with Allen counting aloud, and suddenly let it go. It fell heavily across the wire and the Italian, understanding what was required of him, pulled on the hook until the

chain was well over the top of the fence, then he caught
the hook in the post supporting the wire. Allen spoke into
his microphone ordering the driver to move forward. The
chain tightened pulling at the hook enmeshed in the wire,
and ripping and tearing the strands and posts until a
sufficiently large gap was made through which the tank
could pass. As soon as the tow was unshackled Allen drove
through the gap towards the three Italians. The pillion
rider had been hit in the small of the back by several
bullets. They laid him on his side, but it was obvious that
little could be done for the man. The front of his shirt and
trousers was already soaked in blood. He was gasping for
breath, while dark thick blood trickled from the corner of
his mouth. The driver of the cycle was lying on his back
and moaning. Blood was staining his trousers from a flesh
wound in the thigh. Allen occupied himself by helping the
man out of his trousers and placing his own field-dressing
over the painful but superficial wound. When this was
done he had to force his attention back to the dying man,
who was still gasping for breath. The two Italians from
the first cycle were kneeling by their stricken comrade,
and one was holding his hand and speaking softly in
Italian while the other, using a handkerchief already
soaked and stained, was wiping away the blood and
debris from the gasping and retching mouth.

Allen could not make up his mind. He knew, without
being a doctor, that it would all be over in a few more
minutes, and so rather than cause any further agony to
the man by lifting him on to a tank and starting back for
the squadron, he decided to wait for him to die. The rest
of the troop gathered round, and because they could think
of nothing else they could do to help, they offered cigar-
rettes to the man with the thigh wound and to the two
who were unhurt. The Italians smiled. '*Grazie, grazie,*'

they said, and one produced a lighter and lit the cigarettes for Allen's men before lighting his own. A little while later the dying man drew up his legs in a final spasm of agony, retched as the filthy stuff poured thickly from his mouth, and rolling up his tortured eyes, died and relaxed. Allen, pale and shocked, broke the silence.

'All right, boys, come along, let's have a grave over there by the wire as quickly as you can.' While it was being dug the young gunner who had fired the burst brought his blanket from the tank and with the Italians helped to roll the body into it, then they carried it over to the grave. The wounded Italian was lifted on to the back of Allen's tank, while a cycle with one Italian supporting it was put on each of the other tanks, and in this manner they made their way back to the squadron.

That night Allen lay awake thinking about the afternoon. He began to understand Harvey's feelings, and doubts tortured him as to whether or not he should have stopped the gunner firing. For himself, he would have been much happier if the dead man had escaped. The Italians individually seemed a decent enough crowd, and the two uninjured ones had shown themselves both gentle and sensitive. What a revolting thing war was, he thought. Never had he witnessed anything so horrible and disgusting as the drawn-out death of the Italian. He was certain it was a spectacle that would stay with him for always. Lying there in his blanket, at the war's beginning, he little knew that many other sights and sounds would rival that day's horror for supremacy in his mind.

The days slipped by, and the squadron grew in experience, for although there had as yet been no major clashes with the enemy, the men were becoming self-confident and anxious to get on with the war so that they could return to their homes. So far Davis had been the squadron's only casualty, although several men had reported sick and been sent back to the base. Few of these were genuine cases, and when Major Walters had discussed it with Harvey he had made his views felt. He said, as he thumped the hull of his tank to give emphasis to his words:

'I'm not having any of these windy blighters getting away with it, Pete. I'll speak to the M.O. and tell him to send only the wounded ones back. Why, if he goes on sending chaps back to Cairo at this rate we'll have no one left up here.'

'I'm afraid I disagree, sir. Now that reinforcements are coming out in fairly large numbers we might just as well get rid of the duds, and if anyone tries to work his ticket, well, he's no good to us anyway, is he?'

'We can still make the swine stay.'

'But what good is he? Anyone who hasn't the guts to conquer his fear and stay put to do the job is only a handicap to the squadron. Let him go back to Cairo, that's my opinion. For every one who wants to go back there are twenty keen ones who'd volunteer to take his place and feel it an honour to be allowed to do so.'

Walters grudgingly conceded the point.

Skeffington, after his first unsuccessful visit to the M.O., had now made up his mind to try to stick it out. He loathed every moment spent out on patrol, but he sensed that many in the squadron expected him to go sick sooner or later and so he was determined to disappoint them. He looked bronzed and fit, and the desert sore, since he had looked after it and kept it covered from the flies, had now nearly healed.

2

After the Regiment had spent three months in the desert the colonel announced that it had been decided to grant leave to the squadron. Two officers and ten men were permitted away at a time, and if the squadron was on patrol, replacements were to be made up from the other squadrons. Leave was to last for five days exclusive of the time taken to reach Cairo.

Harvey and Allen had persuaded Walters to allow them to go off together, and at last, sitting in the back of a three-tonner, they bumped their way eastwards across the desert in the direction of the railhead.

Allen said to Harvey as he brushed the flies from his lips:

'Before we know where we are we'll be on our way back again. It's scarcely worth this bloody journey really, is it?'

'My boy, don't you believe it. I intend to live for the next five days. It's going to be five days to remember for the rest of my life. Why, I've been dreaming of this for the last two months. It's all I've had to keep me going. Look out, you Cairo harpies, here I come with my pockets full of money!'

'Don't expect me to spend my time wenching with you,' said Allen looking dusty and miserable.

'You know, you want to try to forget Mary for the next few days. Leave her here in the desert until you come back again. It'll do you a world of good, and if she really loves you she won't give a damn what you do as long as you're enjoying yourself.'

'You don't know Mary!'

'You young lovers make me sick. Why you've never lived, you don't even know what love means.'

Allen began to feel a little resentful. He thought that if what he felt for Mary wasn't love he didn't know what it was. The lorry lurched and bumped. The two dust-covered officers heard the driver revving his engine but the heavy vehicle slowed down and stopped.

The next hour was spent in digging it out of the sand. Allen, his shirt soaked and darkened with perspiration, remarked with a wry grin:

'Christ, we're earning this leave!'

On board the train that was taking them to Alexandria they planned their first meal, and Harvey was amusing himself writing down a menu in his officer's note-book.

'Tomato cocktail for you, Tony?'

'Yep.'

Harvey wrote laboriously against the rocking of the train, his feet drawn up on the leather upholstery, the note-book resting on his knees. He asked:

'What about some prawns in aspic to follow?'

'I was thinking of something more solid, like a whole roast duck with orange and apple sauce and green peas and new potatoes.'

'That's too bourgeois for our first meal. What we want are several small but delicate and tasty dishes.'

'We could split a tin of bully.'

'There you go again; you've got no soul, I'm afraid, my Tony. Here am I really beginning to enjoy myself and you sit there looking like the chief mourner at some bloody funeral.'

'That's an idea. Sole. That's what we'll have.'

'Oh, go to hell!' said Harvey, throwing his book at Allen's head.

At Cairo's main station they put what little kit they carried with them into a taxi and told the driver to go to Shepheards.

They walked up the steps to the entrance, and as they crossed the terrace the immaculately-dressed officers sitting drinking with their girl friends stared almost angrily at the two dusty, sun-blackened officers in their dirty and stained drill with three months' growth of hair on their heads and faces.

In his room Allen's servant from the base was waiting with his kit. Allen was cheered by the sight of the freshly-starched uniform that Saïd had laid out for him on the bed.

'Let's have a bath, Saïd,' Allen suggested, stepping out of the clothes he had not taken off for the last week. 'You can take these filthy things away and burn them; I never want to see them again.'

He went into the bathroom with its tiled walls and chromium fittings. It was something he had often wondered if he would ever see again. He began to play with the taps, turning them on and off, and the sound of running water came musically to his ears.

After he had climbed into the bath there came a knock on the bedroom door. Saïd opened it, and in marched Harvey followed by his servant ushering in a hotel *suffragi* bearing a tray containing glasses and a bottle of champagne.

'Where are you, Tony?' called Harvey.

'Allen Pasha, he bathing,' announced Saïd. Harvey led the procession into the bathroom.

'Just a drop of the old widow to launch the leave with, me boy.' And to the *suffragi* he said:

'Step forward, my slightly sunburned friend, bearing the blissful liquid.'

The *suffragi* grinned, not understanding a word.

Harvey took the bottle and unwrapping the silver paper and wire he forced up the cork with an explosion that shot some of the wine over Allen.

'There you are, now you can tell 'em at home you used to bathe in the stuff when you were campaigning out East.'

He handed Allen a brimming glass, waved the grinning servants from the bathroom, and sat down on the lavatory seat.

'Here's to us, and may we live to rue the day, as they say. If paradise is no better than this I don't think I shall grumble.'

'Cheers, Pete! Good luck, and here's to our leave.'

It was the first alcohol the men had tasted for three months. They quickly emptied the bottle, and Harvey went back to his room, where the barber was waiting.

They dined at a roof-garden cabaret and drank more champagne. Harvey chose his food with considerable care and ate it with great enjoyment, grinning happily. The cabaret was mediocre, but the girls made up for it with their enthusiasm.

'That little one with the fair hair and the big blue eyes, now she looks as though she might have possibilities,' he said to Allen, who was by now beginning to feel the effects of the sparkling wine.

Shortly afterwards the girl happened to come towards their table on her way to the dressing-room, and as she was about to pass ,Harvey grinned up at her.

'Would you like a drink?' he asked. The girl stopped at the table and smiled at the two officers.

'Thank you, I would like.'

Allen stood up and offered her a chair. She was quite pretty and her short skirt revealed long and well-shaped legs.

'I'm Olga,' she announced. 'What is your names?'

She spoke attractive but very broken English; later she told them that she came from Hungary.

'Haven't you got a little friend who would care to join us?' Harvey enquired after a little while.

'I could bring Lila; she is my friend, you see me dancing with her just now eh?'

'Yes, you go and fetch Lila,' said Harvey, and when she had disappeared through the dressing-room door Harvey said to his friend:

'Nice little thing, isn't she: we should have a very sociable evening, don't you think?'

In a few minutes Olga came back with a dark and quite pretty girl of about twenty.

'Zis is my friend Lila,' she said, and the two sat down. The waiter brought more glasses and Harvey poured out the champagne.

Allen danced with Lila, but felt a little embarrassed for she also was wearing her cabaret costume which consisted of a sleeveless tunic and a skirt that reached nowhere near her knees. He felt the eyes of some of the more senior officers, dancing with their wives or unattractive nurses, upon him. Or were they on the thighs of his engaging partner? He was beginning not to care very much, the champagne was giving him courage and making him reckless. He even thought for a moment that Mary would be happy if she knew he was enjoying himself.

When they reached their table, at the end of several dances, Harvey was endeavouring to persuade Olga to spend the night with him.

'You very naughty man,' she was saying. 'What would my mama say if she could hear you? She always warn me about you British officers. Olga, she say, you never listen to these men. They mean very bad for young girls like you.'

'But I'm not asking her, it's her little daughter that I'm putting the question to. What about Lila? Let's make it a foursome.'

'Hold it,' interrupted Allen. 'Include me out, I've had about enough for my first night. After this I'm home to bed alone.'

'Suit yourself, me boy, I could probably keep both of them happy myself.'

The girls laughed, and Olga exclaimed amidst her giggles:

'Oh, you English, what terrible men you are! Are they all like you in England?'

They danced until well after midnight, and drank more champagne. When at last Allen could drink no more and the whole place seemed to him to be revolving, he said:

'Pete, I'm away before I pass out.'

Harvey spoke to Olga: 'Go and get your things and hurry up. We'll take Tony home first.'

Lila said good-bye and thanked them for the evening. She told Tony she hoped he would be better in the morning, then she went off with Olga. Harvey watched them go through the door of the dressing-room. For a moment or so after the door had closed on them he sat gazing at it, the gentle grin playing about his firm mouth and puckering the corners of his smiling eyes as he visualized again the rounded thighs and attractive little rump that Olga had revealed as she ran up the three steps to the door. He sighed, and turned to Allen.

'On your feet, soldier, and so to our virtuous couches.'

'But what about Olga?'

'Little Olga can go to her own couch. Come along.' And he hustled Allen across the floor and into the lift.

By the time they reached the hotel the champagne had done its work on Allen, who never remembered his friend supporting him to his room. Eventually they reached it and Harvey lifted him on to the bed and undressed him, and turning out the light went back to his room to dream, in all its vivid and horrid detail, of the ambushing of the two Lancias.

Allen awoke with a headache and fierce thirst. When

Saïd brought him his tea he was quickly sent off again to find some aspirin. He lay in the comfortable old-fashioned brass bedstead gazing at the Victorian striped wallpaper. He realized he had not been so comfortable for many months, and now he had spoilt his pleasure by drinking too much and making himself ill. He regretted he had wasted one evening of his all-too-short leave.

That morning the two officers went to the Gezira Sporting Club and sat on the terrace watching the bathers in the crowded swimming-pool.

'Feeling better, me boy?' inquired Harvey. 'Because if you're not, just feast your eyes on the little thing in the red costume standing by the spring-board.'

'God, don't you ever think of anything else?'

'Not unless I'm forced to. You know, what you need is a John Collins. It will make the world turn more smoothly for you. It's the vibrations that upset you and spoil your sight. Come along before you commit suicide.'

They went into the cool, crowded bar, and sipped their long powerful drinks.

'This is so pleasant and such a contrast to the last few months that I just can't relax and enjoy it; I keep thinking about going back on Saturday. I wish to God we didn't have to,' said Allen.

'You don't have to; you could always go sick. Tell 'em you get headaches or something like that. Something they can never really check up on. They'd send you off to see a psychiatrist who'd ask you all sorts of intimate questions about your sex life or lack of it, and in the end he'll say you're suffering from battle neurosis. You would be given a job at the base or be sent home to Mary if you wished, and I'm sure she would welcome you. Why, you could probably be married within the next three months if you did that.'

Allen looked at his friend for a few moments. He said:

'And you think I could live with myself if I did that?'

'Well, there would be plenty like you, and at least you've done something towards it. It's not as though you've never been near the front line like most of the people drinking at this bar.'

'You know I couldn't pack it in.'

'Of course you couldn't. If I thought you could I wouldn't spend my time drinking and whoring with you. Your trouble is you don't live. You don't give yourself to the moment. You think of the future with that fertile imagination of yours and visualize all the beastly things that could possibly happen to you, and bang! there goes the present, all wasted. People like you and me, we have no ties, no one dependent on us. We can take each day as it comes and live calmly by the standards we set ourselves. What an opportunity to practise the real art of living and at the same time teach ourselves the unimportance of death. But that's enough philosophizing for one morning. Come on, drink up, let's have some more before lunch.'

After a heavy meal they spent the rest of the afternoon at the pool, swimming, and sleeping in the sun, then at length they dressed and calling a taxi, drove back over the bridge towards Cairo.

'Let's have a look at Groppi's,' suggested Harvey. 'I believe all the Cairo lovelies foregather there for tea. There must be a couple just waiting for us if the short-range desert group haven't already bagged them.'

The band was playing a slow fox-trot and the tiny floor was crowded with uniformed officers dancing with the pretty Egyptian and European girls they were not permitted to take to the British clubs.

Harvey and Allen found a vacant table and ordered tea. Harvey looked around and after a few moments said:

'See that little lovely in the white dress by the pillar over there. I shall offer her the pleasure of dancing with me.'

He got up and went across to the girl, and after a few words was following his partner towards the dance floor. Allen watched the couple moving slowly to the pleasant rhythm of the orchestra. He had no desire to dance. So far he had seen no one worth asking. He envied Harvey's capacity for enjoyment. His friend seemed to drag every ounce of pleasure out of life. He wished he could do the same.

The music ceased and the couples were returning to the tables. Harvey sat down with his partner and grinned across at Allen who remained sitting there alone. Soon the orchestra began to play a tango and Harvey took his partner on to the floor again. After watching them for a while Allen let his glance wander about the room and then for the first time he saw Dolores. She was sitting at a table with two elderly ladies. Her face was small and oval, her eyes dark, but not as dark as her jet-black hair. She was dressed in a frock of a navy blue material which contrasted with the chain of jasmine she wore about her slender neck. All these things Allen noticed besides the fact that she was very young and very beautiful. He looked away because she had caught his stare, and he did not wish to appear rude, but within a minute he was forced to turn his head and look at her again, and as he glanced at her he noticed that she was looking straight at him. He tried to look away but immediately his eyes returned to her face as if drawn by a magnet. And still she looked at him, while her two companions continued their conversation. And now about

her lips was the faintest of smiles, both mocking and pro-
vocative. Allen felt strangely excited, but before he could
analyse his feelings he got to his feet and walked across to
her table and all the way their eyes were fixed upon each
other.

'May I have the pleasure of this dance?' he asked.

She smiled at him and spoke to her companions in a
language which he could not identify. As yet she had not
spoken to him. Now he was following her between the
tables towards the dance floor. She was small, scarcely
more than five feet two or so but beautifully proportioned,
and as she walked her small hips swayed in the tightly
fitting dress. They reached the dance floor, and she turned
to wait for him. He put his arm around her, and she was
soft and smelt of jasmine, and her hair was perfumed. She
smiled at him, and he bent over her, and a lock of her hair
touched his cheek. He looked into her eyes, and then their
cheeks were together as they danced in perfect unison.
For a few moments he tried to gather his thoughts to think
of something to say, but everything that came to his mind
was trivial, and so they danced without speaking. Then at
last she sighed, and as he looked into her face she said:

'I thought that you would never speak to me.'

'Did you want me to?'

She ignored the question. Instead she asked:

'Do you not wish to know my name?'

He listened delightedly to her English, which was
obviously not her tongue but which she spoke with a
charming accent.

'Answer me!' she ordered.

'Tell me your name, then,' said Allen, smiling down at
the pretty girl.

'Dolores. Do you wish me to tell you all my names?'

'Please.'

'Then I will make a beginning. I am Dolores Maria Pilar . . .'

But he did not catch the long list that rolled so sibilantly from her tongue.

'You must be Spanish.'

'Ah, he is clever too.'

'Why do you mock me?'

'What is mock me?'

'Tease me.'

'I don't mean to.'

'Let's sit down for a while. Will you come back to my table?'

'And my mother and aunt, what will they say? You had better come to our table. They will go soon, and who knows, perhaps if they like you a little they may let me stay for a while. That is, of course, if you would wish it.'

'Of course I should wish it,' replied Allen.

She led him to her table and it was only when she was about to introduce him to the two ladies that she remembered she did not even know his name.

The handsome but slightly austere women could speak very little English. Dolores's mother offered him some coffee, and another cup was brought, and then Dolores, smiling at him, commenced speaking to her mother in Spanish. The conversation continued for some time, the other woman occasionally joining in with a few words, and then at last Dolores spoke again to Allen.

'If you wish, I may stay, but only if you will bring me home. It is not far; our flat is in Soliman Pasha.'

The two women eventually got up from the table. They appeared a little reluctant to leave Dolores, but after making her promise to be home early they left, and almost before they were out of the ballroom Dolores moved her chair a little closer to Allen saying:

'Now we can really enjoy ourselves; please tell me again your name.'

'Tony Allen.'

'I shall call you Antonio.'

'I'd rather you didn't; anything but Antonio.'

'You don't like Spanish, eh?'

'Very much, but not Antonio.'

Dolores laughed happily.

'You like dancing?'

'Sometimes.'

'Very well, we shall dance.'

And as they danced he inquired:

'Do you come here often?'

'No, only with my mother and aunt, and that is, how you say, occasionally? You see,' she continued, 'my family, they are very strict, and they do not allow me to come here by myself, but today I see you sitting there alone and you look so brown and handsome, so I tell my mother to let me stay with you for a while. The English officers always behave so well.'

Allen, listening to her, could not make up his mind whether or not she was mocking him. She spoke so quickly and so animatedly in a broken English which was entirely fascinating.

'How old are you?' she inquired.

'Twenty-one.'

'Are you married?'

'No.'

'Engaged?'

'No.'

'Do you have a sweetheart?'

'Yes.'

'Where is she?'

'In England.'

72

'Is it very beautiful there?'

'Yes.'

'But cold and foggy, yes?'

'Sometimes.'

Dolores continued to ask question after question. Allen only had time to answer in monosyllables before she burst upon him with another, until at last she announced:

'Ah, I am so happy!'

'Why?' he asked.

'Because I like it here. I have never been here before alone with a boy friend, such a beautiful one too!'

They were both laughing now.

'By the way, if I may be permitted to ask you a question to make up for all the ones you have asked me, how old are you?'

She hesitated for a moment before replying, then she said very rapidly:

'I am sixteen, but next month I will be seventeen.'

Allen was already completely captivated by the young girl. Such sparkle and vivaciousness was something entirely new to him. It did not exist among the few English girls of his acquaintance. He studied her, and she saw his eyes upon her, and her face became serious. Then Harvey was standing at the table.

He grinned at Dolores and seated himself in a vacant chair. He looked at Allen and said, 'You're not deserting me too, or are you, old friend of mine?'

'I thought you were enjoying yourself, at least you seemed to be the last time I saw you.'

'If you hadn't had your mind on other things you might have noticed her leave well over an hour ago, since when I've been sitting in unhappy solitude.'

Allen laughed and introduced his friend to Dolores. He said:

'I've promised to take Dolores home.'

'It is not necessary,' she interrupted, her dark eyes flashing and hinting of hidden fury.

'No!' exclaimed Allen, sensing the sudden change in her mood. 'What I was trying to tell you', he looked at his friend, 'was that the only way I could persuade Dolores's mother to allow her to stay was by promising to bring her safely home when the dancing finishes.'

'In that case I'd better beat it,' laughed Harvey. 'I'm probably one of those from whom you are supposed to be protecting Dolores.'

'Don't be silly, we'll all go together,' announced Allen, but he knew that the girl resented his friend's intrusion and was very relieved when Harvey insisted, 'No, now that you seem so happily occupied I think I'll pop off and attend to one or two things I've had in mind.' And without giving Allen the opportunity of arguing, he stood up and after shaking hands with Dolores he said to Allen, 'See you later on,' and walked away from the table. When he had gone Dolores asked:

'Is he your friend?'

'Yes, we're in the same Regiment.'

'Have you known him a long time?'

'No, not very long, several months that's all; only since I came to Egypt.'

'He is a cruel man, I think.'

'No, he's not. I think he's quite the opposite of that. He makes a good friend.'

'But he is not good to women; I can tell by the way he looked at me.'

'I'm afraid I wouldn't understand about that, I'm not a woman.'

Now they were laughing again as they walked towards the dance floor and Harvey was forgotten, for Allen was enjoying himself too much to worry about his friend whom he knew to be quite capable of amusing himself on his own.

Soon the dancing had finished and it was time to leave. The man and the girl stood on the pavement outside Groppi's watching the noisy traffic as it swept around the circle where the several streets intersected. Allen tried in vain to signal a passing taxi, but Dolores persuaded him to walk the few hundred yards to the block of flats where she lived. When eventually they reached the building and Dolores was entering the lift he said:

'Perhaps I should say good-bye here. It has been such a lovely evening.'

'No, no, you must take me home, all the way. You promised to my mother.'

'All right, if you insist,' and he was happy to be persuaded.

They stopped the lift on the third floor and walking down a short corridor Dolores pressed the bell of a door leading to one of the suites.

An elderly maidservant answered the summons and they went inside, Dolores leading the way to a spacious lounge, beautifully furnished and appointed. The two ladies whom he had met earlier in the afternoon were seated in comfortable tall-backed chairs. They greeted him with a smile, and Dolores's mother ordered the servant to bring wine. She spoke in Spanish.

'Victoria has been with us ever since I was a baby,' explained Dolores.

'That's not very long, is it?'

'Now you tease me, eh?'

They talked happily, joking with each other while the elderly women looked on scarcely understanding their conversation. The wine was heavy, filling him with con-

75

tentment. The desert, and his first experiences of battle, were far away from his thoughts, and in the pleasant surroundings listening to the gay chatter of his pretty companion he became relaxed and at ease for the first time in many months.

The mother was speaking.

'Dolores, play for us,' and after a little argument in Spanish the young girl took from a corner of the room a beribboned guitar, and idly fingering a few sonorous chords she inquired of Allen,

'Do you know any Spanish music?'

'A little, but I am afraid I don't remember the names. There is one song I know, *La Paloma*. Can you play it?'

'*La Paloma* is not Spanish, it is Mexican, and a very old song. There is a story that when the Emperor Maximilian was to be executed the captain of the firing squad asked him if he had a last request to make, and the Emperor replied that he would very much like to hear *La Paloma* sung once again before he died, and so they fetched a gipsy girl with a guitar and she sang and played it to him. Now I shall play it for you.' But her innocent remark caused an icy chill to strike at the man which was only dispelled by the haunting melody given such expression by the girl's sweet voice.

Harvey was seated on a high stool in a popular bar near the Turf Club.

'Abdul!' he called to the handsome Sudanese with the three scars on each cheek. 'Whisky *moya*, and make it a big one.'

'Coming, sair.'

The drink at his elbow, he studied with glassy eyes the officers crowding the bar, hoping to recognize an acquaintance, but he saw no one he knew. He swallowed the drink at a gulp, and placing the empty glass with a bang on the wooden bar, he ordered another.

Two officers standing behind him were talking.

'You know, it's jolly nice being able to discuss the whole thing over a friendly drink,' one was saying.

'Of course, old man,' said the other who was wearing the G.H.Q. badge on his arm. 'It's the personal contact that always counts. Naturally we're not deliberately going out of our way to upset you people down at the Depot when a little mutual understanding will sort things out. Now, what's the trouble? If there's anything I can do for you, you've only got to ask.'

'Well, old chap, it's about Anderson. I know he did remarkably well at his O.C.T.U. and I must admit it, he's passed out top of practically all his courses at the Depot, but the fact remains, he's a Blue and we're desperately short of good bats at the moment. After all, we're due to play you people in a few weeks' time. Now I'm sure you wouldn't like it said that you posted all our good blokes to the desert so that we couldn't put up a decent side against you, would you?'

'Steady, old boy, you've got us entirely wrong.'

'Well, all we're asking is just to keep young Anderson until we can get someone to take his place and that shouldn't take very long at the rate they're posting them out from the U.K. now. Of course, the chap's as keen as mustard to get up to the desert, but I can't help feeling that this war isn't going to finish tomorrow and so there's no need to rush into it. He'll get his chance, and all in good time, so what do a few weeks matter one way or another?'

Harvey watched the G.H.Q. man lean forward and rest a small note-book on the bar. He took from his breast pocket a tiny gold pencil threaded through a buttonhole on a thin gold chain.

'Anderson, you said, that's the name?'

'Yes, old boy, and it's jolly decent of you, giving us a chance to make a game of it like this.'

'Well, let's hope your Anderson doesn't make a duck after all you and I have done for him.'

'I'll murder the sod if he does. Now, what are you going to have old man? This calls for a little celebration.'

Harvey was about to interrupt. The whisky was having its effect and he had great difficulty in controlling his anger. He thought of Skeffington up there in the desert, hating and dreading every day that dawned, but still with what little courage he possessed forcing himself to stick it out, and Allen, his friend, whose sensitive nature must have rebelled at the bloodshed and the primitiveness of their existence, and poor old Walters and the men, all enduring it for some reason or another while these people here at the base took good care that nothing, not even the war, should interfere with their pleasures. The match was more important than the battle!

'Christ!' he exclaimed aloud, and called for another whisky. He was feeling more and more depressed. He had been looking forward to a cheerful and riotous night out with Allen, but his friend had met a pretty girl and had gone off with her, and was probably by now sitting down to a good dinner in some comfortable home. Good luck to him, too, he thought. Here he was after weeks in the desert, absolutely fed up to the teeth, and wishing only for the company of his own kind. He began to toy with the idea of returning to the squadron before his leave expired. He realized that would be ridiculous, but when he was left to himself life always seemed at its worst. He kept thinking of Vera. They had been happy enough for the first few years of their marriage; then gradually they had drifted apart. His business had occupied his thoughts and energies, he had to travel a great deal and often he was forced to leave her alone for many weeks at a time while he visited other countries in the course of his work. So she had become bored and felt herself neglected until that afternoon when she had met Jackson at the Harris's cocktail party. How well he remembered that fateful afternoon. He was to have gone on there after a conference at the office, but he had been inadvertently held up and then it was too late, so he had telephoned the Harris's and left a message for Vera telling her not to wait for him, and Jackson had driven her home. Three months later she had gone away with him. Only then did he realize what she meant to him. But he had never seen her again except in his dreams, and all the time he remembered her with a tenderness that tore at his heart. He thought of Allen in his youthfulness and innocence protesting his love for Mary. Why, neither of them even understood the meaning of the word, of that he was certain. Love was something that grew out of companionship, and only came after two people had lived together for a long time – all else was passion.

He walked out of the bar, reeling a little as he went. A G.H.Q. officer loudly remarked to his companion as Harvey brushed against him.

'Some chaps need a little discipline.'

'Muck off!' snarled Harvey, and the outraged officer, catching the cruel glint in Harvey's eyes, quickly engaged himself in conversation with his neighbour.

Out in the street Harvey hailed a taxi.

'Do you know Denise's House?'

'Yes, sair, all officers going there,' grinned the driver.

A young Egyptian girl opened the door, and he followed her inside. She led him into a large room with a bar along one wall at which a number of officers stood drinking. A radiogram was playing, and several couples were dancing.

'You want to dance?' inquired the girl.

'No, I want a drink first. You like to have one with me?'

'Champagne,' came the quick request.

He ordered a whisky and a half-bottle of champagne. Leaning his back against the bar he watched the dancers. Most of the officers were in various stages of intoxication. He noticed two midshipmen, probably on leave from Alexandria. Neither looked more than sixteen, but they were very handsome and caused quite a stir among the girls of the establishment. The girls wore evening dress; some were European, others Eastern, all were reasonably attractive and young, and they appeared to be enjoying themselves.

'What's your name?' he asked his companion.

'Amira.'

'Shall we dance, Amira?'

She nestled in his arms as they moved slowly round the room. Her perfume was pleasant. He was beginning to enjoy himself, beginning at last to forget for a while. His mouth relaxed and the tight little lines at the corners were gone. He pressed her close to him and her breasts lost their shape against his tunic. Just before the music ceased she whispered into his ear:

'You come with me, eh?'

She led him by the hand to a room upstairs and locked the door. Then she turned to him, and stretching her arms around his neck kissed him long and passionately on the lips. Moments later she gently disengaged herself from his embrace and unfastening her dress at the back, she lifted it over her head. She was naked except for her stockings and a flimsy white suspender belt that contrasted excitingly with her brown skin. When it was over he paid her and returned to the bar. Towards morning the room was less crowded but the radiogram still played for the few couples who were dancing. He said to the girl with whom he was waltzing.

'Yvonne, what about showing me your bedroom?'

'Come along then, chéri,' and hand in hand they climbed the thickly-carpeted stairs, her skirt rustling as she went.

The sun had scarcely risen when Allen awoke on the morning after his meeting with the young Spanish girl, and it was with some surprise that he realized he had been thinking of Dolores. Before, on awakening, he had always let his thoughts wander pleasantly to Mary. He got up and rang the bell, and ordered the *suffragi* who answered its summons to find Saïd.

When he had bathed and dressed he went into Harvey's room, but it was unoccupied, the bed still undisturbed. He left a note for his friend.

'Sorry I missed you; spending the day with Dolores. See you tonight if you're not too worn out! – Tony.'

He breakfasted in his room, waited on by Saïd; had one more look for Harvey who still had not returned, then went out into the street and walked about until it was time to call for Dolores. He was happy and excited and the minutes did not pass quickly enough for him, but at last he was walking with her down Soliman Pasha towards Kasr-el-Nil.

'Let's take a *ghari?*' he suggested, and when they had found one he directed the driver to Mena House.

It was a beautiful, warm, sunny morning and he sat close to Dolores on the small seat. He wondered if he dare take her hand, which was close to his – and then he thought of Mary and fought against the desire.

Dolores wore a plain white frock and looked extraordinarily young and pretty. He stole a glance at her face and noticed that she was smiling happily. She chattered merrily all the way down the long straight road that led to the Pyramids, firing question after question at him. She wanted to know all about England, his home, his family, his sweetheart, and she listened with interest to everything he had to tell her. Then she took hold of his hand and exclaimed.

'I am so happy, Tony, why can't we do this every day?'

'Well, for one thing the poor horses would soon get tired, and besides one day you'd run out of questions and then you'd become bored with me.'

'Do I annoy you with all my questions?'

'Of course not. I love it, I could listen to your chatter for hours.'

She was still holding his hand when they came to the Mena House Hotel.

They spent the morning in and out of the swimming-pool. She looked very lovely in her black costume, and Allen noticed many admiring glances cast in her direction. Once, in the water, she had tried to push him under, and he had struggled with her and in the flurry of threshing limbs and twisting bodies his hand had burned with the feel of her, but she seemed unconscious of it as she laughed and splashed water into his face.

They had lunch at a table near the pool, letting the sun dry their costumes as they ate. Then they lay on the grass close to each other, and the wine they had drunk and the afternoon heat and the swimming made them tired, and they soon fell asleep and were not disturbed by the shouts and splashes from the pool.

In the late afternoon they left the hotel and walked up the hill towards the Pyramids. They stood to watch a couple of energetic soldiers climbing to the top of one of them; it looked hard work scrambling up from one huge block of stone to the next, but the two men did not seem to worry about the heat.

'What about it, Dolores, shall we try?'

'I'm not dressed for such exercise,' she laughed, looking down at her frock.

They strolled down the path to the Sphinx and gazed at the huge stone figure uncovered from the sand, with the damaged nose that was reputed to have suffered from a ball fired from one of Napoleon's cannons. On the way back it became dark, and Allen wanted to take her in his arms, but the thought of being disloyal to Mary discouraged him and during the long ride home they held hands, silently occupied with their thoughts.

The days passed far too swiftly for Allen, who now spent all his time with Dolores, shamelessly leaving his friend to find his own amusements; in fact, they seldom saw each other for Harvey usually returned to their hotel long after Allen had breakfasted and gone out. Allen was inclined to be a little smug about his friend's nocturnal activities. He disapproved of his heavy drinking and his insatiable desire for prostitutes. He asked himself why Harvey could not find a nice girl like Dolores; someone with whom he could pass the time without recourse to drink and the other thing, but it was something he did not understand and he ceased to worry about it.

It was the last day of their leave. The next morning they were catching the train that would take them back to the squadron. Allen had been spending the day with Dolores, and now they were having tea at Groppi's where he had first met her. He was silent, brooding upon his return to the desert. Dolores knew nothing of this, since for security reasons he had not told her that his Regiment was stationed in the desert, and she understood that he was waiting to be posted somewhere or other. She knew about the security regulations and had refrained from questioning him, not wishing to be embarrassed by his refusing to answer her.

They were dancing, and the band was playing *Stardust*, a melody that was new and haunting. Dolores softly hummed the tune as she danced with her mouth close to Allen's ear as she bent over her. Then he said:

'You do not speak for a long time. Why you are so very serious, Tony?'

For a moment he was silent, then he replied:

'Because after today I shan't be seeing you, that's all.'

'You mean you do not wish to continue seeing me?'

'No, don't be silly.'

'What then? Is it because of your sweetheart?'

'No, of course not.'

'Then what is it? I do not understand.' She smiled up at him. Then it suddenly dawned upon her. She inquired breathlessly:

'You're not going away, Tony?'

'Yes, I am, I'm afraid. Tomorrow morning I'm leaving Egypt.'

She did not speak and he was thinking about what he had told her. It was a little heroic, he thought, the soldier's farewell, but he was enjoying the moment. Then he looked at her but she quickly turned her head away from him, and he knew she was crying, and he could not help feeling flattered until he began to worry about people noticing him with a girl who was in tears. Somehow he got her outside and into a taxi. It was only a minute's ride to Dolores's flat, and she was still crying and dabbing at her eyes with a tiny handkerchief as they were going up in the lift.

'Stop it, Dolores. What will your mother think?'

'She will understand,' she sobbed, and they were the first words she had spoken since he had told her.

'You must not mention it to her. What I have just told you is secret,' and he knew he was being cruel and robbing her of all comfort, and that knowledge gave him a perverse pleasure.

'We had better go back and ride around in a *ghari* until you stop crying,' he suggested, and she nodded agreement through her tears.

He told the driver to go to the Pyramids, intending to turn back when Dolores had recovered. He did not wish to be very late since it was their last night in Cairo and he had promised to meet Harvey for a drink.

'Feeling better?' he inquired, breaking the long silence. They had reached Gezira and still she had not spoken.

'Thank you.'

'Then shall we turn round?'

'You want me to go home?'

'Of course not, but there is so much to do. I must be early tonight.'

'You don't wish to take me to the Pyramids?' Before he could reply she continued:

'Oh Tony, you don't understand. I shall miss you so much. Can't you stay, couldn't you leave the army and get a job? My family would find one for you. Please stay!'

'Don't Dolores, you know that's quite impossible.' He knew he was hurting the girl by showing no sympathy and allowing her to lay bare the secret longings and desires of her young heart, and because he was enjoying the situation he listened to her arguments. Then they were at the end of the road leading to the Pyramids.

He told the driver to wait while they walked up the hill towards the three looming Pyramids bathed in the soft moonlight. Again they were holding hands and this time she clutched his tightly. They stood in an alcove at the base of one of the Pyramids gazing up at Cheops. For a moment they looked solemnly into each other's eyes, then she was in his arms, fastening her soft mouth on his. Allen felt the desire for her surge through his blood and he no longer fought against it. He pulled her down into the sand, and for a while they lay there silently, their lips pressed hungrily together. She sighed as hesitantly and gently his fingers began to caress the soft warm body snuggled in his arms.

'Oh, Tony,' she whispered as she clung to him. 'I love you so much, please say you love me just a little bit.'

'I adore you, my darling,' he murmured, enraptured by the treasure that was his to take.

Much later, as they held each other closely in the *ghari* that was taking them back to Cairo, Dolores asked,

'I wonder if you still really want to see me again, now that I let you make love to me.'

'Of course, I do, my darling,' he answered, but his thoughts were all confused and he wished that the *ghari* driver would make the horses go a little faster, for he wanted to be alone to think things out. The ecstasy he had experienced a little while ago was quickly followed by a sense of guilt. He knew that he would be incapable of facing Dolores's mother again.

Just before the *ghari* stopped outside the block of flats in Soliman Pasha, he put his arms around her and kissed her.

'I'll be thinking of you always, my love. Write to me often, and just as soon as I can get back to Cairo I'll come to you.'

The *ghari* stopped, and she clung to him, the tears streaming down her face.

'Don't cry, Dolores, I promise you I'll come back to you,' he said. At last she took her arms from about his neck.

'*Vaya con Dios querido mio*,' she murmured, then she climbed out of the *ghari* and ran into the building.

3

The squadron continued its patrolling activities in the forward area, and since neither side was yet ready to commit its forces to a major engagement, it had so far sustained no casualties. The men were gaining in experience and confidence, and even Major Walters was becoming more effective as its commander, particularly so after the recent occasion on which the colonel had spoken to him.

'Walters,' he had begun, 'I'm not too happy about your squadron. Very soon, I expect, we shall be seeing some action, not the sort of stuff we've all been going through, but some real tough battles. If the squadron's not up to standard, then both tanks and crews will be wasted. To be quite frank with you, I have several times toyed with the idea of replacing you, but I don't like doing it and it won't be necessary if you tighten things up a bit. Get used to handling the squadron – you've got the petrol now. Practise controlling the whole squadron; if chaps start going off on their own you've lost that control, so see what you can do to improve things a bit.'

That interview had considerably upset Walters, but he was determined not to suffer the disgrace of being replaced, and so he devoted all his energies to mastering his command, and eventually began to succeed. When the time was ready for the attack the colonel was glad that he had given him the chance to make good.

The advance started at first light. The tanks, followed by the infantry in Bren carriers, had moved up during the hours of darkness, and along almost the whole of the front the enemy had been taken by complete surprise.

As it grew light the squadron could be seen scarcely a thousand yards from its objective, the aerodrome, which according to intelligence reports was guarded by an infantry battalion and supported by guns that could be used either against aircraft or tanks.

Major Walters, stimulated by the scale of the offensive, and encouraged by the close proximity of the remainder of the Regiment, was full of confidence. At last he had complete control of the tanks. His voice came over the wireless:

'Hullo Bolo, Bolo calling, speed up and engage targets as you sight them. Over.'

The Italians had been caught entirely unawares. The commanders of the leading tanks could hear clearly above the noise of their vehicles, the shouting and yelling of the enemy as they tried to rouse their sleeping troops. Then the firing started. Italians in slit trenches were using rifles and Bredas against the well-protected tanks which were accurately returning the fire with their machine-guns.

Hargreaves's troop had already overrun the first slit trench, killing and wounding its defenders. Two Italians climbed out, unharmed, from another and began to run towards the shelter of some nearby buildings, but the driver of the tank nearest to them, ignoring the orders of his commander, pressed his foot upon the accelerator, and ran both the men down before they had covered fifty yards. Hearing an agonized shriek the leading man looked round, and seeing his comrade pulped beneath the heavy track he stood still, and raised his arms above his head; but the driver, filled with the flush of his first success was without mercy, and the Italian died, too petrified either to move or cry out.

The artillery began to fire on the tanks, giving away their positions by the bright muzzle flashes.

'Hullo Bolo, Bolo calling, overrun the guns. Over,' came the voice of Walters and the squadron bore down on their targets in a wide arc, every weapon blazing.

One of the tanks had stopped and over the wireless its commander could be heard asking for assistance.

'Hullo Bolo, Bolo Seven calling, have been – ah–h–h. . .' A dreadful scream of fear and agony, horribly distorted by the wireless, was heard throughout the entire squadron.

Captain Harvey immediately ordered his driver to make for the tank, but even as he looked at it, judging his distance, it became a huge brilliant ball of flame surmounted by a spiralling column of thick black smoke. Harvey watched helplessly as its driver frantically flung open the vizor and commenced to struggle out, but the heat quickly conquered the wretched man, and he suddenly collapsed across the front of the tank for all to witness his cremation. Harvey, realizing that there was nothing further he could do for the crew, ordered his driver to speed up and rejoin the squadron, which by this time was well in among the guns. These had by now ceased firing, the crews still alive having surrendered.

Down one of the runways, from the far end of the landing strip, roared the three engines of a Savoia at full boost, its occupants hoping to escape capture, but its course was bringing it every second nearer to the squadron and still it was not airborne. Now almost every tank was firing at it, the tracer floating into the plane along the whole length of its fuselage. Then it was airborne, but as its wheels left the runway a tracer exploded the petrol tank; blazing wreckage was scattered over the desert, sending up the black spiralling smoke in company with Bolo 7.

Most of the infantry battalion were only too willing to surrender, and the men began to collect in a large group with their weapons. Walters signalled to the prisoners to form up and march in the direction of a large yellow marquee. Suddenly small-arms fire was directed on the squadron by some of the airmen who were prepared to make more of a fight for it than the infantry who were supposed to protect them. Allen's troop was ordered to deal with these men while Walters instructed his gunner to fire over the heads of the prisoners, now lying down endeavouring to shield themselves from their comrades' fire which was coming very close to them. There were shouts in Italian from the prisoners, and then with the weapons that had not yet been taken from them they commenced firing at the airmen and at the same time calling upon them to surrender. Thus persuaded by Allen's troop and their own countrymen, the airmen at last gave in, and the capture of the aerodrome was the squadron's first victory.

The infantry had rapidly followed up to disarm the prisoners and take charge of them until they could be sent back to the base. The wounded were accommodated in the yellow marquee and tended by Italian volunteers.

The squadron had lost two tanks in the short engagement. Sergeant Gregson and his crew in Bolo 7 were dead and the tank still burned, assailing the nostrils of the men with the heavy, pungent stench of oil.

Second-Lieutenant Turner's tank had been hit in the early stages of the battle, but since the turret was undamaged that officer had ordered his gunner to continue firing until the action was over; then, when the opposition had been silenced, he had jumped out in company with his gunner and operator to find out what damage had been sustained. The shell had hit the front of the tank right beneath the driver's compartment. The vizor was closed but Turner could see from the wreckage that Norman, his young driver, must be seriously hurt.

'Martin,' he said to his gunner, 'see if you can get through from inside the turret to open up the vizor.'

While the gunner climbed back on to the tank Turner studied the splintered hull, and bending down to look underneath he noticed blood dripping through the jagged hole made by the shell and forming a dark and widening stain on the pale sand.

The vizor was slowly opening, pushed upwards and outwards by Martin's blood-covered hand. Turner saw Norman sitting back in his seat, his face pale and clammy, his lips trembling, the hands still grasping the sticks. He seemed to recognize Turner, and in a voice that was scarcely more than a feeble whisper he murmured piteously:

'Oh, please help me, sir. I can't move, sir. I'm not badly hurt, am I, sir?' He continued to gasp in short plaintive sentences.

'I'm sorry, sir. I can't help it, sir. Oh, don't let me die, please, sir. Please try and help me, sir,' he implored.

Looking closer the men could see the horror of Norman's body. A small shell had penetrated the tank's hull at a point directly between Norman's feet, shattering his legs into a shapeless mass of bloody flesh mixed with the white of blood-stained bone. His shorts were wet with blood and through a jagged tear protruded a little piece of glistening intestine.

'Get the morphia, Martin, before you climb out,' ordered Turner, sickened and revolted by what he saw.

'Don't hurt me, sir. I'm sorry, sir.' Still the voice of Norman gasped on.

'Of course we're not going to hurt you, old chap. Don't you worry, we'll have you fixed up in no time, but first I'll give you a shot of morphia to make you more comfortable.'

Turner sat on the front of the tank and leaning inside he stuck the needle into the wounded man's arm and squeezed hard on the container.

'There's some tablets here too, sir,' announced Martin who was searching in the first-aid box.

'Let's have them as well', snapped Turner, and he pushed two of the tiny white pills between Norman's ashen lips, but already the blood had started to come, forcing the tablets from his mouth, and with a terrified choking gurgle the tortured man collapsed; and falling forward his head struck the vizor opening with a dull thud, and rested there while the blood from his mouth trickled in a thin, uneven dark line down the slope of the tank. A little later, when Turner was quite satisfied that his driver was dead, they lifted out the shattered body and buried it close beside the tank.

The colonel gave orders for the squadron to remain on the aerodrome for a few days until the advance was due to continue, for in several areas the troops were being held up by the stubborn resistance of some of the enemy, and it was not deemed advisable for units to advance independently. The line would go forward as a whole.

Walters walked across to Harvey's tank and found him talking to Allen. The two officers saluted their squadron leader.

' 'Morning, Pete; 'morning, Tony.' Then he continued:

'We've got to do something soon about poor Gregson and his crew. Their tank's cooled down by now so let's get it over. I'm not leaving here 'till we've buried them.'

Harvey looked at Allen for a moment or two before speaking, then he said:

'Tony and I will take care of it, won't we, Tony?'

'Yes, sir,' replied Allen, wishing he had the courage to refuse.

'I'm coming,' said Walters. 'They're my men.'

They took spades from two nearby tanks and Walters and Allen climbed on to the outside of one while Harvey got into the driver's seat, and the little party squeaked across the desert towards the burnt-out hulk. When they reached it they found the unrecognizable body of the driver still lying across its front. Charred, shrunken and cracked, the hairless skull was split open like a roasted chestnut with eyeless sockets and long teeth grinning through the cracked and cindery skin.

Harvey climbed on to the tank and looked down through the open turret. Walters joined him and as they leaned over peering into the burnt-out interior the major retched with the stench that struck up at them.

'Oh, Christ!' he said, screwing up his eyes.

'We'll dig two graves; that's all that will be necessary. There's scarcely anything left now in the turret. I'll go inside and pass them out,' said Harvey, outwardly calm and unperturbed.

Silently they dug the graves, each occupied with his own dreadful thoughts. Allen had not seen inside the turret, and his mind pictured the hideousness of what must inevitably come.

He allowed Walters and his friend to lift off the driver's body which had by now become firmly stuck to the hull, and when Harvey applied pressure to the shrivelled legs, with the shreds of boot and the nails and steel protectors still showing, one snapped off at the groin and Harvey gently laid it down in the grave and returned to the task of getting the rest of the corpse off the tank. Eventually they buried the driver and stood smoking cigarettes before continuing.

'Let's get it over,' said Walters, and Harvey climbed on to the tank and carefully lowered himself into the stinking turret. A cloud of flies swept out, disturbed, brushing Walters's face as he peered down. He jerked his head backwards, looked at Allen waiting beside the tank and nodded his head from side to side with eyes closed, signifying his utter revulsion.

A little later Harvey's head appeared; 'Ready?' he inquired.

Then he lowered it again and Allen saw hands appear holding between them pieces of what had lately been his companions. For a moment as he looked at the thin, sun-reddened arms of his friend he imagined they were stretching out to the skies to witness their horrid burden. Then Walters was receiving it and passing it down to him, and the feel and smell of it remained with him always. When he had placed it in the grave he returned to the tank for the next handful, until at last their gruesome task was completed and they knelt rubbing the filth and smell from their hands with the hard dry sand.

The advance continued and the squadron moved across the desert along each side of the track that led into the town. Soon, in the sunlight, the men could see from their turrets the first white buildings of their objective.

Harvey's troop was out in advance of the rest of the squadron, and as he leaned forward trying to focus his glasses on to the road and desert ahead, he wondered what the next hour might have in store for him.

He was almost level with the first single-storey buildings when the Italians began firing. Harvey saw the small anti-tank guns bunched close together less than three hundred yards from him, sited up the road beside some low houses. By ordering his driver to turn hard left he was able to put the houses on the left between himself and the guns. His other two tanks followed his example before the Italians had done any damage, although as he was reaching the shelter of the houses Harvey heard the metallic thud of steel striking the hull.

Harvey, speaking over the wireless, reported the position of the guns to Walters, and suggested that a troop should be sent along the backs of the houses bordering each side of the road with the object of turning in on the main track beyond the guns and working their way back, try to shoot up the enemy from the rear.

Second-Lieutenant Turner was detailed to take the right side of the houses while Harvey continued along the left. Another troop would come up to engage the guns from the houses where Harvey was at that moment waiting.

Turner, still commanding the tank in which Norman had been killed and which had been repaired by the fitters who had worked throughout the night at their task, took his troop cautiously forward, but when he had advanced a little over a hundred yards he came to a wide gap between the houses and quickly realized that he and his tanks would be an easy target if they attempted to cross it. He signalled back his information and was ordered by Walters to remain where he was.

Machine-gun and rifle fire were being directed on to the approaching tanks from infantry firing from inside the houses, but its only effect was to force the tank commanders to keep their heads well down inside the turrets.

While Turner was halted on the right and Harvey slowly went forward on the left, Skeffington, who had now been ordered up by Walters, reached the comparative safety of the houses where Harvey had first stopped.

Desmond Skeffington was as frightened as ever he had been. How he had managed to get to the shelter of the houses without being hit seemed to him to be little less than a miracle. He felt he would never have the nerve to move forward from his position of safety, and he was now dreading the next order from the squadron leader that must surely be directed at him. While he waited apprehensively for it to come, his driver very skilfully edged the tank right up to the side of the building facing the guns, and Skeffington, wondering what was happening, peeped over the top of his turret and just caught a glimpse of the four guns before ducking his head again, but nothing happened, and after a few seconds he looked once more, and still the enemy had not spotted his tank.

Skeffington eventually fought back his fear sufficiently to tap his gunner on the shoulder and whisper into his ear, although from that distance the enemy could not possibly have heard him through the continuous rattle of the small-arms fire.

Suddenly the turret echoed with the staccato sound of the gun's burst, and the smell of cordite filled Skeffington's nostrils. The gunner had judged his range well and the tracer bullets were causing the guns' crews to take cover behind their weapons' protective shields. At that moment Harvey's troop opened fire and the Italians were forced to turn two of their guns to engage the new menace on their right. Then Skeffington, as though inspired, seized his opportunity and speaking in a voice both calm and confident he ordered his driver to charge down on the enemy guns at full speed. Two of the Italian guns each fired a round at the tank speeding relentlessly down upon them before their crews lost heart and ran for the safety of the stone houses, leaving several dead and wounded lying on the ground.

The tank reached the deserted guns, smashing into them and crushing them beneath the tracks, the driver quite oblivious of the dead and wounded scattered upon the ground among their weapons. At last it stopped and

D

Skeffington, forgetting for the moment the small-arms fire, put his head and shoulders out of the turret as an Italian, resting his arms on a cupboard behind a latticed window, carefully aimed his rifle and pressed the trigger. Skeffington, feeling a stabbing pain in the region of his ear, collapsed on to the floor of the tank and lay there moaning. In the dim light of the tank the operator saw that his commander's face was covered in blood, but there was no room for any examination or first aid and so he took charge of the vehicle and ordered the driver to turn round and get back to the squadron as quickly as possible. As soon as he judged the tank to be out of range of the enemy he told the driver to stop, and together he and Taylor tried to lift out their commander, but Skeffington, having recovered from the first shock of the wound and realizing he could not be seriously wounded, tried to help himself from the uncomfortable floor. At last he was outside and standing shakily on his own feet while his crew, wiping away the blood mixed with oil from the tank, discovered that the bullet had done no more than remove a little of the top of their commander's left ear.

'It's not so bad, sir,' said Taylor, 'a bit of plaster will soon put it right and then the M.O. will fix it up proper.' And after a while they returned to the town which the squadron had by now succeeded in capturing.

The infantry had arrived and were searching the houses. The prisoners were sitting disconsolately in the square and the few wounded had already been dressed and were waiting for the ambulances. Thirty-four Italians who had died in the little battle for the town had been buried, and Walters made the men carry sand and cover the roadway where the guns had been overrun by Skeffington's tank.

Harvey and Allen were sitting smoking in the doorway of an empty, two-storied house.

'It might have been a damned sight worse,' Harvey was saying. 'Only one casualty, our dear Desmond pinked in the earhole, and even he put up as good a show as anyone could expect. You know, I'll be sorry to see him go. This squadron is really becoming a unit, and we're all getting so used to each other and to working together, that I shall almost feel resentful of his relief, whoever he is going to be.'

'When is he leaving?'

'As soon as the ambulances arrive. It's quite a gash; he'd be silly to stay where he can't get decent treatment for it.'

The town was small and possessed no hospital. The civilians had long since departed and the Italians had left the four guns and a few infantry simply as a token force when the main body had withdrawn before the British advance.

Walters was coming towards them so they got to their feet to wait for him.

'What's happening now, sir; is there any news?' asked Harvey.

'We're going to stay here for a night at least before we push on. Skeffington put up a damn good show, don't you think? Now he refuses to go back to hospital; says he'll have it dressed when he can. I know I could order him to go, but I'm damned if I want to lose him now we're becoming such a team.'

'That's exactly what I was saying to Allen just now; we've become very effective.'

'Well, the infantry seem to have taken over so let your men get some rest, but don't allow 'em to go far from their vehicles.' Walters moved on down the narrow street.

'Let's have a look in here,' suggested Harvey entering the house on whose step they had been sitting. 'We might sleep in here tonight instead of under the stars.' Harvey led the way into a bare room with a stone floor.

'This will do,' he said, looking around him. 'We'll get our blankets and stake our claim before the bloody infantry beat us to it.'

Allen pushed open a splintered wooden door that stood ajar and entered a smaller room. There was a rough wooden table and a broken chair, and along a wall stood a tall wooden cupboard. In the small space between the cupboard and the wall there crouched an Italian. Allen saw him immediately and his hand flew to the pistol at his hip, but before he had succeeded in freeing it from its holster the Italian was half-way through the unglazed window. Allen shouted to Harvey, and forgetting about his revolver he grasped the Italian about the legs and together they fell struggling on to the stone floor. The Italian brought up his knee with a vicious jerk into Allen's groin, quickly wriggled free and whipped a clasp-knife from inside his tunic, pressed the spring release and dived at the writhing Allen with a long, thin, shiny blade of steel. It was then that Harvey's heavy boot caught the Italian in the ribs, knocking the breath from his body and temporarily paralysing the man. He let fall the knife and rolled on to his back as Harvey dropped astride him, reached over the Italian's head and seized the weapon and plunged it again and again with sickening thuds into the Italian's unprotected neck.

'That'll teach you, you murdering wop bastard!' he snarled. Leaving the expiring man he turned to Allen and when he saw that his friend was only badly winded, he exclaimed:

'Oh, Christ, I thought he'd knifed you!'

The walls and floor of the little room were bespattered with blood. It had spurted over Harvey's face and hair, making him hideous. And as Harvey lifted his friend to his feet, the last breath rattled in the Italian's throat, causing the blood to bubble from the gashes as he died. Allen struggled free, and leaning out of the window, through which the dead man had so recently sought to escape, he vomited into the garden below.

Men had arrived and were peering in through the doorway at the carnage, reluctant to step into the room that resembled a theatre stage after an evening's performance of Grand Guignol.

Harvey, who was now outwardly calm again said, as he wiped the blood from his face with his sleeve:

'All right, this isn't a peep show. You can bury that if you're looking for a job,' and he indicated the corpse with his foot.

When Walters heard about the Italian he sent for the commander of the infantry company and ordered him to have every building in the little town thoroughly searched all over again and to report to him immediately it had been done.

Three days after the capture of the town the squadron moved forward once more in the wake of the retreating enemy, but it sighted little except occasional burnt-out lorries that had fallen victims to the R.A.F., and large quantitites of abandoned arms and stores. The Italians in their anxiety to put as much distance as possible between themselves and the British forces who were rapidly following them up, wasted little time in destroying the equipment they were forced to leave behind.

Towards midday Walters halted the tanks for an hour's break and maintenance. Close by were two Lancias that had been machine-gunned from the air. One had been completely destroyed by fire, the other had been hit in the engine and deserted, still loaded. Some of the crews walked over to this lorry and climbing into the back commenced examining its cargo and throwing out the crates and boxes to their comrades on the ground.

'Muck me!' exclaimed Trooper Jenkins. 'Here's a mucking basket full of bloody lira. Think of the dames we could mucking buy if we were in ruddy Italy now!'

It was only when they found a heavy box of grenades and began tossing them lightheartedly at any target they could find that Walters interfered and ordered the men to get back to their tanks.

'What's these, sir?' inquired one of the men, showing the squadron leader a large cardboard box containing hundreds of small tubes such as children have in their paintboxes.

The major examined one and replied, 'Prophylactic ointment, and you can leave these here. It will be a hell of a long time before you chaps will have any use for them,' and he walked away leaving Trooper Jenkins to explain to the puzzled man in simpler if somewhat coarser terms.

During the afternoon they sighted six Italian tanks and Walters ordered the squadron to speed up and attack. When the enemy appreciated the superior guns of the advancing tanks they turned tail, and then Walters ordered the squadron to open fire. Lieutenant Hargreaves scored the first hit at a range of three hundred yards or more and the enemy tank instantly caught fire. The remaining five, realizing that there was no escape in flight, turned to face their attackers and, returning the fire, prepared to fight it out to a finish.

Walters ordered the squadron to fan out on a wide encircling front and then directed each troop to engage its nearest tank. The Italians had halted to fire thus making even better targets. Allen, moving slowly forward towards the enemy, spoke into the intercom:

'Driver, steady. Gunner two o'clock, three hundred

yards. Fire!' The gun recoiled and Allen saw the bright red glow low down on the Italian's hull, but the tank did not catch fire. Then a head and shoulders frantically thrust itself out of the top of the turret, but at that instant Musgrove slammed another round into the breach and Brown pressed the trigger. Again Allen saw the red glow, this time a little higher up on the hull and as the head and shoulders of the emerging Italian disappeared into the turret, the tank caught fire. It burst into a huge ball of brilliant flame that reminded Allen of a painting of Abraham beside the blazing altar on which he was about to sacrifice his son, a painting that had hung, years ago, on his nursery wall. The squadron continued to fire until every tank was a blazing inferno, then Walters ordered Harvey's troop to close in to see if there were any survivors, and Harvey found two men crouching in the sand just out of range of the reeking heat of the flaming wrecks. Both were blackened by the oily smoke, but although dazed and shocked neither was seriously injured and Harvey made them climb on to the outside of his tank. Once again the squadron was advancing, leaving behind six straight black spiralling clouds of smoke to mark the spot where it had passed.

The following day Skeffington's troop, which was out several hundred yards ahead of the squadron, came upon a Lancia that had broken down. Without having to fire a shot he took prisoner the twenty men or so who had hoped to escape captivity in it. The fitters, signalled up by Walters, arrived in their three-tonner and quickly repaired the lorry and escorted it back with its prisoners towards the infantry who were following up close behind the tanks.

Shortly after the prisoners had been sent away, three enemy fighters suddenly appeared flying only a few feet above the desert, and almost before the crews were aware of their presence they were attacking. The tanks traversed their turrets and tried to get their guns to bear on the aircraft, but the three Italians flew at such a low level that it was almost impossible to hit them at the speed at which they were travelling. One was concentrating on Turner's tank. First it flew right over the turret clearing the tank's short aerial by what seemed to the crew to be scarcely more than a foot or so. Then, gaining height it turned and dived on its prey, guns blazing, sending fountains of sand rising in a line that led right up to the tank; the men inside heard the smack of the shells hitting the hull and making fragments of the plating fly off and ricochet all about the crowded turret. A jagged splinter struck Turner in the abdomen, and as he fell to the floor dragging earphones in a tangled mass from his wireless set, he screamed in his agony and fear – no longer a human being but a wounded and terrified animal whose only instinct was to escape. He began to fight and claw his way from the darkness to the safety of the blue sky that he could see above the turret's open hatch, leaving Martin his gunner, with his forehead still pressed to the rubber spring pad of the sight, dead in his seat, his left side laid open by a splinter. The operator who so far had miraculously escaped injury, hauled himself out of his hatch and throwing himself to the ground lay cowering in the sand. When Turner, exhausted by the blood that ran thickly down both his legs, at last got his head and shoulders clear of the turret, the aircraft had disappeared and the tanks ceased firing.

Walters, who was nearest to Turner's tank, had seen it hit by the fighter and was now out of his own tank and running towards it. He saw the driver and operator climb out, seemingly unscathed, and a moment later he was greatly relieved to see the commander's head appear and then he noticed the pallid face and the blood on Turner's hands and arms. Before he could reach the tank he saw Turner raise himself to climb out and suddenly collapse across the turret ring, arms and head hanging down, mouth dripping redly. The squadron leader assisted by the driver and operator lowered Turner to the sand, but he was already dead. Others came and they hauled out the gunner, and buried them both in graves a few feet apart. They were the only casualties.

Walters was worried about the aircraft and expected further attacks at any moment now that the news of their approach must have been passed back to the enemy, but although he had his command constantly on the alert, the aircraft did not reappear.

Two days passed and still the squadron continued westwards, meeting no further opposition. The men were weary from the long advance. Walters had driven them by day, and during the hours of darkness they had worked on their tiring tanks and kept guard. No sooner did they drop beside their vehicles to snatch a few minutes' sleep than they were roused again and mercilessly driven onwards. The tanks were also beginning to fail. Engines gave out, wireless sets, and even guns required changing. Two tanks had been left behind, their crews no longer capable of repairing them, and the fitters, those magnificent men who had performed such miracles with the squadron's many mechanical casualties, had reluctantly been forced to admit to Walters that it would take several days before they could hope to have them moving again.

The huge red sun was just about to sink beneath the horizon, and the men were lying in the sand beside their tanks when a scout car approached from the east flying the Regiment's pennant. The little car drove in among the tanks looking for the squadron leader, and then the colonel stepped out with the adjutant, who had been driving, and while the colonel led Walters out of earshot of the men the rest of the officers gathered around the adjutant.

Harvey asked, 'What now? When does this Cook's tour finish? These tanks of ours won't go on very much longer even if we can. You'll have to turn us into bloody infantry if you intend to keep us going many more days. You know all this pushing on and on rather reminds me of the story of the young officer who was practising to drill a squad of men. He was standing at the side of the road commanding the squad to march up and down and then a general suddenly appeared in a staff car and stopped and stood near the officer, watching him. This made the poor chap so nervous that he became speechless and all the time the men were marching further and further away down the road until at last the general could keep silent no longer. "Well, at least do something, even if it's only to wave them good-bye!" he muttered to the embarrassed officer.'

'That's what we're here for, Pete,' said the adjutant. 'We're going to pull out and let the reserves who have been following up on transporters take over. We're to make for a pleasant spot down on the coast and rest and refit. Suit you?'

'Can we tell the men?' inquired Harvey.

'Better wait until old Walters lets you know officially, otherwise the colonel will give me a rocket for not keeping my big mouth shut.'

Then, while they waited for the colonel and Walters to return they discussed the advance and asked after their comrades in the other squadrons and were relieved to learn that the Regiment's casualties had been extremely light.

The following morning, after the men had been given a

full night's sleep, the squadron moved leisurely northwards to the coast and came eventually to a deserted palm-fringed beach that seemed to the tired men as beautiful as any south-sea island. There it halted while the men drove their tanks beneath the trees and camouflaged them with nets threaded with fronds. Then they dug shallow pits and, spreading coloured canvas over the tops, they made comfortable bivouacs that sheltered them from the sun and helped to keep away the tormenting flies. When the tanks had all been put into complete working order again, and guns and wireless sets either repaired or replaced, the men's time was their own and they were not paraded except when senior officers came visiting the squadron to make little speeches congratulating the officers and men.

Towards midday a station wagon drew up in the squadron's lines, and out stepped several officers, including a major-general wearing the G.H.Q. badge. Major Walters hurried forward to greet him.

Harvey, who was sharing a mug of tea with Allen at the troops' mess lorry, exclaimed: 'Who the hell's this? No one is expected as far as I know; probably just looked in to see if he can scrounge a gin!'

At that moment Walters came running towards Harvey, leaving his visitors standing in a little group.

'Get the men paraded as soon as you can. He wants to talk to us,' he panted.

'Who is he?' inquired Harvey.

'I don't know. For God's sake get the men paraded!'

The men were quickly rounded up and made to put on shirts and find their caps, and at last Harvey had them formed up. He marched off to report to the squadron leader.

The group approached. Harvey's voice commanded:

'Squadron, at-ten-tion!' and he handed over the parade to Walters who in turn handed it to the general who ordered Walters to stand the men at ease. When this had been done the general began:

'All right, men, stand easy and keep the flies off. What you've done is beyond praise, and the South Africans have commanded me to thank you for your invaluable assistance. Now you, Major Wallis,' he continued, looking at the squadron leader, and Walters, who was standing close to the general, interrupted in an audible whisper:

'I think you've got the wrong squadron, sir. I'm Walters; Major Wallis is about three miles down the coast.'

'Really, oh, I say, h'mm, careless of me rather, what? Ah, well, better get down there I suppose,' and in the shortest possible time the station wagon and its occupants were disappearing in a cloud of dust.

For two months the squadron was allowed to bask in the Mediterranean sunshine with only the flies and an occasional khamsin to molest it. Replacements for the casualties arrived from the base, and once more the squadron was complete and ready for action. No leave to Cairo was granted, but the men, who constantly grumbled about this restriction, nevertheless appeared to enjoy themselves, so pleasant were their surroundings after the hard weeks in the barren desert.

One morning, shortly after the mail had been sorted and handed out, Harvey, who was sitting on the ground by his tank surrounded by papers and busily engaged in trying to balance his imprest account, noticed Allen walking slowly towards the beach. He called to him but his friend took no notice although it was quite obvious that he must have heard Harvey's shout. Watching him, it was apparent to Harvey that something had happened to upset him, and then he remembered that the mail had just been distributed. His first instinct was to hurry after Allen, but on second thoughts he decided it would perhaps be more advisable to leave him alone for a while, for he knew that if there was anything he could do Allen would sooner or later ask him.

Lying naked in the soft sand, Allen let himself be comforted by the sun's warmth, and the numbness that had overcome him with the reading of the letter slowly began to leave him. He reached for his shirt and took from a breast pocket the letter and read it again – the brief note from Mary's father telling him that his daughter had died in an air raid.

The news of the arrival of Rommel and his Afrika Korps soon reached the squadron, with all its sinister implications, and the men quickly realized that it could not be very long before they found themselves participating in battles that would make the fighting they had already experienced seem like a picnic. In a short while Rommel had becomd a legendary figure, and his name was mentioned invariably with respect and admiration. Every man knew the name of the commander of the German forces in North Africa, although a considerable number of the same men were ignorant of the name of their own commander-in-chief; but all this was before the coming of Monty with the two badges in his beret and the brain and drive that was to reduce the vaunted and *élite* Korps to a routed rabble.

Skeffington was telling an anecdote in his boring and long-winded manner. It was about an officer who had been sent on a patrol mounted on a camel, and after several days had passed, his unit received a faint signal from his transmitting set.

'The message read,' continued Skeffington, 'Send immediate assistance, Rommel captured', and the fellow gave his map reference, but just as his unit was about to inform all and sundry of this wonderful piece of news, a further signal was received which when deciphered read, 'With reference to my last message, for Rommel captured read camel ruptured.'

'Oh, bloody funny!' said Harvey. 'Is that all?'

Skeffington looked a little hurt.

'Perhaps he didn't understand it, old man. I should explain it to him if I were you,' suggested Allen.

The day came all too soon when the squadron was ordered to move to a position well up in the desert where it was considered that the Germans might endeavour to break through the British-held line, but even before Walters was able to get his command up to the area the Germans were on the move. Walters kept the tanks rumbling forward, allowing the men no rest, for when they halted for a few hours the time was spent on repairing and overhauling the vehicles.

The German advance was gaining impetus, and the British positions were being overrun by the speed of the attack and the superiority of the enemy's weapons.

Long before the squadron could reach its destination the Germans had arrived, were in possession and already preparing to continue their successful advance.

It was about two o'clock in the morning when Walters halted the squadron, and shortly afterwards the colonel and the adjutant arrived in the scout car. In front of the squadron the night sky was illuminated at regular intervals by soaring flares bursting into tiny red, green, or blue stars that floated gently back to earth and were extinguished.

The adjutant was speaking to the officers gathered around him while the colonel was conferring with Walters and Harvey.

'That's Jerry,' he said, indicating the flares. 'He's only a few hundred yards out there in front of you, but don't lose any sleep over it. By the way, I've brought up some mail for you boys. It's in the scout car, come along and I'll give it to you.' Allen took the small sack and tipped out its contents on to the floor of the car, the interior of which was dimly lit by a small blue bulb. One bundle was for the officers, the remainder for the men. Allen called to Brown and told him to distribute the letters to the squadron while he handed out those from the other bundle to the officers eagerly pressing about him. He was disappointed that no one had written to him, not even Dolores.

The scout car disappeared into the darkness, and Walters addressed the officers sitting near him in the sand.

'This is it, chaps. This is what we've all been waiting for. Jerry is about a mile ahead of us along a two-mile front packed tight with tanks and guns. We're part of an armoured brigade lined up facing him, and we're going to smash our way through and knock hell out of him. We'll just move forward with the rest of the brigade.'

When Walters had finished issuing the final details of the attack Harvey said to Allen:

'Come on over to my tank, I've got a wee drop of Scotch tucked away against such a time as this.'

Harvey climbed into his turret, and opening one of the small white ammunition boxes of the type that contain the belts of machine-gun rounds, he withdrew a bottle from the straw that had been wrapped about it as a protection against the tank's movement. He half filled his enamel drinking mug from the bottle, then poured in water and passed it to Allen.

'There you are, me boy, get that under your belt. It will help keep out the bullets.'

'Cheers, Pete, and good luck.' Allen swallowed some of the liquid, and returned the mug to his friend who raised it to his lips.

'Jenkins,' called Harvey to his driver, who was lying in the sand beside the gunner. 'Are you chaps asleep?'

'No, sir, can't seem to remember how to, sir.'

'Would you like a drop of whisky?'

'Yessir!'

'Then fetch your mug.'

Harvey poured whisky into the mug, and Jenkins thanked him, and returned to share it with the gunner and operator. There was still a little left in the bottle.

'When you go back give this to your crew,' remarked Harvey, indicating the bottle. They chatted for a little longer, then Allen wished his friend good night and returned to his tank carrying the bottle which he gave to Brown who was engaged in stripping the lock of a machine-gun with the aid of the tiny light inside the turret.

'Here you are, Brown. Share this with Howard and Musgrove and don't let Major Walters catch you.'

'Thank you, sir,' said Brown, eagerly taking the bottle.

'That's all right. Don't thank me, thank Captain Harvey, it was his bottle.'

Harvey pulled his greatcoat about him as he lay leaning against the track at the rear of his tank. He gazed up at the glittering stars that seemed to hang so low in the sky. He took from his pocket a folded envelope and lifted out a limp, sweat-soaked snapshot of a woman. There were even pale bloodstains on it from the Italian he had killed in the town. It was too dark to see the likeness, but Harvey grinned wryly at it for a moment, then returned it to the envelope. Shortly afterwards he fell asleep.

Major Walters lay beside his tank thinking of the coming ordeal. Remembering all that the colonel had just told him, he knew that there could be but few of the squadron left by the end of the day. The colonel had said that the enemy possessed a number of eighty-eight-millimetre guns that outranged anything the tanks carried. It was hoped, however, that the attacking tanks would be close enough to the Germans when the dawn came for the smaller guns to be within effective distance. Walters forced his thoughts away from the dawn to his wife and sons, and was glad they could not see him now. He imagined them sleeping soundly in some far-off bed, and he knew that he would never see them again. His wife would be inconsolable, for she worshipped him and he suffered her grief, and it wrung his heart, momentarily filling his eyes with tears. Sleep deserted him in this his hour of greatest need.

Lieutenant Desmond Skeffington turned restlessly from side to side in his blankets, tortured by fear. He was quite certain that something dreadful was in store for him and that he was being dragged relentlessly towards it, powerless to escape his doom.

Allen, wrapped in his greatcoat, thought of Mary and reasoned that since she was no longer there it mattered little if he survived the day.

It was still dark when Major Walters ordered the squadron to mount and prepare to move forward.

Allen, standing with his head and shoulders clear of the turret, felt the chill of the approaching dawn and adjusted the silken scarf that Dolores had sent to him. All around him could be heard the noise of the engines as they were being warmed up, and occasional flashes from the exhausts lit up the scene. In a short while the darkness gave way to the early morning ground mist. At last, through his earphones came the distorted voice of Walters giving the relentless and irrevocable command:

'Hullo Bolo, Bolo calling. Advance. Over!'

Allen ordered his tank forward, and glancing to his left he noticed Harvey moving his troop on the same course a hundred yards distant. Then the mist began to lift like a curtain rising on a vast sable stage, heralding its sinister and macabre performance. And at that moment the orchestra commenced and the guns were firing. As the mist cleared Allen noticed two hundred yards to his right front a stationary tank that was obviously not of British design, and then climbing from its turret he saw a German in a soft-peaked khaki cap. The German stepped down into a small, open car parked alongside the tank. Allen reacted:

'Enemy car, 3 o'clock, one hundred and fifty yards. Fire!'

The machine-gun chattered, and Allen listened to the spent cases rattling on to the hull of the tank. The red tracer flew toward the man at the wheel of the car. Now the car was moving.

'For Christ's sake, Brown!' yelled Allen, but even as he spoke, the German jerked forward, fell out of the doorless car and lay spreadeagled and motionless on his back. The car continued in a small half-circle, then stopped, and as Allen's tank drew level he could see that the man had been hit in the neck and shoulders. From what Allen saw, he believed that the man was dead, but this time there could be no stopping. He noticed Harvey waving his congratulations, and he signalled back. And then in front of him, barely four hundred yards distant, was the enemy, massed to receive the attack. Large tanks of the same pattern as the one he had passed and which had been knocked out in yesterday's battle, and the muzzles of the dreaded eighty-eight millimetres formed almost an unbroken line stretching all along the brigade's front. There were several

British tanks that had been destroyed the day before. He picked his nearest target and ordered Brown to fire. The enemy was not moving and the tank made a good target. Allen's eyes followed the tracer. He saw the red glow as the armour-piercing shell bored its way into the hull, and was overcome with joy as the tank immediately burst into flames.

'Well done, Brown!' he shouted, and chose a fresh target as Musgrove reloaded the gun. But now the eighty-eight millimetres had commenced firing, and their shells were bursting all about the tanks with vicious cracks that sent jagged splinters screaming through the early morning air.

Skeffington, fighting back his fear which had been heightened by the awful din of the gunfire and the sight and smell of burning tanks, still kept his head clear of the turret.

He gave an order to Taylor, his gunner, and at that second a shell burst a few yards from his tank and the blast blew his head backwards causing him to strike the back of his neck violently against the iron rim of the turret. He was dead even before his long body slumped inertly on to the oily, vibrating floor of the tank, unmarked by the shell, his neck broken. Taylor, his forehead pressed tightly to the sights of his gun, and Malcolm, busily engaged with his task of reloading, never knew of their commander's passing, for a shell pierced its way through the front of the tank, where the plating was thickest, and exploded the petrol tank, setting alight to the vehicle that was to become the funeral pyre of Skeffington and his crew. Andrews, the driver, suddenly conscious of the breath-taking heat that enveloped him, fought furiously to open the vizor that had been jammed by the shell, but the efforts of the screaming man were of no avail. The heat quickly blackened the faded crest painted on the hull until it was no longer visible.

Major Walters ploughed forward, giving clear orders to his gunner who had already scored several hits on enemy tanks, but these successes gave no joy to Walters, and his mouth sagged as he counted the increasing number of tanks that were halted and burning. He was stunned and horrified at the slaughter, but he still moved forward until a bursting shell smashed the tank's right track, immobilizing it, and there he remained directing his gunner and encouraging the remnants of his command until a German artilleryman had the satisfaction of seeing his target burst into a ball of flame and billowing black smoke.

Allen was very close now to the inpenetrable line of German tanks. He was also quite certain that he would never be able to reach them, for the enemy fire was both murderous and accurate. He was amazed that he had managed to survive for so long. He directed Howard and Brown, and with the aid of these activities he built his barrier against fear.

He saw Hargreaves's tank go up in flames and the driver scramble out of his hatch. Hopping on one leg, the other drawn up behind him, he reminded Allen of the gazelle he had seen in the early mornings bounding across the desert searching for the camel-thorn still wet with the precious dew that the rising sun would soon evaporate. The man hopped away from the enemy, seeking refuge from the shells that burst in fountains of sand around him, but after a few more leaps he suddenly disappeared in a cloud of sand and black smoke and Allen passing the spot a few moments later, saw nothing that resembled a human being in the scattered, sand-covered fragments.

A German tank was firing at Allen, and the shells were coming very close as he could see by the tracer that streamed gaily past his head. He directed Brown on to the enemy tank. Brown fired and missed and Musgrove reloaded.

'Come on, Brown, for Christ's sake get it!' he shouted, but it was too late. The German shell bit into Bolo 3, just beneath the gun, shattering Brown's head and sending fragments of his skull and small splinters of steel into Musgrove's chest and stomach. Allen felt the blast of the shell and the sledge-hammer blow as he was hit, then he collapsed in a heap on the bottom of the tank in company with Musgrove, who squirmed and wriggled beside him. For a few seconds he lay stunned, then his senses cleared and his mind struggled to grasp what was happening. He knew that he had been wounded, but he had no idea in what part of the body. He was covered in blood, yet he felt no pain and with each movement his brain was clearing. Just as he was getting to his feet, a second shell hit the tank, throwing him on top of Musgrove who was now shrieking in his fear and pain. Allen noticed the daylight streaming in through the hole the shell had made, then he saw Brown slumped back on his little swivel chair, his headless neck dripping redly from the jagged edges. Allen turned his attention to Musgrove who had now ceased his screaming.

'Pull yourself together, man, and I'll try to help you through the driver's hatch – come on, we haven't got much time left if we want to go on living for a bit longer,' he ordered.

'I can't move, sir', wailed Musgrove.

'Course you can. For Christ's sake, at least make some sort of an effort,' and Allen struck the wounded man heavily across the face with his open hand. Musgrove gathered his failing faculties and assisted by Allen, began to pull himself painfully towards the driver's compartment. For a moment Allen fought to clear the man from the tangle of headphones that were caught about his legs, and all the time his imagination was anticipating the next shell that would set the tank on fire. Cordite fumes filled the turret making Allen gasp and cough as he struggled with Musgrove. The driver's seat was empty and there was no sign of Howard. Somehow or other, with super-human strength, he bundled Musgrove over the back of the seat and then he saw Harvey reaching in with both hands through the driver's open hatch. Never in all his life had he been so glad to see anybody. Inside the tank with Brown and Musgrove, waiting for the shell that would blast him to eternity, he had already felt abandoned by the rest of the world.

'Steady, old boy,' encouraged Harvey as he grasped Musgrove beneath the armpits, 'we'll soon have you out.' He pulled the man through the small opening, and Allen could see Howard waiting to help. In a few seconds Allen jumped through the opening back into the world of daylight, sand and men.

'You all right, Tony?' inquired Harvey.

'Yes, thanks Pete – I'm sure I'm hit somewhere, but it can't be serious, and with all this blood it's impossible to tell just where.'

'Okay. A few yards from the back of your tank there's a bit of a hollow in the ground. Let's get Musgrove over to it, then we can do him up a bit and lie doggo until things blow over.'

They picked up the wounded man, and bending low hurried to the spot that Harvey had indicated. It was a recent bomb-crater, and it offered welcome protection to the little party from the shell splinters and bullets that whined about their ears. As Allen stumbled along, clutching Musgrove's legs beneath his arms, he noticed that his thigh was becoming stiff and starting to ache. As soon as they reached the safety of the crater Howard and Harvey pulled off Musgrove's shirt and shorts. The wounded man was now unconscious and breathing laboriously. There were many small gashes in his chest and abdomen and it was quite impossible to tell how deeply the splinters had penetrated, but the three men bending over their naked companion knew that there was little hope for him. They possessed no dressings, so Harvey placed Musgrove's shirt over the worst area of the wounds to keep the flies away.

'Now, let's have a look at you, Tony. Do you feel Okay? You're beginning to look a bit white about the gills!'

Allen had already discovered a tear in his bloodstained trousers on the outside of his thigh, and he began to pull them off. Then he saw a small hole in the flesh where the splinter had entered and a few inches away the jagged and open area where it had come out. Harvey came over to look at it, and remarked, 'Pretty, but harmless. It's missed the bone. Now let's have that gorgeous scarf of yours – it was just meant for this.'

Harvey took the silk scarf that Allen had removed from his neck and folding it he quickly bandaged the two wounds.

Allen asked: 'How the hell did you manage to be on hand? What's happened to your tank?'

'It went up in smoke like most of the others. I got myself blasted clean out of the turret, and by the time I picked myself up it was just a ball of fire. I couldn't get anywhere near it to see what happened to my boys, but none of them got out. I'm afraid they've had it this time.'

Musgrove appeared to have regained consciousness. He moaned weakly between his laboured breathing and began to twist his tormented body until he had thrown the shirt from him. Howard bent over him, doing what he could to comfort the man, who was now begging for water.

'Don't worry, we'll soon fix you up with a drink,' said Harvey, but the wounded man did not hear.

'Water, water,' he continued to moan in an entreating voice.

Harvey looked at Allen who was also beginning to feel the first pangs of thirst that follow loss of blood. He said: 'That's our immediate problem I suppose. Let's see if your tank's been sent up yet, Tony. If it hasn't, with any luck we might be able to get one of the water bottles.'

They crawled up to the rim of the crater. All round them they could see burning tanks from which poured reeking, oily black smoke. They noticed how close they were to the German lines. They could see the enemy guns and the features of the soldiers manning them. Allen's tank was a good forty feet away, but it seemed more like a mile across the unprotected ground where shells were bursting and bullets and splinters bit viciously into the sand, sending up little clouds of dust that eddied away in the sunlight.

Allen was the first to see the Red Cross flag on the little stick fluttering some distance away.

'They've got a first-aid post dug in over there, Pete,' he said, pointing to the flag.

Harvey looked at Musgrove who had now become unconscious again. He said, 'That's the place for him. It may be a hell of a time until our chaps pick us up, and if they don't we can't make a dash for it before dark. We'd be dead ducks before we covered ten yards, and in any case, in a little while you won't be able to walk with that damned leg of yours.'

As they watched the first-aid post they saw two Germans with large red crosses on their arms hurrying towards it carrying a wounded man on a stretcher, then they carefully climbed into the dugout with their burden and disappeared. A little later the two men emerged with the empty stretcher and hastened away in the direction of one of the guns that had ceased firing, it's long barrel pointing awkwardly and harmlessly into the sky.

'Those chaps have certainly got some guts, running around in this lot,' remarked Harvey.

They saw the two returning with another casualty. Black smoke suddenly grew from the ground in front of them, and the watching men saw them drop the stretcher, and fall on their faces.

'Christ, they've had it this time,' gasped Harvey through his teeth, but before he could speak again the two stretcher-bearers got to their feet, and picking up their burden hurried on towards the dugout.

Harvey thought for a few moments, then he said:

'Howard and I will carry Musgrove over there, that will at least give him a chance of living. This place is too much of a no-man's land for them to worry about taking prisoners, and even if they do try something like that, we can most probably make our getaway after dark. You, Tony, had better stay here. You wouldn't be able to escape with that leg of yours, and you don't want to wind up in a P.O.W. camp. With any luck they'll let Howard and me go, then we'll come back with some water and a dressing for you. If, however, our luck is out, wait until dark, then do the best you can to get back. You're bound to be picked up by our chaps before very long.'

For a while they made their plans, then Harvey pulled off his shirt to hide the fact that he was an officer. At last they were ready to leave. They had chosen their time well, for a lull had occurred in the shelling and the men noticed this with visible relief. Howard got his arms under Musgrove's shoulders, and Harvey took his feet. As they lifted him, the shirt fell off, leaving the man naked and bloody. Allen made to pick it up.

'Don't bother about it any more, he'll be all right as soon as we can get him over there,' remarked Harvey.

'Good luck,' said Allen, as the two climbed awkwardly up the steep wall of the crater bearing the wounded man.

Harvey made no reply, saving his breath for the task ahead of him.

Allen dragged himself to the parapet and watched them as they made their way to the dugout. He saw them stop once and lie down to rest for a few moments, then they got to their feet and hurried on. Miraculously, the shells had almost entirely ceased to fall in their area. When they were getting close to the first-aid post, the German medical orderlies reappeared with the empty stretcher, and Allen heard Harvey call:

'Hey, Fritz! Come and give us a hand.'

The two Germans stopped, and one grinned and pointed downwards with his forefinger at the entrance to the post, then they hurried off with the stretcher in the direction of their own lines.

Carrying Musgrove feet first, Harvey led the way into the dugout that served as the German aid post. About a dozen men, swathed in bandages and in varying stages of consciousness, were lying on blankets, while a little distance away from them were three still figures covered with ground-sheets. In a corner was a long narrow table over which was spread a rubber sheet, and on it lay a wounded man.

A young German doctor, bronzed and wearing only a pair of brief khaki shorts, was attending to him, assisted by a medical orderly. For a moment the doctor stopped what he was doing and glanced up in surprise at the two Englishmen. Then he smiled and in English, which he spoke in a pleasant but typically German accent, he said:

'Come here.' Indicating with his forceps a spot on the ground near the table, he returned his attention to the man on the table. After a few moments he spoke in German to the orderly who commenced to bandage the wounded man's arm and shoulder, then putting down his forceps and washing his hands in a bucket, the doctor came over and looked at Musgrove who was unconscious and breathing with difficulty. After a rapid examination the doctor stared at Harvey and shook his head.

'Not good,' he pronounced, pointing to one of the larger punctures just above Musgrove's navel.

The doctor spoke to the orderly who had nearly finished bandaging the man on the table, then, while he waited, he picked up a packet of cigarettes from the table on which his bottles and instruments were spread out. He offered it to Howard and Harvey who each took a cigarette.

The orderly had now finished bandaging the patient and was trying to help him off the table, but the effort was too much for the wounded man who suddenly collapsed in the orderly's arms. Harvey, who was nearest to the table, quickly placed his arms beneath the inert man, and lifting him clear of the table, placed him gently on a blanket at the end of the row where the other wounded were lying. The doctor smiled approvingly. 'There is not much help here,' he sighed, and as the two Englishmen placed Musgrove on to the vacated table, the doctor poured cognac into a tiny glass and gave it to Harvey.

'You drink – is good,' he said. Harvey took a sip, and offered the glass to Howard, but the doctor stopped him.

'You finish, I have more.' And when Harvey had emptied the glass the doctor refilled it, and passed it to Howard. Then he went to work on Musgrove, but apart from giving him an injection and cleaning and covering the wounds, there was little he could do. At last they lifted Musgrove from the table, and put him on a blanket with the other wounded.

While the doctor had been attending to Musgrove several more wounded had been brought in by the two stretcher-bearers. Among them was a British infantry corporal whose leg had been blown off just below the knee. The man was pale, but courageously cheerful. He told Harvey that a shell had burst right above his weapon pit, killing outright the two men with him. When he discovered that a fragment of the shell had completely severed his leg, he had calmly removed the lace from his boot, and using it as a tourniquet, had wound it round his groin.

Harvey began to worry about Allen. The din of the gunfire had started up again and it was now late in the afternoon. Many wounded had been brought in, and he and Howard had been assisting the tireless doctor in his efforts to help them. He began to think how they might get away before the troops arrived to take them prisoner. He saw that Howard still had his pistol strapped to his side. The Germans had been far too occupied to notice this fact. A little later Harvey was able to signal to Howard to conceal the weapon in his pocket.

While Harvey was wondering whether it might not just be possible to walk out of the dugout and run for it, he heard a heavy vehicle approach and stop. A few moments later several Germans came in, bearing empty stretchers upon which they lifted the wounded and carried them outside. The doctor looked at Harvey and smiled. He seemed to read his thoughts. He said, 'You can stay and help me until it gets dark. You have been good; I will not look when you go.'

For a moment their eyes met and held, then Harvey turned his attention to Musgrove who was being lifted on to one of the stretchers. The unconscious man's face was shrunken and bloodless, he scarcely breathed, and Harvey knew that in a few hours he would be dead. There was nothing more they could do for him now. The Germans raised up the stretcher and carried it away.

Howard picked up a water bottle that one of the wounded had left behind him. He shook it and discovered that it was still fairly full and catching Harvey's eye, he quietly slipped the strap over his shoulder.

Allen watched the last of the torturing sun as it quickly sank from sight in the western sky, and he knew that in a very little while it would be quite dark. Most of the day he had lain peering over the parapet of the crater towards the entrance to the dugout. He had seen four lorries bearing large Red Cross flags arrive at the post to carry away the wounded, but he was fairly certain that Harvey and Howard had not yet been taken away. His wound had stopped bleeding, but it ached abominably and every time he tried to move to a more comfortable position a burning spasm of pain made him almost cry out. The sun had drawn all the moisture from his body and he was parched with thirst. Several times he had toyed with the idea of crawling to the dugout but he knew that if he succumbed to this temptation it would mean the end of his freedom until the war was over. For a while, before his leg had become too stiff to move, he had tried to summon up the strength to crawl out to the tank, but he doubted if he would be strong enough to climb inside to search for the water bottles once he had managed to reach it. Then the Germans solved the problem for him by shelling his tank until it caught fire. The blast of the shells and the heat of the burning tank drove him to seek shelter at the very bottom of the crater. When he crawled up again, he noticed that nearly the whole of the Regiment's tanks were burning. The few that had survived had withdrawn to hull-down positions, and were still firing at the enemy who had also lost sufficient tanks to deter him from advancing any further – at least for the time being.

Just before darkness closed down Allen saw a Volkswagen stop outside the dugout. Three men got out, two of them with light machine-guns slung over their shoulders, the other looked as if he might be an N.C.O. Allen saw them enter the post and his heart sank, for he was certain that they had been sent to escort Harvey and Howard to the prisoner-of-war cage. A few moments later his worst fears were confirmed, for coming out of the dugout was the N.C.O. followed by one of the armed men and then he saw Howard's bare head.

Harvey watched the daylight rapidly fading through the entrance to the dugout. He whispered to Howard who was standing close to him.

'Any moment now we'll have to be going. Just follow me.' Scarcely had he said this when they heard a vehicle draw up, and a few moments afterwards an N.C.O. and two armed men came in. The N.C.O. saluted the doctor and spoke in German. After a little while the doctor said to Harvey:

'I'm sorry but you will have to go with these men. The stretcher-bearers have informed them that you were here. I have told the corporal that I would like you to stay and help, but he says he has orders to take you back immediately. There is no more I can do.'

The doctor looked genuinely sorry. Even the escort looked not unfriendly. They had not bothered to unsling their weapons. The N.C.O. saluted the doctor and led the way out followed by one of the guards. Howard followed, and Harvey and the other guard brought up the rear, for in the narrow entrance there was room only for one at the time. Just as Howard was stepping out into the desert, Harvey shouted 'Tackle him,' then he suddenly turned, and threw himself on to the guard who was following behind. Howard grasped the man in front around his legs, and tripped him on to his face. The N.C.O. swung round in astonishment, only to face the menacing barrel of Howard's .38. He already had his hobnailed boot on the fallen guard's head, pressing his face into the sand.

Harvey whispered hoarsely behind him, 'I've got my bloke's squirt-gun, he'll be quiet for some time. Keep your chaps covered while I see if I can start the car. As he passed the prostrate guard, he stooped to pick up the fallen machine-gun and handed it to Howard. Then he climbed into the open vehicle and in a few seconds he had succeeded in getting the engine going. By this time Howard had made certain that their late captors were unarmed.

Howard climbed in beside Harvey, still covering the Germans with the machine-gun. The car moved off. In the distance Harvey could see Allen waving and cheering from the top of the crater. In a matter of seconds Howard had leapt out, and picking up Allen who was holding Harvey's shirt, he placed him on the back seat and they were off again, shouting and cheering and heading back to their own front line, Allen's thirst and pain forgotten.

In the fading light they could see some distance ahead, the outlines of several tanks. Harvey spoke to Howard sitting beside him. 'We don't want any trouble now, particularly from our own chaps. Stand up and wave a white handkerchief.'

'I haven't got one, sir.'

'Then take mine.'

Harvey, with a certain amount of trepidation, drove towards the nearest tank. He was very relieved when no one fired on the Volkswagen. Howard was waving the handkerchief and shouting, 'Don't shoot,' as he noticed the tank's turret, with its threatening guns, traverse lazily in their direction. A face peered over the turret's rim, then a voice inquired,

'Is that you, Harvey?'

'It sure is!' the driver of the Volkswagen yelled.

Captain Bennett, the second-in-command of 'C' Squadron raised himself out of the turret and dropped wearily to the ground. He walked across the few yards to the halted car. Then he noticed Allen, blackened and blood-encrusted from head to foot, lying full length across the back seat.

Harvey climbed out of the car and said, 'He's got a nasty thigh wound, but it's not too bad. He'll be all right if we can get him back to the M.O.'

The stars were hanging low above the desert; occasional orange flashes of gunfire flickered across the night sky, while to the west, at frequent intervals, coloured Very lights soared heavenwards to burst into tiny balls of brilliance.

Bennett said, 'We'll call up R.H.Q. and get them to send up the M.O.'s carrier. It will be quicker and safer than wandering back on your own in this thing. They'll be up in no time.'

Within the hour Allen was lying on the operating-table at the Field Ambulance. The M.O. had given him an injection and was busying himself stitching up the larger gash in the wounded man's thigh from which the splinter had emerged. Allen, dazed by the shock of the wound and the consequent loss of blood, no longer felt any pain. The drug made him feel slightly intoxicated.

He asked, 'What's happened to the rest of my squadron?'

'We'll tell you all about that in the morning. You've had quite a day of it, I should imagine. Now if I were you I should concentrate on getting some rest.' Almost before the M.O. had finished speaking, Allen had fallen into a deep sleep, oblivious of the needle that was skilfully drawing together the gaping flesh.

Harvey and Howard stopped the Volkswagen in front of Brigade H.Q.; they were soon directed to the Staff Captain. 'Glad to see you back, Pete,' he welcomed when he saw Harvey. 'You can get some rations from that truck over there – it's the Brigade Mess. They'll be able to fix your man up and tell him where he can sleep. When you've had some food, come back here, and I'll lend you one of my blankets. I expect you can do with some sleep. Anyhow, I should hurry up and get a little if I were you, the brigadier will want to see you as soon as it gets light. He's got some dark scheme in his mind for organizing what's left of the brigade into a regiment, or even a squadron if necessary. In the meantime, however, if it gives you any comfort, there's practically a complete brigade in reserve on their way up on transporters. They should be here before it gets light. From intelligence reports, if they mean anything, Jerry has completely run out of tanks for the time being. There's supposed to be nothing behind him worth worrying about for at least thirty miles. We've got an infantry battalion, skulking about out in front there to stop him recovering any of his tanks while its dark. By midday tomorrow, we should be pushing forward again.'

Harvey slept fitfully. Although, he was utterly exhausted the sound of gunfire awoke him at intervals, and once during the night he heard the comforting vibrating rattle of transporters bearing their heavy but welcome burdens through Brigade H.Q. on towards the front to reinforce the gravely depleted armour. He was awake and on his feet almost before the first signs of dawn had appeared in the eastern sky. The staff captain found him sipping tea from a borrowed enamel mug.

'It's all right, Pete, the new brigade is up in position. They'll be pushing forward as soon as it gets light, and when the divisional commander is satisfied that the new attack is a success he's going to order the withdrawal of our Brigade – or what's left of it.'

Harvey finished his tea. He said, 'Just the same, if it's Okay with you, I think I'll drive the old Volkswagen up and see if I can take over an N.C.O's tank. I don't feel right hanging about back here with nothing to do while there's still some of the Regiment up there.'

'Suit yourself, old boy, I expect they'll be glad to see you, but mind how you go.'

Harvey found a petrol dump and refilled the Volkswagen's tank. As the light began to grow from the east he drove rapidly towards the battle area. On the way he passed the returning transporters. His spirits rose as their numbers increased. Then he came to the tanks, stretching in a line from north and south as far as the eye could see. He heard the powerful staccato bursts of their engines as the drivers nursed them into life, and then they were moving forward to finish the destruction that yesterday's battle had begun. The shelling had commenced, and the Germans were clinging tenaciously to the ground they had won in their rapid advance, but the tanks swept forward, their guns blazing, supported by the battery of 25-pounders located behind a ridge, a half-mile to the rear. The noise was deafening, the sand ahead became a sea of black shell-bursts, and even as Harvey watched, the first tanks had broken through the German lines. In a little while the battle began to die down and B Squadron, and the rest of the regiment, were avenged.

Relentlessly the brigade swept westwards, smashing into the retreating enemy and leaving in its wake burning tanks, wrecked guns and the broken corpses of the men who had remained at their weapons. Behind it followed the motorized infantry, that with skilful use of mortar, grenade and bayonet, rapidly dealt with the small pockets of suicide troops that had been left behind in hastily-dug trenches to slow up the British advance.

Late in the afternoon the survivors from the Regiment went out with a recovery unit to bring in the tanks that might still be made serviceable. Bodies were gently lifted out and buried in shallow graves close to the tanks in which they had died. The padre, wearing his surplice, drove in a jeep from group to group, murmuring a few words of the burial service beside each tank.

Harvey, at the wheel of the Volkswagen, went out to the area where B Squadron had fought. Not a single tank had survived the battle. He watched the men handing out the charred and unrecognizable remains of Major Walters and his crew. For a few moments he stood beside their communal grave, staring down at the blanket. He was no longer sickened by the horror of the scene. Gazing at the blackened cinders, he only saw them as once they had been – men he had known intimately, men caught up in the toils of war who had laughed and cursed, and in fighting for a cause, had lost the toss and died.

He drove across to Skeffington's tank before the recovery unit could reach it, and climbing on to the scorched and blistered hull, he peered down into the darkened ruin. Then, with no one to see, he gave a last salute to the man who had endured so much in his efforts to overcome the agony of terror.

A little later he halted the car beside the first-aid post where he and Howard had carried Musgrove. The little Red Cross flag no longer fluttered in the gentle evening breeze, for a large shell had burst over the dugout, blasting in the walls. He noticed fragments of the operating table and several torn bodies, while wedged upright in a corner of the trench was the head and torso of the young German doctor. Harvey turned and walked slowly back to the car, and climbing in, drove off to find his own tank. It had been completely burnt out. One of the tracks lay in the sand, blasted from the sprockets by an 88 mm. Jenkins and the rest of his crew were still at their action stations, small and unidentifiable skeletons except to Harvey. He remained standing beside the tank until the recovery party reached it, then he helped lift out the bodies of his men. When it was all over and the padre had gone on to the next tank, Harvey drove back to Brigade H.Q. On the way he was conscious of the happiness that suddenly flooded over him with the realization that he was still alive to feel the warmth of the sun and enjoy the cloudless blue of the sky. A fly feasted irritatingly at a cut on his arm, and he brushed it away with his open palm. Yesterday, he would certainly have killed it.

Allen felt much better. His thigh, although still rather stiff, no longer pained him, while the immediate effects of shock had almost passed off. His one desire was to get away from his more seriously-wounded companions in the field ambulance.

The overworked M.O. bent over Allen's leg. 'This is coming along very nicely. We'll soon have you on your way to a decent hospital in Cairo. I expect you'll be glad of a bit of rest back in civilization.'

'How long will it be before I can leave here, Doc?' he asked.

'Oh, in a day or two, I hope. We're a bit short of ambulances, and I've got to get the more serious cases away first. You can try walking about on this if you like, to see how it goes.'

Allen's spirits brightened when later in the day he saw Harvey come in to the tent.

'How are you, Tony? How much longer do you intend to stay malingering in this joint?'

'I'll be away just as soon as they can find an ambulance for me. Doc tells me it may take a day or two.'

Harvey studied his friend for a moment or so, then he asked:

'Are your nerves ready to take a bit of a shock?'

Allen looked startled. 'Now what's the matter?' he inquired.

'Oh, don't look so worried, it's not all that bad. I've just been given orders to reform B Squadron, and if you're fit enough, you're to be my second-in-command.'

'You mean they've given you a crown?'

'That's right, and you can consider yourself a captain.'

Allen began to feel very satisfied with life. 'Tell me more,' he ordered.

'Well, what's still left of us is going back to some nice comfortable barracks in Cairo, and after a short time of rest and relaxation, we're going to re-form the whole Regiment and take over some brand new tanks that are supposed to be on their way out to us.'

'What sort of tanks?'

'I'm not so sure about that. Probably American ones. Why, are you so particular?'

Allen laughed. Harvey continued: 'I'm driving back to Cairo in the Volkswagen. The rest of the Regiment are going back in three-tonners, and I'm afraid they won't require many of them for what's left of us.'

Allen thought for a moment, then he said, 'When are you starting back?'

'When I leave here. I've got nothing left to pack any more.'

'Neither have I, if you see what I mean.'

The two looked at each other and grinned.

Harvey said, 'We'll pinch a pillow or two and make you as comfortable as possible. If you find it's too much for you, I can drop you off at one of the staging hospitals.'

'Don't you worry, Pete. I'll be fine. Why, I'd even start walking back to Cairo to get out of this place.'

'What's the M.O. going to say?'

'Nothing. He's far too busy in the theatre at the moment.'

Allen still wore his bloodstained shirt and slacks. He had no other clothes. Clutching a pillow and supported by Harvey he limped out to the Volkswagen and climbed in, and in a few moments they were heading eastwards down the track towards the Nile valley.

For several hours they kept going. They passed a number of vehicles loaded with troops, and many tanks and guns on transporters heading towards the front line.

At last Harvey asked, 'How's the leg, Tony?'

'Not too bad. The pillows help quite a bit. But I'm damn glad we're not crossing the Sahara in this thing.'

Harvey smiled. He said, 'The next camp we come to we'll stop and try to scrounge some grub. I could certainly do with a cup of tea to wash the dust out of my throat.'

Late in the afternoon they came upon several lorries that had halted for the night just off the track. Near one the men had built a fire and were preparing their evening meal. Harvey stopped the car close to the group. The men crowded around the Volkswagen, pointing at the palm tree and swastika, the insignia of the Afrika Korps. Then someone noticed Allen's bloodstained clothes and the sweat on his face.

'Are you all right, sir?' a corporal inquired.

'Yes, I'm fine, but I could do with a drink if you've got one to spare.'

While the men were fussing about Allen and questioning the two officers concerning the recent battle, a young lieutenant walked over from one of the lorries and joined the group. Harvey explained to him that they were on their way back to Cairo and had stopped in the hope of getting a meal. In no time at all Allen was lying comfortably in the Lieutenant's camp bed, drinking tea laced with rum. A medical orderly had looked at his wound and put on a fresh dressing. Soon the stars came out and the little camp settled down for the night. Harvey, wrapped in borrowed blankets, lay in the sand close to Allen's bed.

The camp broke into activity as soon as it became light. Harvey and Allen breakfasted on fried tinned sausages washed down with scalding tea. A quartermaster brought a new shirt and slacks for Allen, the Volkswagen's tank was refilled, and in a little while the two officers said good-bye and headed towards Cairo as their hosts started up the lorries and continued their journey towards the front.

Harvey drove throughout the day, halting only for a short while at a petrol dump to refuel. By four o'clock in the afternoon, they were only fifty miles west of Alexandria. Harvey said:

'What am I going to do with you, when we get to Alex?'

'Take me to the Cecil and help me to the bar. Then you can go and look for a field cashier and collect some ready money. After that you can go and buy yourself a couple of crowns, and some pips for me, and we can start celebrating our hard-won and well-deserved promotion.'

'The proper place for you is hospital with that leg. That's where I'm taking you, my boy.'

'Not bloody likely, you aren't. If they once get me inside I'll be there for days. It's getting better all the time. A few hours whisky treatment and I'll be as right as rain. Don't you worry, the first moment I notice it's getting worse I'll tell you. If I go to hospital now you'll get another second-in-command, and without my military genius to rely on you'd be out of your depth before you'd ever started.'

'You're delirious, Captain Allen.'

'Say that again, Major Harvey. Even in your coarse voice that sounds like music to my sensitive ears.'

'You're delirious.'

'No, you dim-witted clod, the captain part, I mean.'

4

The Cecil Hotel was fairly full when Harvey and Allen arrived. The reception clerk studied his book while the officers waited impatiently. 'I'm afraid I've only got one room vacant at the moment. If you two gentlemen would not object to sharing for the night?'

'That's good enough for us. We'll be off first thing in the morning,' stated Harvey.

Harvey took the key and followed Allen to the lift. He noticed his friend was limping badly and was obviously in pain.

There were two beds in the room. Allen made for the nearest one and dropped wearily on to it, too exhausted to raise his injured leg from the floor. Harvey came across to him and gently lifted the leg on to the bed. He saw that Allen was pale and sweating.

'Let me get you out of your things, you'll be more comfortable. Besides, I'd like to see your leg.'

'Look, Pete, for God's sake stop fussing around like an old woman, and muck off and get hold of some money. Then we can buy a drink which is what I want more than anything else at the moment.'

Harvey grinned and said, 'Okay, I shan't be long.'

He went out of the room, closing the door gently behind him. He walked down the stairs and entered the bar. The large room was full of officers. He looked around for a few moments until he found what he was looking for – a man wearing R.A.M.C. badges on the lapels of his tunic. The doctor was drinking with three other officers. Harvey approached the little group. He said to the M.O.:

'Excuse me, sir, but could I have a word with you?'

A few moments later Harvey opened the door of their room.

'Tony, I've brought someone along to look at your leg.'

137

Harvey and the doctor helped Allen out of his clothes. He lay naked on the bed, a thermometer sticking out of the corner of his mouth.

The doctor untied the stained bandage and examined the wound, which had been bleeding. He took the thermometer from Allen's mouth and said, 'You ought to be in hospital with this leg. I could order you to go, but we'll give you a night's rest here and see how you look in the morning. I'll go and get a few things from my room and fix you up. In the meantime, we'll ring down and order you some food.'

'What did you want to get him for?' asked Allen when the doctor had gone.

'Don't be an ass, Tony. I'm not taking any chances with you. Suppose, for instance something went wrong and you lost your leg, how do you think I'd feel about it? It's my responsibility.'

After a few minutes the doctor came back with fresh dressings. While he attended to the wound, he said:

'When you've eaten something, take this tablet I'm going to leave for you and you'll have a good night's sleep. Fortunately you've got no temperature so there's no infection. If there was you'd go straight into hospital.'

A waiter knocked on the door and brought in Allen's dinner. Harvey and the doctor waited until he had finished eating. They watched him swallow the pill, then, when the dishes had been removed, Harvey said, 'Now off you go to sleep Tony, I'm going to find the field cashier, then I'll have some dinner and a few drinks. I won't disturb you when I come in, so see you later on.'

'Have a nice time, Pete, and thanks for everything, Doc.' murmured Allen sleepily.

'Don't thank me, old man,' exclaimed the M.O., 'It's all in the day's work. See you in the morning.'

Outside the room the doctor said: 'You won't find the field cashier tonight, he closes shop at five. I can let you have a couple of quid until the morning. Anyhow, come along and have a drink with me – you look as though you could do with one.'

'I certainly could, and it's very kind of you.'

When they reached the bar the doctor's companions were still there. Harvey was introduced and given a drink. The doctor insisted that he join the party for dinner. After the finest meal Harvey had eaten in months he was persuaded to go back to the bar with his new-found friends, where they remained drinking while a *gulli-gulli* man produced a live chicken from Harvey's ear and a snake from the doctor's pocket. They stayed drinking until well after midnight, then Harvey walked a little unsteadily up the stairs to his room.

He noticed that Allen was in a deep sleep, so quickly undressing he climbed into bed and switched off the light.

The following morning Allen awoke feeling bright and cheerful after a long night's rest. While he was having his breakfast in bed, the doctor knocked and put his head round the door.

'Hullo! Can I come in and have a look at my patient?'

'I really think you've done the trick, Doc,' remarked Harvey. 'I'm sure he feels much better than I do after last night with your friends. It was quite the best evening I've had for some time.'

The doctor took Allen's temperature and put a fresh dressing on his wound. He noticed it had stopped bleeding.

'Well, what about it, Doc, can I go on to Cairo today?' inquired Allen, a little anxiously.

'Do you really feel up to it? It's quite a journey you know.'

'Sure I do. I'm a new man this morning.'

'Well, if I give in to you, will you promise me to go straight to a doctor when you get there?'

Harvey interrupted. 'He'll go to a doctor; I'll be responsible for him.'

'Okay, you can go.'

'Can I have a bath now?' inquired Allen.

'No, you certainly cannot. Not now I've taken all the trouble to put that dressing on. You keep your leg out of the water until they remove the stitches.'

The M.O. remained chatting for a while as they helped Allen into his clothes, then Harvey said: 'You wait here, Tony, while I pop off and get some money. I'll get the car filled up and settle for the room, then I'll be back for you. I shan't be very long.'

Soon they were speeding along the black, sun-baked road that ribboned across the desert. When they reached the Half-Way House, Harvey stopped the car. 'Here you are, Tony,' he said, removing the three gilt stars from his own shirt, 'you can have these now.' He put in their place the epaulettes with the two new crowns he had taken from his pocket.

'Thank you for my pips, sir,' remarked Allen. 'Let me be the first to salute you, sir.'

Harvey returned the salute. 'That's all right, Captain Allen, now let's go inside and wet them before you get us both demoted.'

It was still light when the two officers drew up outside the three-storied brick building that was to be their mess.

'This looks good after what we've been used to,' said Allen. 'I could quite happily spend the rest of the war in a place like this.'

'Don't you worry, you won't. I give us a couple of months at the most, then we'll be off again. Bigger and better battles, that's what the boys at G.H.Q. have in mind for us.'

In a few minutes Allen was stretched in an armchair in a cool room that overlooked a well-kept lawn studded with short palm trees. Saïd, his servant, had been expecting him and had already brought his kit from the store and unpacked it. The sight of the clean and freshly-starched uniforms gladdened Allen's heart.

'Saïd, you one-eyed old rascal, you don't know how glad I am to see you again,' greeted Allen.

'Master good man. Allah keep him,' smiled Saïd happily.

Later in the evening Harvey came into the room. 'Well, old man, what did the M.O. have to say?' he inquired.

'Everything is going fine. I've got to go along to the M.I. room in the morning and have the stitches taken out. He says that I must take it quietly for the next few days, but that there's no need for me to go to hospital.'

'Good. Have you done anything about Dolores yet? Do you want me to ring her up, or go and see her?'

'No, I don't think so, Pete. We'll just wait and see how things go for a bit.' Allen could not make up his mind about Dolores. He badly wanted to see her, but he knew exactly what would happen if he gave way to the temptation, and he had already come to the decision that he did not love her enough to marry her. He thought that the solution to his problem was to stay away from her as long as he could, and leave the rest to the future.

'Okay, just as you say, but a little feminine relaxation would probably be just the thing for you.'

'Well, we'll see. Now what about our new squadron. Is there any news?'

Harvey lit a cigarette and studied Allen for a few moments. 'You know,' he said, 'you want to take it easy for a while. After all, it's not just you and me against the whole bloody Axis. I have seen a few other troops around this place besides us.'

The men of B Squadron marched up and down the parade ground obeying the raucous commands of S.S.M. Roberts. After a while he halted the weary, sweat-soaked men, and addressed them:

'Some of you new people from the depot may have been told that once you're posted to a fighting regiment you can relax until you get to the desert. Now is the time to forget it. In fact, this morning I shall make it my pleasure to help you to forget it. Before we've finished with you you're going to be a credit to the Regiment although it looks as if I'll have to become a magician to do it. Look at yourselves, you miserable lot of perishin' misfits, mincing around like a crowd of nancies with boils on your arses. You aren't training to be ballet dancers, you're training to be soldiers in B Squadron, the best squadron in the Regiment. At least, it was until you had to be inflicted on it. Now pull yourselves together, you poor weary Willies and we'll try again.'

The three reinforcement subalterns who had newly joined the squadron stood in the shadow thrown by the barrack block. Edward Palmer, fair-haired and a little under average height said: 'In all my long experience of army life I've yet to hear a warrant officer say something original. What a depressing thought it is when one realizes that all over the world sergeant-majors are saying exactly the same things at the same time only in different languages. How horrible it must sound in Japanese. To my mind that is the most revolting lingo in the world – even worse than Welsh.'

'I get bored stiff standing around watching this sort of

thing,' remarked Holmes. 'Can't we sneak back to the mess for a game of snooker?'

Fraser looked at his watch. 'It's nearly twelve, come on, let's leave the poor sods to it.'

The trio walked quickly away in the direction of the mess, the S.S.M's harsh voice becoming fainter and fainter as they went.

Lieutenant-Colonel Rankin, the Regiment's new commanding officer, sat at his desk studying the records of service of his squadron leaders, while Major Peck, his second-in-command, stood watching him.

'I say, Peck,' exclaimed the colonel, 'look at this. Harvey is a territorial. I would have preferred a regular for B Squadron, wouldn't you?'

'I know it is a bit unusual, but although I say it myself, Harvey will do you as well as any regular could. He's had a lot of battle experience and that's what really counts at a time like this. Besides, poor old Walters was a territorial and he turned out pretty well after all's said and done.'

'I suppose you're right,' the colonel grudgingly conceded, 'but there isn't a single regular in B Squadron. We shall have to keep our eyes on it.'

'Don't you worry, sir. They'll manage very well.'

The colonel put the reports into the safe and locked it. He said: 'I wish they'd tell us when we can expect our tanks. I've been worrying them down at G.H.Q., but nobody seems to know anything. I know just what will happen. We'll be kept hanging about here with nothing to give the chaps to keep them out of trouble, then all of a sudden the tanks will arrive and they'll send us straight up to the blue without ever having a chance to get in some decent training with them. Anyhow, we're wasting our breath discussing it. Let's go over to the mess and I'll buy you a gin.'

Major Harvey stared across his desk at the three officers standing to attention. He said in a cold, impersonal tone:

'At twelve o'clock this morning, or a little before, I went to have a look at the squadron doing drill. There was no officer present. Would you mind telling me where you were?'

Fraser began to speak: 'Sir, we'd been there since the men started this morning. I thought – "

Harvey cut him short. 'I don't wish to know what you thought, I want to know where you were.'

'I went to the mess, sir,' answered Fraser who had now gone very pale.

'What about you two?' snapped Harvey. They answered together:

'In the mess, sir.'

'You mean all three of you were lounging about in the mess while your men were sweating it out on the parade ground?' There was no reply.

In a milder voice Harvey continued. 'The men very seldom like their officers, but they do occasionally respect them. If you carry on like this they'll very quickly despise you. For the next three days you can all three of you consider yourselves confined to barracks. You will spend the whole of the day with the men. If I catch any of you in the mess except at meal times you'll be for it. That's all.'

The three men saluted and marched out.

'I don't think I'm going to like our squadron leader, the silly jumped-up bastard,' muttered Palmer.

'Never mind,' said Fraser. 'I'm afraid it was my idea to beetle off this morning. We did rather lay ourselves open to a rocket, but I must confess I didn't expect he'd keep us in like a lot of little schoolboys. What are we going to do with the troops? We can't just hang around them all day like a lot of poor relations.'

'I shall lecture my troop on cultural subjects, and in the evenings I shall let them take it in turns to read aloud from Browning and Keats. Perhaps I may even get them to put on a Greek play,' announced Palmer.

'It might be an idea to tell them something about our civilian jobs or our hobbies,' suggested Holmes.

'There's nothing I could tell my chaps about my favourite pastime that they didn't know already,' Fraser said.

The tawdry night club was crowded with other ranks. A band was playing, and men danced with the hostesses or with their Continental girl friends. At a table sat five other ranks from B Squadron who had survived the recent battle.

Lance-corporal Binney poured some beer into his glass and pushed the bottle towards Merriman. He said, 'What's the bloody squadron coming to, I'd like to know? Having us drilling all the morning in that ruddy heat. Anyone would think we're entitled to take it easy for a bit after what we've been through, but not bloody likely. No leave, no bloody nothing. I tells you, its all on account of these reinforcements. Just because of those muckers, we're being treated like a lot of ruddy recruits.'

Pettigrew muttered: 'That sod Roberts. I'll do him one of these days, and those three little twerps they've just given us dressed up as officers. What bloody use are they going to be, I ask you?'

Merriman said, and his speech was slurred by alcohol: 'Even Harvey's different now he's got the squadron. I s'pose it's gone to his head, 'cos he seemed a good enough bloke in the desert.'

Gadd was watching a pretty little dark girl who was dancing with an Australian. He said: 'Look at that bit with the Aussie. I'm going to ask her for a dance.'

Gadd stood up and walked to the dance floor, swaying slightly as he made his way between the crowded tables. He waited until the dark girl and her partner moved round to him, then he suddenly smacked the Australian heavily on the back and exclaimed: 'Excuse me, chum.'

'Beat it, Pommy. The lady doesn't want to dance with you,' the Australian snapped, looking threateningly at Gadd.

'Who the hell are you calling a Pommy?' asked Gadd, spoiling for trouble.

'On your way before I get tough with you, Pommy,' was the Australian's reply.

Gadd drove his left fist into the Australian's stomach, then as the winded man doubled up, he stood back and with all the force of a full right arm swing, hit him on the jaw. The unconscious Colonial fell backwards on to the dance floor and lay still. The dark girl screamed and darting at Gadd, drove her nails into his face, but he quickly grasped her wrists and holding her arms behind her back with one hand, he kissed her on the mouth, at the same time caressing her bottom with his free hand. The girl fought to free herself, spitting and biting like a frenzied cat.

In a matter of seconds the dance floor had cleared and the band ceased playing. Three Australians rushed at Gadd, and the first to reach him dived at his legs in a flying tackle. Gadd swung his arms to try to save himself. His fingers touched the girl and grasped her dress which came away in his hand in a crisp, tearing sound. Then he was on the floor with the three men on top of him.

'Hang on, Gaddy boy, we're right with you,' yelled

Pettigrew, as the men from B Squadron dashed to their comrade's assistance. The little dark girl, clad only in her panties and brassière, was making unsuccessful efforts to retrieve her torn frock which was still caught about Gadd's legs, but the flying feet and struggling bodies kept her away and she began to cry in her distress and humiliation. The whole place was in an uproar. Men were fighting in little groups throughout the club. Others were contenting themselves by throwing bottles at the struggling soldiers or at the glasses and bottles in the little bar. A flying chair hit a screaming woman as she ran for shelter, knocking her to the ground, but she quickly scrambled to her feet and made for the exit where a number of girls were pushing and struggling with each other to get through the narrow entrance. The battle still raged after the women had fled. Two M.P.'s came through the entrance swinging their truncheons. Cat calls, yells and bottles greeted them and they hastily retreated to summon the riot squad. A few minutes later an officer and twenty men arrived each armed with a wooden stave. Chairs and bottles greeted them but they were quickly through the entrance and spreading out into the club. The riot squad were all hefty men who seemed to be enjoying their work. They went from group to group, tapping the fighting men on legs and arms with skilful and paralysing blows. In a little while some forty men were lined up on the dance floor, while all around soldiers lay unconscious or sat rubbing aching limbs.

S.S.M. Roberts stamped into Major Harvey's office and saluted briskly. Harvey sensed immediately that something was wrong.

'What is it, Sergeant-Major?' he inquired.

'Sir, five men from the squadron are in the detention barracks at G.H.Q.'

'Who are they?'

The S.S.M. reeled off the names of the prisoners. He was still standing stiffly to attention.

'Stand easy, Roberts. What have they been up to? Do you know yet?'

'Yes, sir! Drunk and assaulting in a bar. They started a brawl and smashed up the place. We've got to send an officer with an escort to bring them back.'

'Aren't they all old B Squadron men?'

'Yes, sir.'

'You'd better send someone to ask Mr. Fraser to come over here. Then I want you to detail an escort with a five-tonner.'

'Very good, sir.' Roberts stepped back and saluted. Just as he was going through the door, Harvey stopped him.

'And Sergeant-Major, make sure there are no reinforcements on that escort, do you understand?'

'Yes, sir.'

Lieutenant Fraser stood beside the truck, waiting for the five men he had just signed for to be marched from the cells. In a little while they emerged from the building surrounded by their escort. Fraser's fastidious nature was shocked by their dishevelled appearance. They were unshaven and bareheaded. Their drill uniforms were creased and torn and stained with drink and vomit. There was little truculence left in their bruised bodies as they climbed sullenly into the back of the vehicle.

As soon as the party returned to the Regiment the men were marched in front of their squadron leader. Harvey studied the faces of the five men as the S.S.M. was reading the charge. When Roberts had finished, Harvey spoke:

'Have you anything to say?' he asked. The prisoners looked straight to their front, and were silent.

'Not only are you a disgrace to the squadron,' went on Harvey, 'but you've set a sorry example to the reinforcements, and, if it means anything to you, you've let me down. I happen to have taken a great pride in the squadron ever since I came to it. I liked to think it was perhaps the best in the Regiment, but no one else is going to think so now after your behaviour last night. I can't deal with you; it's out of my hands. You're remanded for the C.O. That's all.'

The S.S.M. shouted the orders:

'Prisoners and escort, left turn, quick march!'

In a few seconds Harvey was left alone, staring blankly at the wall in front of him. He smiled wryly, wondering how anyone could possibly hold him personally responsible for what his men did on their night off; but they were his responsibility. He knew that the colonel would drive that point home.

The following morning the R.S.M. read the charge, the adjutant and Major Harvey standing to attention beside the colonel's chair.

'Do you accept my award?' inquired Colonel Rankin as he glared at the five men. The accused signified that they did.

'Very well, you will be confined to barracks for the next three months or until the Regiment returns to the desert, whichever is the earlier, and the damage you caused will be stopped out of your pay.'

The prisoners were marched out, and Harvey prepared to leave.

'Just a moment, Major Harvey. I wish to speak to you alone,' said the colonel. There was no friendliness in his voice. The adjutant quickly saluted and went out, closing the door behind him.

'Major Harvey,' the colonel began, 'I am disturbed by this incident inasmuch as it reflects on the whole of my Regiment. My confidence in your capacity to command your squadron is not a little shaken. What you appear to need is more experience in keeping control of your men, and for that I have in mind a little plan. You will draw rations for the entire squadron and take it on a ten-day exercise into the desert east of Cairo. Teach your officers navigation and your men desert craft. Generally toughen them up and although you haven't any tanks, treat them as if they were under battle conditions. Get them out of here by tonight, keep within thirty miles of Cairo and maintain constant wireless contact. Is that understood?'

'Yes, sir,' replied Harvey.

'Right, you will have plenty to do, so get on with it.'

Harvey saluted and went out. He was burning with shame and anger at the colonel's injustice. He silently cursed the colonel and the five men as he walked back to his squadron office.

S.S.M. Roberts was waiting for him, nursing a file of papers under his left arm while he saluted with his right.

'Never mind those now,' snapped Harvey as Roberts started to say something, 'get the squadron paraded.'

'But some of the men are on courses and at lectures, sir.'

'Sergeant-Major, I don't want any 'buts' from you. I want the entire squadron paraded here just as quickly as you can do it. Now get on with it.' Roberts flushed a little, then hurried away while Harvey picked up the 'phone and arranged for vehicles and rations.

In a little while B Squadron was lined up on the parade ground outside Harvey's office. Lieutenant Palmer reported to his squadron leader that all the men were present, and Harvey went out to address them:

'As the result of the behaviour of five of you men the

150

entire squadron has been ordered into the desert for a ten-day exercise as punishment. Perhaps when you return you will think twice before disgracing the squadron again. That's all! Sergeant-Major, will you take over please?' Harvey went back to his office as the men received their instructions.

When Harvey drove over to the mess to collect his kit, he stopped at Allen's room to tell him what had happened. He found his second-in-command resting fully dressed in an easy chair. When Harvey had finished, Allen said:

'I'm coming with you, Pete. I should feel lost without the squadron around.'

'Don't be silly. You're excused duty with that leg of yours. Just concentrate on getting yourself fit again. I shall need all the help you can give me when we come back.'

Allen argued a little, but Harvey was adamant, and in a little while he left.

Late that morning, when B Squadron in its trucks had moved out into the desert, Allen walked across to the M.I. room. The doctor looked at his thigh, from which the stitches had been removed.

'There's nothing wrong with that, Tony,' the M.O. announced. 'In a week or so the stiffness will have disappeared and you'll be fit for duty again. In the meantime don't use it too much.'

'Do you think I could go out to the squadron, Doc?'

'Definitely not, you're to stay here until I say so.'

Allen walked back to the mess feeling rather bored. He dropped into a chair, and picking up a magazine passed the time until lunch was served. Afterwards, he went back to his room to sleep through the heat of the afternoon. He had just undressed when there was a knock on the door.

'Come in,' he answered.

An orderly put his head around the door.

'Colonel's compliments, sir. He wants to see you in his office.'

'Thank you,' replied Allen, and the orderly closed the door.

Allen quickly dressed himself, wondering why the C.O. wanted him.

Colonel Rankin greeted him coldly. 'Why aren't you with your squadron, Allen?' he inquired.

Allen concealed his surprise. 'I'm excused all duties, sir.'

'Then you're not much use to us, are you?'

'I don't know, sir. My leg is almost healed. In a few days I shall be able to return to duty, I hope.'

'You don't see my point, I'm afraid. This is a fighting unit. We can't afford to carry passengers. If you're not able to do your job someone else must take your place. If the M.O. says you're to be excused duty, then I must put someone in your place. In the meantime you had better go to the Base Depot. When you're passed as fit again, and should there be a vacancy for you, no doubt you will be able to return to us. I'm sorry, Allen. I'm sure you see my point.'

As Allen walked back to the mess he kept muttering under his breath, 'You bastard, you rotten bastard.'

On the evening of the same day that B Squadron had been despatched to the desert and Captain Allen to the Base Depot Colonel Rankin, wearing a smart gaberdine uniform, was attending a dance at the Gezira Sporting Club. He had swallowed several gins and was feeling extremely pleased with himself. He thought that he had earned his night's relaxation after the busy day he had spent in re-organizing and putting new life into the Regiment. Discipline was what was needed to put the

Regiment into shape. It had grown slack in the desert, and the men and some of the officers too, seemed to have the idea that they could do just as they pleased now that they had come back from the fighting. He intended to make it his job to disillusion them as quickly as he could on that score.

The band struck up a Paul Jones and he took his place in the circle. When the music stopped, he found himself looking down into the smiling blue eyes of a W.A.A.F. officer. In a few seconds the band started again, and they were dancing.

Lieutenant-Colonel Martin Rankin was a very handsome young man. Tall and dark, with a large black moustache, he looked the very image of a regular officer. His pretty partner was not unaware of his attraction nor was she averse to his attentions, and so it was that later in the evening she accepted his invitation to dinner. When the dance finished the Colonel called a taxi and on the short journey back to the little W.A.A.F.'s hostel, he slipped his hand over her's as she agreed to meet him on the following evening. Just before she stepped out of the taxi she looked at him quizzically, a half-smile about her full red mouth. Rankin kissed her on the lips and felt his kiss returned, and then she was gone.

Lieutenant Fraser was taking his turn to navigate the squadron. It was very hot and the sun beat down on the open trucks as they bounced and bumped across the rough stones and patches of soft treacherous sand. Major Harvey, who was following in the rear of the squadron, noticed that one of the vehicles was stuck in the sand. He drove across to it and saw the five culprits working frantically with shovels and sand mats in their efforts to free the wheels, which had sunk inches deep into the sand. Binney, no longer wearing his lance-corporal's stripe, was issuing instructions. Harvey halted his vehicle clear of the patch of soft sand and walked over to them.

'Stop what you're doing,' he ordered. 'I'll back my truck as near as I can to you, then you can connect your tow-rope to mine. We'll put the sand mats under my back wheels. That should get you out. Hurry up!' The men did as Harvey had ordered, and in a few moments they were free of the sand. Harvey smoked a cigarette as they unshackled the tow-rope. Suddenly his eyes twinkled and his mouth widened into a grin as he watched the sweating men.

'You silly buggers,' he remarked to the weary group. 'You've only yourselves to blame. Do you think I enjoy being out here when I could be sitting comfortably in Cairo?'

The men looked sheepishly at each other, then Gadd said: 'I'm sorry about the other night, sir, honest I am. In fact all of us are for what we did. We didn't think it would make trouble for everyone like this.' Pettigrew, dirty and sweat-stained added: 'It won't happen again, sir.'

'It had better not,' agreed Harvey. Then he asked: 'Why are you chaps all in the same truck? Why don't you spread yourselves round the squadron and give the new men the benefit of your experience?'

'Well, sir,' replied Binney. 'We'll do that in a day or so, but just for the moment we're not so popular as we might be, so we're sticking together for protection like.'

When Harvey had driven away, Merriman remarked:

'Old Harvey's not a bad sod for an officer. I'd sooner 'ave 'im than a lot of other muckers I've known, s'truth I would.'

'You'll soon change your bloody mind when he comes

chasin' after you again,' commented Burnett. 'You're like a bloomin' lot of schoolgirls in love with their blinkin' mistress. Oh, please Major Harvey, I'm ever so sorry. I'll never be naughty again, sir.'

'Ah, shut up, Burnett, we don't want to listen to your ruddy views. Not in this 'eat we don't,' ordered Binney.

Allen lounged in an easy chair in the ante-room of the Base Depot Mess, overcome by boredom. He was also worried about his future with the squadron. He doubted very much if the colonel would replace him before B Squadron returned from its penance, but of this he could not be sure. One thing was certain: he was going to get himself passed fit for active service before the squadron came in again.

There were well over a hundred officers at the Depot. About a quarter of these belonged to the permanent staff while the rest were either on courses or awaiting posting. Like Allen, there were also several officers recuperating from wounds and illness.

A young lieutenant limped into the ante-room, his leg encased in plaster. When he saw Allen, he smiled across the room at him.

'I'm ready for a beer, going to join me?' invited the officer, whose name was Fellowes.

A waiter brought a bottle and two glasses; Allen sipped his drink. He said: 'That's better, this place is beginning to get me down.'

'How long have you been here?' asked Fellowes.

'Two days!'

'God, I've been here nearly two months. I've got to stay here until they take this damned plaster off, and that won't be for another month at least.'

'What do you do with yourself all day?' asked Allen.

'Just lounge about and remember the better days. I've tried to persuade them to let me do a bit of instructing, but they won't hear of it. It's against union rules. I suppose they think I might be capable of taking over some fit person's job, in which case he'd be shot off to the desert to do some fighting and that would never do.'

Allen laughed. 'Are they really as bad as that?' he asked.

'Much worse, old man. Of course, there are some genuine exceptions who spend half their time trying to get back to their regiments, but very few succeed. As far as I can see, most of the others are determined at all costs to keep clear of the fighting. They are known locally as the Short Range Desert Group. Talk to 'em and you'll soon find out for yourself. Instructing is their very life. It's all they ever speak about. I believe they're pretty good at it too; they've got to be, there's so much competition.'

Allen ordered more beer as Fellowes continued: 'They creep around the commandant and the staff captain, and if they think their number's up, then off they go to the M.O. with some obscure trouble that he can't quite put his finger on, and then they're downgraded as medically unfit for the desert. Allergic to sand or some such bloody nonsense. You should have been down here a few weeks ago when it looked as if old Rommel was coming visiting here. The long faces and subdued voices when cruel rumours whizzed around the place that every officer who could fire a rifle was to be sent up to the desert. The commandant even had 'em out on the ranges for an hour a day. That old boy's got a sense of humour and no mistake. The funny thing is, you know, most of them would be absolutely useless in the field. No self-respecting regiment would dream of keeping them for more than a day. They'd be posted straight back to Cairo.'

'Oh, surely it can't be quite as bad as all that?'

'All right, if you don't want to believe me just you wander around the place and see for yourself. It will be an eye-opener for you, mark my words.'

One afternoon, when Allen had been living at Depot for a week, Fellowes came into his room.

'Come on, Tony,' he said, 'let's get out of this God-forsaken place and go and have tea out at Gezira.'

As the two officers were making their way towards a vacant table on the club's crowded terrace, Allen suddenly noticed Colonel Rankin sitting with a very attractive young girl in W.A.A.F. officer's uniform. Rankin was looking very pleased with himself, thought Allen, and then the colonel saw him before he could look away, and beckoned to him.

'Well, Allen, how are you getting along?' inquired Rankin in his heartiest manner. As Allen was about to make some perfunctory answer, the colonel went on: 'This is Miss Grenfell.' Then he turned to the girl and said: 'Peggy, I want you to meet Captain Allen. He's one of my young officers. At the moment he's enjoying a spot of sick leave. He got himself shot up in the desert a few weeks ago.'

The girl smiled pleasantly at Allen and said: 'I do hope you're managing to enjoy yourself.' Allen liked her soft, expressive voice. He replied, not looking at Rankin:

'I find it rather dull with nothing to do. I shall be very glad to get back to the Regiment.'

The colonel was in a gay, expansive mood. 'When do you think you'll be passed fit to return to duty?'

'Within the next two days for certain, sir.'

'That's fine, then, you'll be back before your squadron

returns. Ring up the adjutant and ask him to arrange for transport when you're ready to rejoin us.'

'Why, thank you, sir,' Allen replied, unable to conceal his surprise.

'That's all right, Allen, we shall all be very glad to have you back again.'

Allen was scarcely able to believe his ears. He remained chatting politely for a few moments, then he excused himself and rejoined Fellowes.

'Keeping up acquaintances with the senior ranks, eh?' remarked Fellowes with a grin as Allen sat down. 'Well, it never hurts, you know, to keep in with the right people.'

'That happens to be my C.O., and what's more, he's just told me I can go back to the Regiment as soon as the M.O. gives me the all clear.'

'Is he the bloke you were telling me about who got you sent to the Depot?'

'Yes, he's the one. Anyhow, he's changed his mind, and that's all I care.'

'I wonder why,' mused Fellowes. 'Perhaps that pretty little popsie he's got with him is having a softening influence on him, or then again, maybe he realizes that the Regiment can't function without you.'

'Whatever it is,' laughed Allen, 'I feel a new man again.'

'Well, I hope sometimes, when Jerry is throwing everything he's got at you, you'll remember your old pal Fellowes eating his heart out at the Base Depot.'

'Don't be stupid, you'll be away yourself in a few weeks.'

'Rot, old boy, I'll be here until the end of time. I can feel it in my water.'

When the men of B Squadron, dusty and sunburnt, returned to the Regiment, Captain Allen was there to meet them. He noticed how fit the reinforcements looked; even the three new officers had already developed an air of efficiency. Later, as he was walking back to the mess with the squadron leader, Harvey remarked: 'You know, Tony, I quite enjoyed it out there. As a matter of fact, I believe, everyone did, once they'd got used to it, of course. I know we didn't have any tanks, but I do believe we've got a damn good squadron again. You wait and see. By the way,' he added, 'how's our C.O. been getting along?'

Allen told of his temporary banishment to the Base Depot and of how he had met the colonel at Gezira.

'Funny chap,' remarked Harvey, when Allen had finished. 'Let's hope he'll be all right.'

'Tony, have you seen Dolores yet?' he went on to inquire.

'No, that's all over as far as I'm concerned. Nice little thing, but a bit too young for me.'

'Still thinking of Mary, eh?'

'Sometimes, but that has nothing to do with it.'

'I should hope not!' exclaimed Harvey.

The weeks passed by, and then came the disappointing news of a fresh thrust by Rommel. Before the British could stop him, his spearheads had reached the Sollum area. Tobruk had been by-passed and this meant that the garrison could now only be supplied by sea, which was no easy matter since the harbour was small and littered with wrecked ships. Stukas were always lurking close at hand to dive bomb the laden ships once they were within a few miles of the harbour.

At last the Regiment received its long-awaited tanks, and then Lieutenant-Colonel Rankin led it to a barren training area some forty miles from Cairo.

The days were spent on the gunnery ranges, or on

tactical exercises, and in a very short time the Regiment was once again ready for action.

One evening shortly before dusk Major Harvey brought the squadron into camp after a whole day's 'wireless scheme'. He climbed wearily out of his tank, and after dismissing the men, walked across to the little tent that served as the squadron's mess. Waiting for him there he found a letter from Vera. The sight of her handwriting caused a spasm of tightness in his chest. The envelope was postmarked Cairo, and had been posted only three days ago.

'My darling,' he read, 'you will, no doubt, be surprised to learn that I am here at Maadi. Six months ago I left Henry for good. The memories of those days and nights that you and I had spent together soon made everything else seem impossible and cheap. I believe he's now married; anyway, I don't hear from him any more, and it's all quite finished. I never loved him, Pete, although perhaps just for a little while I believed I did, but I know now that it was only the excitement of something new. I pay all the time for my folly and weakness, and my thoughts are full of you. I worry day and night about you, and if you are in danger. I must confess that I couldn't bear to face life without the hope that one day, no matter how far distant, we might come together again.

I'm now in the A.T.S. and I've just arrived here in Egypt. I shall be in camp at Maadi for some time. What a wonderful thing it would be if one day they came and told me that my husband was here, waiting to see me.

Ever yours,
Vera.'

Harvey read the letter twice, then putting it into his pocket, he walked out of the tent and went off to look for the colonel. He found him drinking gin with Major Peck in the H.Q. mess. Rankin greeted him: 'Hullo, Harvey, what brings you over here? Come and have a drink. What would you like?' Harvey curbed his impatience.

'Thank you, sir, may I have a Scotch?'

For a few moments the three officers talked about the day's exercise, then Harvey said: 'Excuse me, sir, but do you think I might have a word with you on a private matter?'

'Of course you may, my dear chap. Come outside for a moment.' The colonel sounded very affable, and Harvey thought that he had seized an opportune moment for his request. Outside the tent it was now quite dark. The still air carried the occasional sound of the men's voices from the distant cookhouse.

'Now, what's the trouble?' inquired Rankin.

'There's no trouble, sir,' replied Harvey, then he went on: 'I hate asking favours, but my wife has just arrived in Cairo. I haven't seen her since I left England, and I was wondering if you'd give me permission to go and see her tonight. She's only over at Maadi. I would be back at dawn tomorrow.'

The colonel answered quickly: 'It's quite out of the question, Harvey. I should have thought you would have known better than to ask for such privileges. We may leave at a moment's notice. Why, I might get the order at any time to move the Regiment and how can I do that with one of my squadron leaders in Cairo? Apart from all that, we've got to think of the men. They've also got wives whom they haven't seen for some time. How are they going to feel about officers who get their wives out here and then go off to see them whenever they feel like it.

No, Harvey, I most certainly can't agree to your request. You'll have plenty of opportunity for seeing her before we leave here, I hope, but you can't go tonight, not while the rest of the Regiment is confined to camp. Is that quite clear?'

'Yes, sir,' replied Harvey, endeavouring to keep the resentment out of his voice.

'Then let's forget about it for the time being. Come back in and finish your drink.'

'Thank you, sir.'

As soon as he could, Harvey escaped from the R.H.Q. mess, and stifling his disappointment, went back to his tent to write to Vera.

The following morning, just as Harvey was preparing to lead out the squadron on a short tactical exercise, a despatch-rider stopped his cycle at the squadron leader's tank to tell him that the colonel wished to see him immediately.

'Ah, there you are,' said Rankin, as Harvey came into the tent and saluted. 'I've got some good news for you. You're to take your squadron to Alexandria to embark for Tobruk. The rest of the regiment will probably be following you, but at the moment there's very little shipping space. You'll be on your own now, at least for a bit, so it's up to you to see that the squadron puts up a good show. Do you understand?'

'Yes, sir.'

'Right. Now for details. Transporters will be here in about an hour to move the tanks. You won't be taking any soft vehicles with you as there isn't room in the ship. You'll find those when you get to Tobruk. You and the rest of your officers and men will be taken to Alexandria in A Squadron transport. Be ready to leave here in two hours and until you're on board the ship your destination will remain secret. Is that clear?'

'Yes, sir.'

Colonel Rankin stood up and offered his hand to Harvey.

'Well, that's about all, except good luck, and we hope to catch up with you soon.'

'Thank you, sir.' Harvey saluted, and turning on his heel walked out of the tent. The pleasure he felt at having his own independent command compensated to some extent for the disappointment that came to him with the knowledge that it would still be a very long time before he saw Vera again. But deep down, in the bottom of his heart, he was glad of the respite to think things over.

5

Major Harvey stood on the dockside watching his squadron march up the narrow gang-plank on to the deck of the little coaster that was to transport the men to Tobruk. A little further along the dock the tanks were being hoisted aboard another ship. The coarse and noisy comments of the troops caused a grin to spread around Harvey's lips.

'Cor, did you ever see such a muckin' tub?' one of the men shouted. 'They must think we're no muckin' use for anything. They're going to take us outside the 'arbour and drown the lot of us.'

The two vessels put to sea as darkness fell. Smoking was forbidden, and each man had orders to wear his life-jacket at all times. Now the men knew where they were going and throughout the night they were silent and tense, for all were aware of the dangers of this short sea voyage.

Harvey was on deck as soon as the first red rays of dawn arose from the eastern horizon. As it grew lighter he saw the second ship, the one carrying the tanks, ploughing through the sea about half a mile astern. A little later he was able to make out the loom of the land a few miles off on the port beam. It had become light again, the no-smoking order was relaxed. Harvey took out a cigarette, and lighting it, leaned on the wooden rail, enjoying the beauty of the morning. It was there that Allen found him, when he came out on deck.

'Well,' remarked Allen, noisily breathing in the fresh morning air, 'this is all very pleasant. A Mediterreanean cruise is just what we need. Unfortunately, it will all be over before we can begin to enjoy it.'

'I don't think you'll be enjoying it very much when we get near Tobruk. Not if Jerry sees us. He won't be very keen on the idea of us reaching the harbour.'

'You're being extremely pessimistic on this beautiful morning. They'll probably be giving us air cover when we get into the danger area.'

'I hope you're right, Tony, but I have my doubts. Anyhow, let's have a walk around and check up that the men are wearing their life-jackets. The alarm will sound for boat drill soon, and we'd better make sure they know what they're supposed to be doing.'

'Okay, sir.' Allen studied Harvey's face for a moment or two, then he said: 'I must say, Pete, you're looking remarkably anxious this morning. It's not a bit like you. Were you seasick in the night?'

'Don't be silly, Tony. I suppose it's the feeling that now I've got the squadron I want to keep it all in one piece. I'm beginning to understand how old Walters must have suffered.'

Palmer, Holmes and Fraser were sitting in a corner on the crowded deck playing liar dice when Harvey found them. For a few moments he stood over them unobserved, watching the game; then Fraser, happening to glance up, noticed him and got to his feet, the other two quickly following suit.

'Sorry to break up the game, but I'd like you to spread yourselves around the ship just in case anything happens.'

When Harvey had moved away, Holmes stooped down and picking up the dice, dropped them into his pocket.

'That's a cheerful thought to leave us with on such a beautiful day,' he said with a wry grin.

'I shall now make my way to the foredeck, fall the men in in three ranks and teach them the breast stroke,' announced Palmer.

'But you can't teach anyone to swim without water,' remarked Holmes.

'My dear Frank, when you get to know me better you

will realize that I can put my hand to anything. I shall teach them by numbers, and as for water, why there's gallons and gallons of it all around us. Besides, they'll get the idea just by looking at it.'

Shortly before midday the raucous sound of the klaxon echoed throughout the ship. The men hurried to their stations, wearing life-jackets and steel helmets. Guns pointed menacingly into a clear blue sky, but there was nothing to be seen. After the initial burst of activity the men stood still, straining their ears to catch the sound of aircraft. For several minutes the silence was only broken by the natural sounds of the ship moving through the calm waters and the clang of a hobnailed boot on the steel deck, then a hoarse voice muttered:

'There it is, I 'eard it then.' And faintly from the sky came the pulsating throb of an engine.

The men shuffled their feet and tightened their life-jackets. The momentary tension was relieved by coarse witticisms that brought howls of laughter.

Suddenly, orders were shouted from the bridge, the crews of the Oerlikons pointed the muzzles of their guns at a shiny speck high in the sky and opened fire. The men watched the tracers mounting in wide arcs towards the target that was well out of range.

Binney pushed back his tin helmet and spat on the deck in disgust.

'Those ruddy Navy gunners. They couldn't hit a muckin' house; not even if you held it on to the end of their ruddy gun for them,' he muttered, and those who heard him sniggered.

Now both ships were firing at the plane, which turned in a wide circle and made off towards the north. The chatter of the guns died away as the plane became smaller and smaller in the distance. Soon the all-clear sounded from the bridge, and as the men wandered away to relax once more on the sunny decks, the hot guns were cleaned and reloaded, and fresh supplies of ammunition were brought up from below.

One of the ship's quartermasters climbed down the companion way from the bridge and made his way across the deck to Harvey.

'Captain's compliments, sir, and would you step up to the bridge.'

''Morning, Major,' greeted the captain as Harvey reached the top of the companion way. He was a stocky little Welshman, with keen blue eyes and a determined thrust to his bristly jaw. He was not the type of man to stand on ceremony. 'Well' he continued before Harvey could speak, 'I suppose you know what that plane was hanging around for just now, don't you?'

Harvey nodded. 'A recce aircraft.'

'That's right. By now he's given his pals our course and before long we can expect the Stukas. You'd better stay on the bridge with me from now on, then you'll be in the picture, and if necessary you'll be in a better position to issue orders to your men. If we run into trouble they're to keep their heads down and not get in the way. Nobody jumps overboard until I say so, is that clear?'

Harvey felt a little resentful about the last remark. He said: 'Most of us have been in action before, sir, there won't be any panic among us.'

'Good,' grunted the captain. He seemed to soften for a moment as he pulled a packet of cigarettes from his pocket and offered one to Harvey. 'I've done this run three times now, and every time we've been Stukaed, but so far, touch wood, the worst has been near misses. Mark you, it's unpleasant while it lasts, but I expect we'll tie up in Tobruk tomorrow as per schedule.'

'I sincerely hope so. I'm not much of a swimmer,' said Harvey with a smile.

The ship ploughed westwards throughout the afternoon. The men were tense, as with straining ears they sought to catch the beat of an engine, while with anxious faces they searched the skies for the enemy.

The ship's bell sounded four o'clock, and as the noise of the last stroke died away the roar of aircraft could be heard by everyone on deck. The klaxon echoed through the ship and the guns opened fire. The tracer pointed to the black plane with the peculiar shaped wings of a pre-historic bird. The watching men saw the three bombs leave its undercarriage as the plane flattened out of its dive just in front of the ship. The first bomb hit the water and exploded about fifty yards off the port bow, the second was closer and landed in the water amidships, while the third came screaming down heading straight for the poop deck. To the amazement of those who still had the courage to watch its progress, it missed the after rail by inches and exploded in the sea astern.

A second Stuka roared out of the sun, but this time the gunners had the range, and the tracer bit into it. Black smoke belched from the fuselage and trailed behind it. Then orange flames enveloped it and without releasing its bombs it continued its dive, and hitting the water less than a hundred yards from the ship, it disappeared in a flurry of foam. The third Stuka came out of the sun in a scream-ing dive towards the ship carrying the tanks. Again the tracer leaped to meet it as the three bombs fell, and the pilot pulled out of his dive, and peeled off in a steep climb away from his target, exposing the black crosses on his wings. There was a flash of flame as the bomb struck the deck. Black smoke and debris rose high into the after-noon sky. Another flash and yet another, and the doomed ship's outline faded into oily black smoke topped with flame. The two planes had almost disappeared, the sound of their engines came faintly, but across the half-mile of sea the screams and shouts from the burning ship were all too audible.

Harvey watched the grim face of the captain as he stared astern through his glasses. The chief officer, who was also watching the burning wreck, put down his glasses and said,

'It doesn't look as if they're getting their boats away, sir.'

'No, Mr Watts,' answered the captain through clenched teeth. 'It doesn't look as if they've got any boats left to get away.'

The small group on the bridge saw the bows of the burning ship rise high out of the water. A little later, across the distance came a dull rumble as the ship's engines dropped out of their fittings and fell aft, together with the tanks as they burst through the holds. Then the bows slipped gently back into the water in a little area of foam, steam and smoke.

'She's gone,' muttered the captain, and still looking through his glasses, said: 'There are a few survivors swimming towards a raft.'

The ship steamed on, deserting the men in the water. Soon the troops began to crowd the rail, staring back at the spot where the ship had sunk. They were murmuring among themselves, and then someone shouted:

'Aren't you going to pick 'em up, mister?' In a few seconds a dozen voices were shouting up at the group of officers on the bridge.

'Major, if you've got any control over your troops, keep them quiet,' snapped the captain, whose face was drawn and angry.

Harvey left the bridge, and with the help of his officers and Sergeant-Major Roberts he had the men paraded. They were still muttering when Roberts called them to attention. For a few moments Harvey looked at the sullen faces, then he said: 'Those men, once they are on the rafts, will soon make their way ashore. It's only a few miles off, and the tide is drifting them in. This part of the coast is still British so they'll most probably all be back in Alex tomorrow. The captain of our ship has orders to get us to Tobruk. Much as he would like to go back and pick those people up it's his duty to keep going whatever happens, so don't make it more difficult for him. We've lost our tanks, but at least we've got something to be thankful for – we're still afloat, and if, and when, we get to Tobruk, then we can make it our job to see that Jerry pays for what has happened this afternoon. I don't want to hear any more remarks as to what you would do if you were in the captain's place. He knows what he's doing, and he's doing it bloody well, so let's have no more nonsense. That's all – you can fall out again.'

The men went back to the rail, but they could see nothing now of the survivors. They were already far astern. But the troops no longer muttered threateningly towards the men on the bridge.

Shortly after dawn the little ship entered Tobruk harbour and hurriedly disembarked the men of B Squadron. As Major Harvey stepped ashore, a staff captain came towards him and saluted.

'The brigadier sent me down to meet you, sir. I hope you had a good trip up?'

'It might have been worse,' Harvey replied.

'Good,' the staff captain went on. 'You're going to a little spot about two miles out of the town – or rather what's left of the town. I'm sorry about transport, but we're so short of petrol up here that I'm afraid you people will have to walk. I've got two men here who will lead the way. Your drivers had better stay here until the tanks arrive.'

'I'm afraid the tanks won't be arriving. The ship that was bringing them was sunk yesterday afternoon.'

'That's bad. The brigadier will be very disappointed.'

'I'm sorry about that,' remarked Harvey. There was the ring of asperity in his voice.

The squadron leader spoke to Captain Allen, and a few minutes later he watched his men marching up the steep hill away from the harbour. Then he said to the staff captain, who was waiting close by. 'Right, now you can take me to the brigadier. Let's break the bad news to him and get it over.'

The brigadier was living in a small cave on the outskirts of the town. An army blanket nailed to a piece of wood across the narrow entrance served as a black-out curtain at night and a door in the day-time. When Harvey and the staff captain arrived at his H.Q. they found him sitting in a camp chair outside his cave busily lathering his cheeks. The staff captain introduced the squadron leader.

'Sir,' he said, 'this is Major Harvey, who was expected up with the tank squadron.'

The brigadier held out his hand to Harvey. 'Glad to see you,' he greeted. Harvey went straight to the point.

'Our tanks were sunk on the way up, sir.'

The brigadier, who had begun to fit a blade into his razor, put it down on the little wooden table and looked up at Harvey for a few moments.

'Did you lose any of your men?' he inquired at last.

'No, sir, they were in one ship, the tanks in another.'

'That was fortunate, I'm very glad about that. Pity the

tanks have gone though. We could have done with those. However, just as well they didn't send a whole regiment as I asked.'

The brigadier adjusted his little chromium-plated hand-mirror and began to shave. Then he said: 'It may be some time before we get any more tanks through, so you'll have to get down to some infantry training.'

The men of B Squadron grumbled about their new role, but Harvey and the rest of his officers kept them at their work from dawn until dusk, while only a mile or so away the enemy was probing the defences along the whole length of the perimeter. The guns were never silent, and at night the sky was lit up by their bursts and the multi-coloured stars of the Very lights.

One afternoon, about a week after the squadron had been in Tobruk, the brigadier sent for Harvey. The squadron leader found him sitting at a table outside his cave studying maps and air reconnaissance photographs. Several other officers in stained and much worn uniforms were standing around holding maps and notebooks. When the brigadier eventually noticed Harvey, he said:

'Ah, there you are. Sorry to tell you, but we've no tanks for you yet. How's the infantry training going?'

'The squadron is coming along very well, sir.'

'Good, do you think you could use it in a defence position out on the perimeter? You won't have much opposition out in front of you – at least, not for the moment.'

'I'm sure I could, sir.'

'Splendid, you'll have a little support until you get used to things, but we're a bit thin on the ground and I've got to keep every inch of the perimeter covered.'

The brigadier looked around the group of officers,

'West,' he exclaimed, 'there you are. Go with Harvey and show him where to put his men. Tell him all you can about what's going on.'

'Yes, sir,' answered Major West. Harvey liked the look of the tall fair-haired young company commander. They saluted the brigadier. As they walked away together, the infantry officer remarked:

'You must feel pretty browned off at being turned into foot-sloggers.'

Harvey grinned, 'We haven't got much option, have we?' he replied. 'Anyhow, things are a bit sticky up here; we've got to be prepared for anything. What's it like where we're supposed to be going?'

'Oh, not too bad. We've been out there for a fortnight. We've got nice little trenches and weapon pits on a bit of hilly ground. Jerry can't get his tanks anywhere near us and his infantry have a lot of open ground to cross before they can begin to winkle us out.'

'What sort of tanks have they got, do you know?' asked Harvey.

'Mark IV's, I think. In fact, I know they are. You can see them at a distance in the day-time patrolling up and down, just out of range of our anti-tank guns.'

'Many of them?' inquired Harvey.

'No, there are only eight that I've counted. They've been there for several days now; always the same ones. But you've got nothing to worry about from them. You wait until you see the place. You'll be as snug as a bug in a rug!'

'Hope you're right,' Harvey said, with a rueful smile.

That evening, shortly after dusk, Major Harvey led B Squadron out to its defensive position. The men climbed into the trenches and weapon pits that the company they were relieving had vacated. Bren guns were set up and sentries posted. Half the men slept while the other half remained on duty.

The night sky flickered with the flashes of the heavier artillery that momentarily illuminated the desert with the brightness of day. The silence was continually violated by the thunder of the guns, but the men who were not on duty scarcely noticed it as they lay in the sand, muffled up in their greatcoats against the chill of the desert night. No shells fell near them, no German patrol was reported, and when the dawn broke through not a single shot had yet been fired by the squadron.

Soon, hot tea from the hay-boxes was passed round and the men drank this with their hard rations of biscuits and corned beef.

One by one the officers reported to their squadron leader, then, after a brief chat, they returned to their positions. When Allen reached Harvey's trench, he found his squadron leader searching the skyline ahead of him with his binoculars. After a little while he put them down and greeted his second-in-command.

''Morning, Tony. Well anyway, our first night here was quiet enough.' He picked up his glasses again, and went on peering into the misty distance ahead.

'See anything?' inquired Allen, who was now adjusting his own glasses.

'Yes, I think I can,' murmured Harvey. 'Take a look about eleven o'clock. There's some dust going up. Can you see it?'

'You're right, Pete. They're tanks moving on to the ridge. You can see them now. Got them?'

'Yes, I wonder how far away they are?'

'A good two miles – maybe more,' answered Allen. 'Look,' he went on, 'there are eight of them. They're fanning out broadside on to the perimeter.'

'That's right,' said Harvey, 'those are the boys that chap West told me about yesterday. He said there were eight of them. Take a compass bearing on the spot where we saw them appear, and we'll mark it on the map. Let's see if they turn up in the same spot tomorrow.'

While the two officers were marking out the position of the enemy, the tanks were quickly spreading out broadside on to the squadron until they covered at least a mile of the front, but they did not approach any closer. A little later Harvey and Allen ducked involuntarily as what sounded like the roar of an express train passed overhead.

'That's one of ours,' remarked Harvey, and they saw a small fountain of black smoke rise from the sand some distance from one of the enemy tanks. The two officers were startled by the report of the gun that was dug in on the hill some distance behind the squadron, then the far-off crack of the exploding shell came to them from across the desert.

'I'm afraid they're well out of range,' said Harvey, 'but at least it should encourage them to keep their distance.'

Throughout the day the eight tanks were seldom out of sight of B Squadron. At intervals the guns inside the perimeter would open fire on them, but the enemy was wise enough to keep just out of range. No German infantry appeared, and still the squadron had not expended one single round of its ammunition.

As soon as it became dark the cook's five-tonner arrived with a hot evening meal, and then, when fresh sentries had been posted and the watches changed, the squadron settled down for its second night as an infantry unit.

In the early morning, as it began to grow light, Harvey and Allen leaned on the parapet of their weapon pit, watching through their glasses as they waited for the tanks to appear.

'Here they come!' announced Harvey. 'I can see the dust now. Look, Tony, they're coming on to the ridge in exactly the same spot as we saw them yesterday. What do you make of that?'

'It means that they laager just below the ridge,' answered Allen.

'Right,' agreed Harvey. Then he went on: 'And when we used to go out on patrol and stop for the night, what did we do?'

Allen thought for a moment then he replied, 'Keep the tanks fairly close together, post an officer and a few men about the place, then the rest of us would get down to some good solid sleeping.'

Harvey continued with his questioning. 'Did we leave anyone inside the tanks, do you remember?'

'Oh, well, we might have posted lookouts, say, perhaps, in two tanks out of the squadron,' said Allen.

'And suppose we had been suddenly surprised by a determined enemy, what would the lookouts in the tanks do about that?'

'Give the alarm,' was Allen's reply.

'Anything else, Tony?'

'No, I don't think so. They couldn't fire the guns. There would be no one else inside the tank to load for them. Besides, unless they were very cool lookouts, they'd probably be too surprised to think of anything for a moment or so.'

For a while both officers were silent, then a grin spread over Allen's face.

'By God, Pete, with a bit of luck we could do it, you know. What about having a crack at it tonight?'

'I'll have to ask the brigadier. If we went off on our own and our luck happened to be out, he could court-martial me for deserting my post, and besides, if we don't tell anyone they'll shoot up the tanks when – big question mark – we come back. By the way, how many chaps in this squadron could climb into a Mark IV and drive it smartly away?'

'Well, I could, for a start, and that leaves me another seven to find.'

Harvey thought for a few moments as he gazed towards the German tanks now clearly visible on the distant ridge. Then he said: 'Send for the Three Stooges. Tell them to pick out twenty-five men who would be likely to volunteer for such a party. Only ones handy with a Sten or able to chuck a grenade will do. You stay here and take over the squadron while I find the brigadier.'

As Harvey climbed out of the trench and brushed some of the sand from his greatcoat, Allen said: 'And the best of luck to you, Pete. Make it a good story because I believe we could pull it off.'

'You're right, I'll make it a good story. Between you and me, I've just about had a bloody 'nough of marching and living in trenches to last me for a lifetime. The sooner I get back into a tank, the happier I'll be, and there's not much wrong with Jerry's Mark IV.'

The brigadier did not keep Major Harvey waiting for more than a few minutes. When he saw the squadron leader he wrinkled his brow in surprise.

'Hullo, I thought you were supposed to be out on the perimeter. What brings you here?'

It did not take Harvey more than a few moments to explain his presence at Brigade H.Q. While he listened, the brigadier lifted himself out of his camp chair and thrusting his hands deep into the pockets of his whipcord slacks, he paced up and down in front of Harvey as he listened to the plan. When the squadron leader had given the broad outlines of his intentions, the brigadier remained thoughtful for a little while, then stopping in front of Harvey he said: 'That's a pretty ambitious plan. I admire your courage, but do you really believe you can bring it off?'

'Yes, sir, given a little luck.'

The brigadier was silent as he thought a little longer, then he went on: 'Show me here on this map where these tanks of yours park at night.'

Harvey looked at the map for a few seconds, then picking up a chinagraph pencil he put a dot on the talc that covered the map.

The brigadier shouted to one of the orderlies to fetch the Intelligence officer. While they were waiting for him to arrive the brigadier said to Harvey:

'We've got a Mark IV somewhere around here. You can bring back your men, then they can see how it starts and how the guns fire. That is, of course, if I decide to let you go.'

A few moments later the Intelligence officer came running up. 'See this spot,' said the brigadier, pointing to the mark that Harvey had made on the map. 'Let me know if there are any infantry or guns in the area. If necessary, get a recce plane over the place, but leave it as late as possible. Give me the latest information at sundown. Understand?'

'Yes, sir.'

The I.O. noted the map reference in his note-book and hurried back to his duties.

'All right, Harvey,' said the brigadier at last. 'Take a truck and go and fetch your volunteers. You'll find out where they've put the Mark IV. Go and practise in that. Whatever you want, if we've got it, you can have, and if the Intelligence reports are satisfactory then I suppose

I'll have to let you go. Your second-in-command will remain with the squadron. I'd rather you took only one other officer with you if you can manage. In fact, I'd rather you didn't go at all, and sent your second-in-command, but I know that's asking too much since all this is your bright idea. Come and see me at dusk. You won't have my consent before then, is that understood?'

'Yes, sir.'

'Good, now off you go and get yourself organized.'

When Harvey returned to the squadron, all was quiet. He saw Captain Allen coming towards him.

'I can see by your face it's Okay, Pete.'

'Yes, Tony, but it still depends on tonight's Intelligence reports. They're going to find out what else is lurking about out there before they hoist the off signal. Anyhow, before I say any more, I'd better tell you that the brigadier has refused to let you come. The second-in-command will stay with the squadron. Those were his orders so there's no argument, I'm afraid. You'll be in charge while I'm away.'

'Yes, sir,' answered Allen.

'Now,' said Harvey, 'which of the Three Stooges shall I take? Who do you suggest, Tony?'

'If it was me, then I'd plump for young Teddy Fraser.'

'Good. He was my choice too. Let's send for him.'

When Fraser climbed into the trench, Harvey explained. 'As you no doubt know by now, we're going to have a crack at bringing in those tanks out there. I've got to take either you, Holmes or Palmer with me. You'd better go and decide among yourselves who's coming. Toss a coin or dice for it. I want the chap who's coming with me back here as quickly as possible.'

'Yes, sir,' said Fraser, and rapidly climbed out of the

trench. Within five minutes he was back again. With an air of apology he announced: 'I'm afraid I'm the one, sir. Hope you don't mind.'

''Course I don't mind, Teddy. I'm glad to have you with me!'

It was the first time the squadron leader had addressed Fraser by his Christian name. The young lieutenant felt very proud at that moment.

The raiding party drove back to Brigade H.Q. and located the captured German Mark IV. Each driver made quite sure he knew how to start up and drive the machine, while the rest made themselves familiar with the mechanism of the machine-guns that were mounted inside. Then, while the twenty-five men gathered round, squatting in the sand, Harvey seated himself on the front of the tank and explained the plan he had formulated. Afterwards, they split up into two parties, one commanded by the squadron leader, the other by Lieutenant Fraser, and practised attacking the imaginary tanks. When this had been done to Harvey's entire satisfaction, they went off to the arms dump to draw their weapons. Each man carried a Sten gun with spare ammunition and hand grenades. Three men in each party drew anti-tank bombs to deal with any vehicles that could not be captured. In addition, both Harvey and Fraser wore Very pistols. Several men also carried Commando knives. When the last detail had been completed the squadron leader gave instructions to a sentry to call him at 6 p.m., then with his men he lay down in what shade he could find to get a little rest before the raid began.

The brigadier poured whisky into two tumblers and handed one to Harvey. 'Here's luck to you. When you get back, come straight to me. Don't be too late because

I don't suppose I shall get much sleep until I know how the party went.'

'Right, sir,' replied Harvey, and finished his drink. The brigadier came out into the night with him. For just a moment he rested a firm hand on Harvey's shoulder as they both looked up at the bright night sky.

'The moon will be down by the time you are ready to attack. Well, off you go,' and very gently he pushed Harvey on his way, making it impossible for the squadron leader to turn and salute.

The men filed through a narrow gap in the barbed-wire fence that marked the perimeter. They moved silently, the sand muffling the sound of their footsteps. The night was dark now except for the occasional gun flashes which lit up the desert around them, but they were still too far away to be visible to the enemy. Trooper Binney cursed as a loose strand of wire caught in the sling of his Sten gun, dragging it from his shoulder. Lance-Corporal Merriman, who was close behind, staggered into him as Binney stooped to retrieve his weapon.

'Look where you're bloody going, you clumsy sod,' snarled Binney.

'Well, get a muckin' move on,' grumbled Binney, 'you're holding everybody up.'

Lieutenant Fraser put an end to the argument: 'Shut up, no talking,' he whispered.

As Major Harvey marched at the head of his group towards the enemy he began to have doubts about the success of his enterprise. He wondered if he had thought up a hare-brain scheme on the impulse of the moment. He forced his mind away from the coming attack.

As a particularly brilliant flash of gunfire lit up the desert he flung himself to the ground. The men behind him dropped automatically, while fifty yards away on his right flank Lieutenant Fraser and his party were also lying flat in the sand. Quickly they picked themselves up and marched on.

At last they came to the ridge on which the tanks had first appeared in the morning. The soft sand had been torn up by the heavy tracks, causing several of the men to stumble in the darkness. As had been pre-arranged, both groups halted at the foot of the ridge while Lieutenant Fraser and Trooper Burnett removed their weapons and heavier equipment. They climbed swiftly up the ridge and disappeared over the top in search of the tanks, leaving Major Harvey and his men to wait anxiously for the information they were to bring back.

Free of their heavy equipment, Fraser and Burnett moved easily and silently to the top of the ridge, where they lay straining their ears. For nearly a minute they waited, but there was no sound from the enemy. Fraser thought that they must be either extremely silent, or much further away than they had estimated. He tapped Burnett on the shoulder and together they swiftly climbed down the far side of the ridge and hurried on. Several times they stopped to listen, but all they could hear was their own breathing and the distant and heavy gunfire, while sometimes, from the north, the staccato burst of a machine gun rattled across the darkness.

Fraser glanced at the illuminated dial of his wrist watch. It was a quarter-past eleven. Counting stops, he judged that he and Burnett had covered nearly a mile and a half since leaving the squadron leader. He decided to go on just a little further then, if he still had not located the tanks, he would bear right and return to the ridge at a point west of where he had left Harvey, for there was still the chance that the enemy might be laagered in that area.

In the darkness they felt themselves climbing a slope, then both dropped flat as suddenly they heard voices from nearby. For a few moments Fraser was too excited to move, then controlling himself, he began to think clearly once more. Signalling to Burnett to follow, he slowly crawled the short distance to the top of the ridge and looked down to where the sound of voices could be heard. After a few seconds he caught the glow of a cigarette as a man drew on it. Straining his eyes, now well accustomed to the darkness, he was able to make out the dim shape of tanks below him. The voices had now ceased, but the dull spark of the cigarette was still visible to the watching pair. Fraser and Burnett waited a little longer, then moved on to a position just below their side of the ridge. Very soon it was apparent that the tanks were lying up in a small, almost circular, hollow with two narrow entrances. Fraser thought to himself that it was hardly the sort of place he would choose in which to park his tanks at night. Then they heard the unmistakable metallic sound of a weapon as it struck some part of a soldier's equipment. They heard it again, and this time it was much nearer. Barely fifty yards away, a distant gun flash lit up the figure of a sentry patrolling the rim of the hollow. His beat was bringing him nearer to the two Englishmen, who swiftly and silently slithered down the far side of the slope and hugged the sand as the man drew closer until he was almost above them. There the German stopped, while the two men below scarcely dared to breathe wondering if the sentry had seen them yet, not daring to look upwards as they waited for the burst from his machine-gun. But no shots came, and after a few moments the German moved on and away from the two perspiring men cowering at the foot of the ridge.

Lieutenant Fraser thought that the raiding party was

going to have a difficult task ahead of it. Something would certainly have to be done about the sentry and any others who might happen to be on watch when the attack went in. Twenty-five men would have a very limited chance of gaining the rim of the hollow without being spotted, no matter how stealthily they approached. And, if they were detected before they could initiate the assault on the tank crews, the alarm would be given, the enemy would rush into their tanks, and Harvey and his men would never have a chance.

After a little while, Fraser took a prismatic compass from his pocket, and quickly setting it, he got a fix on one of the brighter stars. Nudging Burnett, they hurried back to Harvey and his anxious party, and on the way, the young lieutenant conceived a plan to deal with any sentries who might be patrolling the crest of the slope.

Captain Allen stared through the darkness towards the area where the squadron leader and his men would shortly be going into action, but he could see nothing. All was quiet out in front of the squadron's perimeter.

'What time do you make it, Holmes?' he asked the officer standing in the trench beside him.

'I make it five minutes past twelve. Something should be happening any moment now,' he replied.

The minutes slipped by while the men in the trenches waited anxiously for their comrades in the raiding party to start the attack.

Lieutenant Holmes looked at his watch for the hundredth time. It was nearly a quarter past one.

'Maybe they can't find them,' he said, but before Allen could think of a suitable reply, two Very lights soared into the night and burst into Roman candles that glowed brilliantly as they dropped slowly back to earth. Immediately following the Very lights came the flashes of hand grenades, and then, after what seemed ages to the waiting men, came muffled explosions and the far off chatter of Sten guns.

'Christ, there they go,' exclaimed Allen through clenched teeth, 'Good old Pete, let 'em have it.'

The men of the raiding party were lying flat in the sand about fifty yards from the hollow in which the German tanks were laagered, while Lieutenant Fraser and Trooper Gadd crept cautiously forward to deal with the sentries. Gadd, who was stronger and tougher than most of the men in the squadron, had been selected to accompany Fraser on this vital part of the operation. Side by side they crawled almost to the top of the slope and peered down into the hollow. They heard a man snoring and the grunt of another as he turned in his sleep. Fraser, however, was straining his ears, hoping to catch a sound of the sentry. For a long time he peered into the darkness, and then at last his vigil was rewarded. On the far side of the slope's crest, silhouetted against the background of the night, was a faintly discernible figure. Nudging Gadd, Fraser pointed. A second later Gadd vigorously nodded his head.

The sentry remained silently immobile, and Fraser cursed under his breath. He had no desire to crawl all the way round the rim of the hollow to deal with the man, and it would be taking too much of a chance to risk crawling up to the German. He would be almost certain to hear them. While Fraser was weighing up the chances, the sentry moved off again on his beat. Fraser estimated that it would take the German about four minutes to draw level with them, provided he did not stop on the way. The two men waited, tightly grasping wicked looking Commando knives. Fraser fought to control his impatience as the sentry sauntered slowly across the ridge towards them. The hand gripping his knife began to ache and he relaxed his grip, trying to overcome his tenseness.

The sentry was barely five yards from them now, and in a few seconds he would pass within three feet of them as they lay crouched on the slope. Fraser could see him fairly clearly. He noticed the sub-machine gun slung over his shoulder, and the German-type steel helmet and great-coat. The sentry broke wind noisily as he drew nearer, and then he was level with them. The two men held their breath, flexing their muscles, but the German did not see them, and then he had passed on, leaving them behind him.

With a panther-like movement Gadd shot to his feet, took two swift, silent paces, and flung one muscular arm around the sentry's throat, pressing hard against the wind-pipe, while with his right arm he drove his knife with all the force he could muster into the German's side, twisting the handle as the steel sank home.

The sentry made scarcely a sound as he went limp, but Gadd, still supporting him, dragged him off the crest and, helped by Fraser, crushed his face into the sand for the few seconds that he took to die.

Again the two men crawled to the top of the slope and looked cautiously about them. Everything was as before; the men still slept beside their tanks unaware of their sentry's fate. Fraser made certain that there was no one else on the rim before he gave the thumbs-up sign to Gadd, signalling him to return to Major Harvey and report that it was now time for the men to move up to the crest.

A few minutes later the twenty-five men were in posi-tion, peeping over the rim to the hollow where the Germans still slept, oblivious of the enemy's presence.

Suddenly, the darkness faded away as the squadron leader discharged his Very pistol into the night sky above him. The explosion of the cartridge echoed round the hollow, then the little balls of brilliance floating gently above the waiting men illuminated the scene with all the brightness of day.

The watching men looked down upon the eight tanks, the furthest being less than a hundred feet distant. Beside each tank, stretched on ground sheets and covered by blankets, slept their crews. Immediately the Very light soared into the sky an urgent voice screamed, '*Macht, dass ihr in eure Tanks kommt.*'

Then the attack began. A well-aimed burst from a Sten gun silenced the man with the hauptmann's insignia who was shouting orders to the surprised men as he leapt on to his tank. Already he had grasped the turret's rim when the bullets struck his back. Quickly his fingers lost their grip, and he tumbled backwards into the sand where writhing convulsively for a few seconds, he died. Now all the men of the raiding party were either firing their Stens or tossing hand grenades at the sleeping and bewildered Germans who were struggling to their feet encumbered by the blankets still wrapped around them, while overhead the flares hung in the sky casting their light on the slaughter. The Germans were easy targets as they tried to climb into their tanks.

Major Harvey pulled the pin from a hand grenade and lobbed it into a close group of five men who had been sleeping beside their tank, and were now fighting desperately to free themselves from the large tarpaulin that had protected them against the night's cold. One of the Germans screamed as the grenade landed almost at his feet, a high-pitched yell of abject terror that momentarily unnerved Harvey as he waited for the explosion. Then another of the little group without a second's hesitation threw himself down upon the bomb as it detonated with a muffled crack, blowing the man to pieces, but his sacrifice was in vain, for the two men who were still on their feet after the explosion toppled on to their sides as a burst of Sten gun fire caught them.

A few of the Germans were running round in little circles their arms high above their heads as they begged for mercy, but the bullets quickly found them. The raiding party were taking no prisoners this time; they were too short-handed to deal with them. Harvey fired another Very light into the sky, but there were no more targets left to engage. About each tank lay little groups of men in the awkward postures of violent death. The Germans had managed to fire a few rounds from the weapons they carried at their side, but they were silent now and none of Harvey's men had been hit.

'Take six men, Teddy, and see what's down there. We'll keep you covered,' shouted Harvey to his lieutenant.

Grasping a Sten, and followed by a half-dozen men from his party, Fraser hurried down the slope towards the nearest tank. Lying beside it were four dead Germans. A horrible choking noise was coming from the back of the vehicle, and when they looked they found one of the tank's crew on the hull behind the turret. He was lying on his face, his buttocks high in the air, drowning in his own blood. The young lieutenant wanted to help the dying man, but while he stood thinking what he should do he was startled by a burst of gunfire coming from beside him. The German still lay in the same position on the tank's hull, but when the firing ceased the dreadful gurgling had stopped. A coarse voice muttered: 'The poor sod's better off now, sir.'

Feeling sick, Fraser moved on to the next tank. As he

drew nearer he saw the bodies lying around it, and then little streaks of orange flame sailed towards him.

'Look out!' yelled Harvey, but the warning came too late, and those watching from the safety of the crest saw Fraser and four of the men collapse limply into the sand in front of the tank whose machine-gun had now ceased firing. The two survivors had reached the safety of the tank's hull, and were watching with apprehensive eyes the slow traverse of the machine-gun as it began to swing in their direction.

'Oh, Christ,' muttered Harvey to himself as he tried to think clearly. He wondered how many men were inside the tank; if it had a driver, then he knew that the raiding party was finished.

'Stay where you are,' he shouted to the two men who were sheltering under its hull where the machine-gun could not reach them. Then he remembered the anti-tank bombs. To the men near him he ordered, 'Keep the hatches covered, don't let them open up. Now let's have one of those anti-tank bombs, and I'll soon fix 'em.'

Clasping the bomb, he ran under cover of the slope until he had reached a point at the rear of the tank. There he waited for a few moments until the last flare had died away. Crouching low, he ran down towards the tank, regardless of the fact that any of the other seven might still have gunners inside, waiting to strike with their weapons.

He reached the back of the tank, and bent low while he regained his breath. One of the survivors began to speak, but Harvey motioned him to keep silent. Quickly he searched the armour of the hull, trying to select the most vulnerable spot in which to place the bomb, and then he saw the turret slowly traversing. The three men crawled quietly round the tank, keeping out of the way of the approaching machine-gun, and as they went Harvey noticed the little circular piece of plating that covered the filler cap of the fuel tank. Hurriedly glancing about him, and judging the position of the machine-gun, he seized a grenade that one of the men was still carrying. He signalled to them to run for cover while the gun was still pointing away from them, reached on to the hull, and lifting the armour-plated cover he undid the filling cap. Placing the grenade over the space where the cap had been, he pulled out the pin and ran for the shelter of the next tank, his mind willing success to his effort.

A few seconds later the grenade exploded, and then flames lit up the scene around him. He saw the turret hatch of the flaming tank thrust upwards and a head and shoulders appear, then it seemed that every Sten gun in the raiding party opened fire. Harvey remained under cover. But in a few moments the firing ceased and he was able to run across to Fraser and the men who had fallen with him.

Harvey knelt beside Fraser's crumpled body. He looked at the young ashen face across which the shadows cast by the flames were flickering, and noticed that the lieutenant was still alive. A little later Fraser opened his eyes, and seeing Harvey he smiled wanly up at him.

'Where is it, Teddy?' I'll get a dressing on you. You'll soon be all right, old man,' comforted Harvey.

'Don't worry about me, sir. I've had it. Go and see to the rest of my men.' Fraser's voice was scarcely more than a whisper.

'Absolute nonsense. Everyone feels like that when they've been wounded. Let's get your pullover off; then we can see where you've been hit.'

But Fraser was no longer listening to his squadron leader. 'Oh, mummy,' he softly murmured. He shuddered slightly and died. Harvey got up and went in turn to each of the four men lying near Fraser, but they were all dead. Then the ammunition began to explode inside the burning Mark IV, and he quickly returned to the top of the slope where the rest of the party was waiting for him.

The burning tank blazed like a beacon illuminating its seven companions, and silhouetting in grim relief the corpses strewn around them.

Harvey gazed down upon the macabre scene as he planned his next move. Quickly scanning the turrets of the intact Mark IVs, he noticed that on each one the hatches were still open. He felt justified in assuming that there were no men inside them. In any case, he knew it was time he gave a positive command again.

'All right, chaps,' he shouted, 'split up into crews and take over the tanks. Careful how you go, but I don't think you'll find any more opposition down there.'

In a few minutes the raiding party had occupied the seven tanks without any further trouble. When each commander had reported to the squadron leader that his fuel tanks were full, Harvey's spirits rose as he suddenly became aware of the opportunity that was his to seize.

To his gunner he said: 'Off you go and tell all the tank commanders to come back here at once.'

When the six men had gathered around Harvey's Mark IV, he said:

'Your tanks are all topped up. That means that a lorry has been up here tonight with the stuff. Therefore there must be some more Jerries not so very far away. I propose to go on a bit and look for them. They won't be expecting us and when they see their own Mark IVs they probably won't suspect our evil intentions until we're right among them. I suggest that you scrounge around and find a few Jerry hats then we'll really look the part. We'll stay here until just before dawn and in the meantime we might make a start on burying these people.' The squadron leader indicated the prone figures near his tank.

'There are several wounded lying about the place, sir,' announced one of the tank commanders. 'What are we going to do about them?'

Harvey thought for a moment then he said: 'Patch 'em up as best we can and leave all the water we don't need with them. That's as much as it's possible to do for the time being, I'm afraid.'

The men took shovels from the tanks and dug five graves into which they placed the bodies of Lieutenant Fraser and the four men who had died with him. By the time the graves had been filled in Harvey was becoming increasingly impatient. 'I'm afraid we'll have to leave the Germans. It's going to take us too long to bury them now,' he said as he walked across to the wounded who had been carried to the edge of the slope and laid in a little group. Harvey noticed that two of these were unconscious and scarcely breathing. The remaining three, although grimacing in pain, had only minor leg and arm wounds that had already been roughly dressed. None of these spoke English, so it was impossible to converse with them. The squadron leader satisfied himself that there was enough water near them and that they had been made as comfortable as circumstances would permit. He walked back to his Mark IV and climbed into the unfamiliar turret where trooper Thompson was examining the wireless set.

'Have you touched the dials yet?' asked Harvey.

'No sir, but I'm sure I know how the thing works.'

'What I meant was, it's possible these tanks are already netted on the same wavelength. Make a note of it and we'll send Manley round to the other tanks and ask them to switch on. It'll be much better if we have wireless control.'

Trooper Manley, who was sitting in the gunner's seat getting the feel of the machine-gun took the dial readings and, climbing out of the turret, hurried off to the nearest tank.

As Harvey watched, Thompson put on the headphones and switched on the set. The batteries were working and the wireless receiving set hummed into life.

'Hullo Bolo, Bolo calling, report my signals,' intoned Thompson into the microphone, and in a little while the rest of the tanks began to come in on the same wavelengths.

Suddenly, above the mush of the radio, the dull report of two shots echoed round the little turret, and a few seconds later came the sound of screams above the bursts of Sten gun fire.

Harvey pulled himself out of the turret and dropped into the sand, but already the noise had died down.

'What the hell's going on?' shouted the squadron leader, anxiety ringing in his voice.

'It was one of the wounded, sir,' someone called, 'he got Manley with a pistol.'

Harvey hurried to the group standing around the spot where he had left the wounded Germans, then he saw some of the men standing around a body; when he got closer he could see that it was Manley. One glance was sufficient to tell him that the gunner was already dead. A bullet had entered the side of his throat and had torn a large hole where it had come out just below the chin, and Manley had bled to death in what must have been a matter of seconds.

One of the men said: 'He was climbing on to this tank when a bloody German shoots him with a pistol. We couldn't do nothing for him, sir. He'd gone by the time we got to him.'

Harvey cursed himself for not having made certain the wounded had all been searched for weapons. To the men standing near him he said, 'Well, go and make sure no more of the wounded have arms, and do it properly this time, understand?'

There was a short silence as the men looked at each other. No one moved to obey Harvey's order, then one of the men said: 'It's all right now, sir, the wounded are all dead. We must 'ave 'it them accidental like when we got the sod who did poor Manley.'

Harvey felt too weary to go into the matter further. He said: 'Bury Manley over by the others, then get back to your tanks.'

By the time the squadron leader was satisfied that his little command was ready to move as an effective fighting force, the first light of day was already appearing in the eastern sky. Speaking into the microphone, he gave the familiar order:

'Hullo Bolo, Bolo calling. Advance!' and a few moments later the tanks rumbled out of the hollow and headed towards the enemy.

Major Harvey pushed back the soft-peaked cap he had taken from one of the Germans and looked around at the six Mark IVs that were spread out on either side of him. They were travelling slowly, but even so a filmy cloud of dust hovered in their wake and Harvey knew that the enemy would be able to see it long before the tanks became visible.

The squadron leader's spirits had risen now that he was on the move again. He thought of the eight tanks he had just taken from the enemy at a cost of an officer and five men. It had not been such a high price after all, he reasoned, particularly as they had entirely wiped out the

German crews, and with any luck they were going to inflict further casualties on the enemy before very long. Leaning his elbow on the turret, he peered through his binoculars into the distance ahead, but as yet there was no sign of Germans. Putting down the glasses, he looked below into the turret. Thompson was making a small adjustment to the wireless set while Burnett, who had taken the place of Manley, was sitting with an arm resting on the gun that was ready to open fire as soon as any targets appeared over the sights. Catching the men's glance for a moment the tank commander smiled encouragingly at them, then once more he stared ahead, searching the bleak expanse of desert for some sign of the enemy.

It was just before six o'clock when Major Harvey caught his first glimpse of the enemy. About a mile and a half to his right front he had noticed several dark shapes standing out against the desert's background. For some time he stared at them through his glasses, trying to make out what they were. As his tank drew nearer to them he saw that they were large trucks. He counted four of them. Signalling with his arms to his tank commanders, he indicated the vehicles, then speaking over the inter-com, he directed Taylor, his driver, to head towards them. As he drew nearer, the squadron leader was able to make out a number of men in German uniforms standing near the trucks, then he saw that they were unloading something from the vehicles. Some of the men were looking towards the Mark IVs, but they did not appear to be particularly disturbed by their appearance. A few moments later Harvey saw an open Volkswagen detach itself from the group. Whoever was in it was coming to meet the tanks.

Harvey looked at the six heads surmounting the turrets of his small command, each topped by a German cap. He tightened his lips into a little line as he smiled grimly to himself with the thought that a lot of people were going to get hurt in the next few minutes. Into the microphone he said:

'Hullo Bolo, Bolo calling. Prepare to engage targets but don't open fire until I give the order. Over.'

The Volkswagen was only a couple of hundred yards away now. It was making straight for the leading tank which was Harvey's.

The squadron leader lowered himself into the turret and took something from the wireless operator, then he quickly straightened up once again to watch the approaching car while clutched in his right hand was Trooper Thompson's last grenade.

The occupant of the little car waved to Harvey and the squadron leader returned the greeting with his left arm. The German made a half circle until he was alongside Harvey's Mark IV. Now the German was shouting something at Harvey which the Englishman was unable to understand. Harvey grinned down at the young fair-haired German lieutenant and thought that he seemed to be a pleasant, cheerful and efficient young man – the type of fellow he would have been happy to drink with before the war on his travels abroad. And all the time his tanks were getting closer and closer to the trucks. Suddenly, the German realized he had been fooled. Harvey watched the doubt in the man's blue eyes turn to fear, but before he could control the moment's fear sufficiently to react, Harvey was ready for him. With a quick movement he had drawn the pin from the grenade and leaning over the turret he lobbed it across the short distance into the front of the Volkswagen where it fell with a rattle on to the floor boards at the driver's feet. Harvey ducked into the turret as the grenade exploded. Into the microphone he intoned slowly and without any trace of emotion: 'Hullo Bolo, Bolo calling, engage the enemy. Over.' Switching to the inter-com he said: 'Gunner, twelve o'clock, two hundred yards, lorry. Fire!' He leaned out of the turret again to watch the effect of the firing. He noticed the Volkswagen burning fiercely about fifty yards behind him. Again he had completely surprised the enemy. He watched the Germans collapsing in the sand as they ran for their weapons. There was no need to give further directions to Burnett. He could choose his own targets now for there was no shortage of them amongst the bewildered enemy who were desperately trying to oppose the tanks with small arms fire directed from slit trenches. Occasionally, from one of these trenches a stick bomb would come sailing through the air, but they had no effect on the thick hulls of the Mark IVs.

The squadron leader was now standing inside the turret, his forehead pressed to the sponge pad of the periscope, for it was no longer safe for him to keep his head and shoulders outside. There were too many bullets flying about, and the tank crews could hear them rattling harmlessly on the steel plating.

Harvey, his hand gripping the power traverse lever, swung the turret around so that he could get a complete view of the battle area, but now the only Germans he could see were either dead or wounded. Those that remained alive were in the slit trenches, and he had to think up a way of dealing with them before he and the rest of his men could climb out of their tanks and destroy the boxes of stores and ammunition he could see stacked on the ground near the lorries. He saw that one of his tanks was already tackling this problem. As Harvey watched through his periscope, he saw that the tank was now straddling the narrow trench, then slowly it began to turn and as it did so the track bit into the lip of the trench, collapsing the walls on to the men sheltering below. One of the Germans reached up, trying to pull himself out of the caved-in trench, but as he sought to obtain a grip on the crumbling sand the tank's track came down on his arm pinning it to the ground. The man shrieked in his fear and pain, then the side of the trench gave way beneath the tank's weight and the heavy track slipped down, tearing off the man's arm as it crushed him and the rest of the men in the trench to a lifeless mess.

Other tanks were now dealing with the slit-trench opposition in a similiarly effective manner. A Mark IV on the squadron leader's right flank had just lurched across one of the trenches and the driver was beginning the turn that would break down the sides of the trench, when suddenly one of the Germans sprang out of the refuge and grasping a loose strap at the rear of the tank, he began to haul himself on to the hull.

Before Harvey could shout the orders to his gunner Burnett had already opened fire, for he also had seen the man leap on to the tank, but before he found the range the German had pulled an object from his belt and reaching up had dropped it through the open hatch into the main turret below. In the same movement he dived headlong into the crumbling trench beneath him.

Harvey screwed up his face, willing the bomb not to explode as he stared towards the tank's hatch. A puff of flame followed by a lot of black smoke belched upwards through the open hatch as the tank, still moving, settled heavily down on the men already half buried. Then, as if nothing had happened, the driver revved his engines and the tank climbed out of the crumpled grave, its squat nose and gun pointing high into the coloured early morning sky. It trundled off to the next trench, and now only occasional thin wisps of dark smoke trailed from its open turret.

'Hullo Bolo, Bolo calling. Close down. Over,' ordered Harvey, and a few seconds later he saw the hatches being lifted and lowered on all the tanks except the one upon which the German had so recently climbed.

In a little while the slit trenches had been dealt with and the squadron leader, satisfied that the enemy could inflict no further damage, ordered his tank to stop alongside the one with the open turret. Climbing out, he dropped to the ground and shouted to the driver who still had his vizor closed.

'Open up,' he yelled.

In a few moments the steel vizor swung outwards and upwards revealing the oily and perspiring face of the driver.

'Whose tank is this?' Harvey asked. 'Don't you know you've had a bomb in the turret?'

'It's Corporal Merriman's tank, sir. I 'eard them yell just before the bang, sir. Nobody give me any orders after that so I just carried on like.'

'Well done,' praised Harvey. 'I'd better have a look inside. Go to the other tanks and tell the men to get out and see if anything can be done for some of these wounded Germans. I also want to know what is in these lorries. Hurry up, we don't want to be here very long.'

The driver hurried off towards the nearest tank. For a few moments Harvey stood watching him, steeling himself against the horror of the turret. He turned and quickly hauling himself on to the hull he looked down into the wreckage of the turret. One glance persuaded Harvey that there could be no life down there, yet he forced himself to climb into the dripping and slimy chamber to make certain nothing could be done for the torn and naked objects that only a few short minutes before had made three vigorous young men in the prime of life. Harvey noticed with surprise that the ammunition in the racks round the turret had been untouched by the stick bomb. It looked to him as if the three men had absorbed the greater part of the shock and blast of the explosion.

He climbed out of the turret and dropped to the ground, drawing in deep breaths of fresh air as he tried to rid himself of the sickly smell and taste of torn bodies. He noticed his hands and clothes were wet with blood and he picked up handfuls of sand with which he rubbed the worst places.

One of the tank commanders came up to the squadron leader as he finished cleaning his hands.

'We've got ten prisoners, sir, all wounded. Each one's been properly searched this time.'

'Good,' replied Harvey. 'We'll see what can be done for them in a minute. Have you been able to find out what's in the lorries?'

'Yes, sir. It's mostly petrol but there are also some boxes of small-arms ammunition and hand grenades.'

Harvey thought for a few moments, then said, 'I wonder if the Boche is setting up a supply dump here?'

'It looks like it, sir. We've found a place near a pile of petrol cans where they've started to dig a large trench.'

A little later, after the squadron leader had inspected the trucks, he called the tank commanders together and spoke to them.

'First of all,' he began, 'I want all the petrol put back on the trucks. The ammunition that's been unloaded we'll destroy, the rest stays on the trucks. We'll leave the wounded here – they'll be picked up before the day is out. If you can find a couple who are not too badly hurt then we'll take 'em back for interrogation, but make sure there's one chap left here who can walk around and dish out water to those who can't move. I think after that we'll return to our own lines with the trucks and the seven tanks. I don't propose to do anything about Corporal Merriman's tank for the moment. We'll bury them when we get it back. The crews will have to split up a bit otherwise we shan't be able to find drivers for the trucks. In any case we shall all be keeping close together, and if any trouble turns up it will only take a second for the drivers of the trucks to nip back inside their tanks.'

As soon as Harvey had finished speaking the men hurried off about their duties. He walked across to the little groups of wounded Germans lying in the sand.

'Anyone of you speak English?' he inquired.

'I speak a little,' replied one who was nursing a blood-stained arm.

'Good. Well you can tell the rest of your men that we're going to leave you here. You'll have plenty of water and we're going to bring you over your blankets. You'll be picked up by your own people within a few hours. When you've told them all that, you can get to your feet and walk over to the nearest lorry and sit in the front seat. You're coming back with us, understand?'

'Yes,' replied the German sullenly.

The squadron leader called to one of the men. 'Keep an eye on our friend. He's coming back with us.'

'Yes, sir.'

The German sneered at Harvey as he struggled to his feet. 'What harm we can do now?' he asked. 'Are you afraid of the wounded? Why not murder us all? It is easy with the tanks and you Englanders are so brave, yes?'

Harvey turned on his heel and walked away towards the trucks. The wounded German had upset him, but he knew that if he had adopted less rigorous methods his casualties would have been higher. As it was they were quite high enough. If you are going to fight a war, he reasoned, then you cannot afford to risk the lives of your own men by going out of your way to spare the enemy. At that moment he caught sight of Trooper Gadd bending over a German corpse as he transferred the watch from the lifeless wrist to his own. Harvey momentarily wished he possessed Gadd's indifference to slaughter. The trooper noticed the squadron leader watching him, and a guilty look spread over his callous features.

'Seems a waste to leave it 'ere, sir. If I don't take it some other sod will.'

'You're probably right, Gadd,' replied Harvey as he moved on, then he turned round and said: 'You know, back in Germany a watch like that would fetch enough to pay for a man's funeral.' But Harvey knew his words were wasted, almost before they were spoken.

It was while the men were hurrying to reload one of the trucks with the petrol cans that the Messerschmitt appeared. The plane skimmed over the area of the recent battle, then banking steeply as he climbed into the sky, the pilot prepared for a second run over the scene. He could not have failed to recognize the crumpled bodies of the dead Germans, or the little group of wounded lying in a neat line. Seeing that the plane was coming back, the men left the petrol and ran to the safety of their tanks. Already, one of the gunners was firing at the aircraft, and even if the pilot had failed to notice that there was something odd going on below him, he could not possibly have missed seeing the hostile red line of tracer leaping up at him from what should have been one of his own tanks. The Messerschmitt roared over the raiding party for the second time, but the pilot had left it too late to open fire, and as he passed overhead and away every gun that could be brought to bear on the black and white plane chattered angrily up at it.

Harvey watched from his open turret as the Messerschmitt climbed unharmed into the blue sky. He thought to himself that the time had now come for him to return to the squadron. The Germans would be wise to him, and before long other tanks and aircraft would be out after him, seeking their revenge.

A few minutes after the disappearance of the Messerschmitt, Major Harvey led the seven tanks and the trucks in the direction of the perimeter. They were travelling fast, and raising a large cloud of dust. The squadron leader, glancing back, was no longer able to see the little group of wounded Germans he had left behind. Each tank commander anxiously searched the sky, expecting at any moment to see the enemy's planes. They strained their ears, but the noise of the tanks deadened all other sounds.

At regular intervals the squadron leader gazed about at his little command and counted the tanks. They all appeared to be running well. He kept two fingers crossed that he would get them safely home, together with the captured trucks and the wounded prisoner. Some distance ahead of him he could see the gap in the perimeter wire through which he would have to lead his charges, then happening to glance up a little, he saw the plane gliding down towards him. His apprehension was instantly stifled by the sight of the red, white and blue roundels on the fighter's wings. The tank commanders were waving their caps as the plane flew alongside, rolling its wings in friendly greeting. The coming of the Spitfire gave new heart to the weary men, although they could no longer see it through the dust cloud into which it had dived.

The squadron leader led the way through the gap in the wire. The tanks were bunched together in a tight line as they came in from the flanks to pass through the narrow opening in single file. Harvey looking back, frowned as he saw how close together they were, but he hesitated to give the order to spread out again. It seemed such an unnecessary waste of time, but suddenly three Messerschmitts plunged through the dust cloud and dived at the tanks, their cannons churning up the desert into fountains of sand.

In a few seconds the attack was over and the planes were climbing steeply out of danger, but when Harvey raised his head out of the turret again, two of the Mark IVs were already blazing fiercely, and one of them had stopped right in the gap, blocking the way to those behind it. Harvey, realizing it would be impossible to move the burning tank, and that it would take too long to tear a fresh gap in the wire, signalled to the vehicles on the far side of the perimeter to carry on along the wire until they could find another opening.

Meanwhile both the drivers of the burning tanks had scrambled out of their hatches and were running towards the petrol truck which was slowing down to pick them up. Harvey looked at the main turrets of the two casualties hoping to see more of the men make their way to safety, but he knew now that it was too late, and that the heat and flames had claimed their victims.

The Messerschmitts had completed their climb and were turning to make their second run, but by this time the remaining tanks and trucks were spreading out as fast as they could. Again the cannons ploughed up the sand and the tanks' commanders ducked their heads into the turrets, but everyone heard the petrol truck explode into a towering sheet of red flame and black smoke. Again Harvey counted his tanks as they scuttled out into the desert. He was relieved to see that the five were still on the move, then he looked at the blazing wreckage of the petrol truck wondering how many men had died with their German prisoner, for he knew that no one could possibly have escaped from such an inferno. Even if the flames had spared them, the heat would have suffocated anyone within a few feet of the explosion.

The squadron leader clung to the turret hatch as Taylor, his foot pressed down hard on the accelerator, drove the tank over the rough desert. He searched the sky for the Messerschmitts and saw that they were otherwise engaged. A flight of R.A.F. fighters were now occupying all their attention, but the Germans had the faster planes, and giving way to superior numbers and the fact that they were running short of ammunition, they broke off the fight and sped away to their aerodrome.

After the departure of the Messerschmitts the R.A.F. fighters remained in the area until Harvey had shepherded the remnants of his little force safely back to the British lines, while down by the wire the two Mark IVs still sent their colums of black smoke straight up into the still air. The scattered wreckage of the petrol truck had long since ceased to smoulder.

The squadron leader watched the last Mark IV as it rumbled and squeaked its way up the slope towards the spot where the raiding party had halted. He gave the order to switch off and dismount. When the men were fallen in, he hurried to count them, but of the two officers and twenty-five men, there now only remained one officer and thirteen men. Harvey was relieved to discover that only two men had been lost in the Mark IVs that had been hit by the Messerschmitts. They were the tank commanders, and happened to be the only occupants of the turret. The rest of their crews were driving trucks or other tanks.

The brigadier was leaning against the rocky wall of his cave, hands thrust deep into the pockets of his slacks, as he stared at the grimy and weary major who occupied his camp chair and was drinking his whisky from an enamel mug.

'Well, Harvey, although I gave my consent, I never really believed you'd pull it off. You seemed keen to have a crack at it, and as things are a bit desperate up here at the moment, it was a chance I felt I had to take. Twenty-five men on their flat feet and they go and capture eight of Rommel's bloody tanks! I'll bet he'll be pretty sick when he hears about this if anyone over there has the nerve to tell him!'

'We were lucky, sir. I'm pretty sure we'd never get the chance to pull that one off again,' Harvey said.

'You must be pretty worn out after that lot. Go and have a good sleep. Take a truck and drive down to the beach with the rest of your party. You've earned twenty-four hours' leave. When you come back you can give me a report on what took place. You can also put in a couple of names for decorations. If what I say still carries any weight, I'll get you a D.S.O. for what you've done. Now, off you go and get some rest.'

The survivors of the raiding party had returned from the beach where they had been relaxing in the sun and the warm blue waters of the Mediterranean, and were once more with the squadron on the slope overlooking the perimeter. From the slit trenches they could still see away in the distance the two burnt out Mark IVs they had been forced to abandon by the gap in the wire when the Messerschmitts had attacked them.

All was peaceful out in front of the squadron. There was no sign of the enemy. Far to the north came the sound of big guns, and the almost inaudible rattle of machine-guns, but the men of B Squadron were relaxing in their trenches while the sentries stared out across the empty blue haze.

Grouped around the squadron leader's trench were Allen and the two subalterns. They were listening to Harvey's description of the attack on the Mark IVs.

'Young Teddy put up a marvellous show,' Harvey said. 'If it hadn't been for him we might never have located the tanks in the first place, and the way he and Gadd dealt with that sentry! He never made a sound when they got him, and the Germans were only a few yards away.'

When Palmer and Holmes had returned to their men, Allen said, 'By the way, you remember when you sent Fraser off to toss up with Palmer and Holmes to see who should go on the party?'

'Yes, of course, I remember. Why?'

'Well, only just that he never mentioned it to them, that's all. I found out because of something Palmer said after you'd gone. He was a bit worried about you not taking him as he seems to think he was senior to Teddy Fraser. He wondered if we were dissatisfied with him or something like that.'

'Palmer and Holmes are both good blokes. I'm glad to have them with the squadron,' remarked Harvey, but his thoughts were hovering over the shallow grave where Fraser lay.

Allen was staring at the unfamiliar figure approaching their trench, then his eyes noticed the collar.

'Christ, Pete!' he exclaimed, 'It's a God-botherer. What the hell does he want out here?'

The little man in the chaplain's uniform stopped in front of the two officers and saluted the squadron leader.

'I'm Davidson,' he said in a soft voice. 'I was posted to the Regiment the day after you left.'

Harvey shook hands with the cheerful-looking little Welshman, then he introduced him to his second-in-command.

'Have you come up with the rest of the Regiment?' inquired Allen.

'Oh, no. They won't be up for a week or so yet. I thought that I'd be of more use up here. I'm horribly good at scrounging, and I expect there are a number of things you and your men need that I may be able to put my hands on.'

Allen grinned at Harvey and winked an eye. Both men had taken an instant liking to the little man from South Wales who had now sat down on the edge of the trench.

'That's better,' he remarked with a sigh of relief. 'I had to walk out here, and I'm afraid I'm not very used to it at the moment.'

'Where's your kit?' asked Harvey. The padre indicated the haversack he had taken off and placed at his side. 'I don't need much,' he said apologetically. 'My bedding roll is coming up on the ration truck with a few odds and ends I've picked up for the men.'

'The only thing they're interested in is beer,' cut in Allen, and quickly realized it was hardly the remark to make to a chaplain.

'I'm happy about that,' said the padre with a smile of complete innocence, 'because that's one of the things I've brought. Twelve dozen cans. It's quite safe. I got someone to stencil 'essential stores' on the crate so no one will pinch it.'

'I'd like to see Colonel Rankin's face if he happens to be here when that crate is opened,' said Harvey with a smile.

'You're not going to like this very much, particularly

208

after all you did to get hold of the bloody things, but there's no point in beating about the bush. And I may as well tell you now that the tanks you brought us back are going to a regiment up on the north of the perimeter.' The brigadier drew a deep breath after the long sentence, and paused to look at Major Harvey whose face was paling with disappointment.

'You mean, sir, that we're still to be infantry?'

'I'm afraid so, at least for the time being. You see, the regiment that's going to get your Mark IVs badly needs replacements. Fortunately, it's still got the crews, but tanks are the problem now, and they've just got to be replaced. I don't break any security when I tell you that they've stopped reinforcing us by sea, which means that we aren't going to get any more tanks for the time being. So, rather than let you operate with only five, I have decided to hand them over to a regiment that's desperately in need of them to bring it nearly up to strength again.'

There was an awkward silence while the brigadier looked at Harvey, then the squadron leader said:

'Very good, sir, we'll carry on as we were.'

The senior officer was conscious of the flatness in the other man's voice. He felt very sorry for him but he had made up his mind, and a few seconds later Harvey saluted and walked away from the cave. He was wondering what his men would think when he broke the news to them of what had happened to the tanks they had so dearly won.

B Squadron had settled down to the monotony of the trenches. A week had passed since the raiding party had captured the Mark IVs, but although the fighting was becoming fiercer around the northern edges of the perimeter, so far the enemy had attempted no major attack on the squadron's front.

The sun was rapidly sinking beneath the western horizon and Harvey and Allen were taking advantage of the last few minutes of daylight to search the area in front of them with their glasses. Beyond the wire stretched the desert. There was no sign of the enemy. To the north the two officers could see the constant flashes of the heavy guns, while the muffled thunder of the exploding shells was ever in their ears.

'It's getting worse, Pete. God forbid that I should ever talk like a defeatist, but if the ruddy Boche keeps it up like this much longer, then I'd like to know what exactly happens to us. We're not getting any more supplies, yet all the time Jerry is building himself up for the big attack and then what do we do?'

'Sufficient unto the day is the evil thereof,' quoted Harvey. The two men looked at each other for a moment and then they both grinned.

'——!' snorted Allen.

'That's no way to talk to your superior officer,' admonished Harvey.

'——!' repeated his second-in-command.

That night there was little sleep for anyone. The Germans were probing the British defences with their heavy artillery, and the falling shells rent the darkness with orange flames and ear-splitting explosions, while the jagged fragments of shells screamed through the hideous night like tortured souls in hell, turning to water the bowels of the men who grovelled in their trenches and weapon pits as they bargained with God to spare them in return for promises to lead a purer life.

Just before dawn Harvey gave the order for the squadron to stand to. The men were tired after a sleepless night. So far there were no casualties, although a number of shells had fallen near the trenches.

As the first light of day appeared Harvey looked through his glasses and saw that the desert in front of the perimeter was no longer empty. A number of Mark IVs had taken up positions just inside the wire through which they had cut their way during the hours of darkness. The squadron leader could also see groups of Germans busily digging weapon pits while the lorries that had brought them up to the wire were already disappearing in a cloud of dust.

Harvey put down his glasses and looked at Allen.

'It's our turn today, Tony, by the look of things.'

Allen was still leaning on the parapet of the trench peering through his binoculars. After a few seconds he said:

'They've got some guns down there too, and what's more they're pointing right up at us, and all we've bloody well got are small arms. Why the hell did they have to go and take our tanks away. At least we could hit back with them. As it is, we haven't an earthly.'

'Nevertheless, old boy, we've got to stay here until either they pull us out or we've had it. In the meantime, let's get cracking and loose off at the bastards. There's no point in letting them have it the easy way. We might as well knock off as many as we can while we still have a chance.'

In a few seconds the squadron area echoed with the high-pitched voices of men shouting commands, and then the rifles and Bren guns burst into life as fire was concentrated on the enemy down by the wire. Almost immediately the Germans retaliated with their heavier guns and the shells began to burst among the trenches, forcing the men to stop firing and crouch for shelter in the corners of their funk holes.

As soon as B Squadron ceased firing the Germans

climbed out of their own trenches and, bending low so as to make as small a target as possible, they began to run up the gradual slope towards the British lines; and all along the perimeter the big guns were belching forth their salvoes of jagged steel that ploughed up the desert into fountains of sand and black smoke.

'Come on, Tony!' yelled Harvey above the din of the exploding shells. 'If we don't get the men firing again, we'll be overrun in the next few minutes.'

The two officers climbed out of the trench and ran through the squadron lines, yelling encouragement to their frightened men, and in a little while the Brens were firing once more and taking their toll of the advancing enemy.

From positions behind the squadron a troop of 25-pounders was laying down a devastating barrage on the Germans as they massed together near the gaps in the wire, then the Mark IVs began to move forward, the infantry sheltering behind them.

Away on the squadron's right flank several anti-tank guns were engaging the advancing Mark IVs, and a ragged cheer was heard above the sound of bursting shells as the leading tank was hit and set on fire.

The Germans appeared to be concentrating their attention on the squadron's front. Shells were landing among the trenches sending up fountains of sand and torn fragments of rock that rained on the men crouched desperately over their weapons as they concentrated on bringing down the approaching infantry. There was nothing the squadron could do to impede the progress of the tanks.

Major Harvey looked anxiously around him. The leading Mark IVs were scarcely four hundred yards from the forward trenches, and although the anti-tank gunners had now succeeded in stopping two of them, there still remained the six relentlessly squeaking their way forward to destroy the squadron.

A shell burst on the edge of a trench and Harvey ducked involuntarily with the explosion. As the sand and stones rained down he heard the hideous screams of wounded men and then, while he was wondering if he should forsake his position and run to the help of men in the trench, he saw the little padre calmly making his way to the hole in the ground from which the screams were coming.

Captain Davidson, the Regiment's chaplain, was an old man compared with the rest of the men of B Squadron. He was not far off fifty, and all his life had been spent in the mining villages of South Wales. He was a soft-spoken, quietly-mannered man who worshipped God and loved his fellow men. Violence and brutalities he understood together with all the weaknesses of the miners who were his parishioners, yet always his sensitive spirit was revolted by these things, and whenever his onerous duties would permit it, he would wander across the green, deserted hills and pray aloud for his strength to be renewed, and sometimes he would sit on the mountainside, staring across to the Severn Sea while he composed little poems praising God's handiwork. He had married shortly after being ordained, but his wife had died in her first confinement and the child had died with her. When the war started he thought that perhaps his services might be of more use in the armed forces than in the valley, and so he had eventually found himself posted to the Regiment.

He was frightened by the noise of the battle as he crouched in a slit trench, sheltering from the deafening explosions and whining splinters, and then he heard the screams coming from the ruined weapon pit. His sense of duty overcame fear, action gave him courage, and he hurried to help the wounded men. When he reached the crater where the shell had burst, the sight that met his eyes made him want to turn and run.

'Oh, God, give me strength,' he prayed as he forced himself to climb into the wrecked trench where a legless man, whose uniform had been blasted off by the shell burst, jerked spasmodically on his back round and round in a slow and painful circle, screaming:

'Kill me, oh, please kill me, oh, please let me die!'

Davidson dropped beside the partially disembowelled man, and raising the tortured man's head, supported it on his knees.

'Oh, kill me, Padre,' pleaded the dying man, but he had ceased screaming and his voice was growing weaker. Blood poured from him in streams with each movement he made.

'Patience, my son,' whispered Davidson as he held the man tightly to him. 'God in his infinite mercy will comfort you now. Peace, my son, as we both pray to Him to forgive us our sins and grant us the life everlasting.'

Before the padre could finish, the man struggled in the arms that held him so tightly, then suddenly he stiffened and relaxed. For a few moments more the officer prayed aloud over the dead face, then from inside his shirt he withdrew a little cross which he placed for a moment on the pale lips as he administered the last rites. When it was done he gently lowered the dead man's head on to the sand, then he gave his attention to the three other shattered and lifeless bodies that lay sprawled around him.

The anti-tank guns had claimed two more Mark IVs and B Squadron's accurate fire with the Bren guns had kept the German infantry at a distance. The open ground out in front of the trenches was littered with the corpses of Germans who had died before they could reach Major Harvey and his men. The enemy's artillery had concentrated on the squadron's area and by midday it was obvious to the squadron leader that he would have to withdraw his little command to the higher ground behind him where rocks and little caves offered better cover from the tanks and bursting shells than the more or less open ground which they were trying so desperately to hold. Ammunition was getting scarce, and Harvey listened with a feeling of helplessness to his officers' reports of the increasing casualties.

In one of the trenches three men were taking a devastating toll of the German infantry as they strove to reach the squadron. Gadd mouthed obscenities as he worked his Bren gun with a cool accuracy.

'You don't 'ave to kill the bastards, just hit 'em in the belly and they dies in slow agony,' he muttered to Pettigrew who leaned at his side firing a rifle.

In the bottom of the trench lay a dead man, a small blue rimmed hole through his forehead where a bullet had struck, and beside him, whimpering with fear and trembling uncontrollably, crouched one of the reinforcements.

Taylor rammed a fresh magazine into his Sten, and as he did so he glanced at the terror-stricken man.

'Get up and fight, Marshall, you windy bastard! Go on, or I'll give it to you now.' He threatened the man with the loaded weapon. Marshall, wide eyed and with wet, trembling lips stayed where he was.

'All right, I'll give you until I count three, then if you're not on your gun, you'll have it where it hurts most.'

Gadd swung round and grasping the barrel of Taylor's Sten, knocked it upwards.

'Leave the poor sod alone. He can't help it, he's mental. Don't waste time, we've got mucking visitors,' he muttered as he turned back to his gun.

'He gives me the creeps,' grumbled Taylor, 'I can't do me work with 'im whining and moaning. 'E'll have me like 'im soon.'

'Shut your mucking trap and leave him alone, do you hear,' Gadd shouted as he fired his gun at the Germans.

'Getting soft in yer old age, ain't you?' sneered Pettigrew. 'I feel like Taylor about it. Make 'im fight, or give it to 'im.'

'Shut up, the both of you,' muttered Gadd. Then he turned to Marshall.

'Come on, Marshall, old pal,' he coaxed. 'Give us a 'and with the loading, and we'll soon 'ave this lot finished, then we can all go and have a nice rest and a cuppa tea.'

'I can't, I can't,' cried the frightened man.

'All right then, you just stay there nice and quiet like till it's all over,' comforted Gadd.

'Come on, let Daddy Gaddy dry your little isy pisies,' mimicked Taylor, but Gadd turned on him and gave him such a look of cruel venomous hate that Taylor quickly looked away and went back to his gun.

'They're laying off. They've 'ad enough,' shouted Pettigrew as the German infantry wavered and fell back under cover of the remaining Mark IVs, leaving scores of dead and wounded littering the ground out in front of B Squadron's trenches.

In a short while the firing became only sporadic in the squadron's sector, and ambulances drove up to take away the wounded who had been collected from the trenches. A little later the ambulances went out, well within the range of the Mark IVs which had halted by the wire, to pick up the wounded Germans. Several were hopping and crawling back towards the wire, refusing the British offers of assistance.

The padre in his bloodstained uniform came to the trench where Gadd and his little party were resting after the battle. Marshall still crouched there trembling in the same position he had maintained during the attack. He seemed incapable of speech.

The padre murmured over the corpse that the men had lifted out of the trench, then he got up and looked down at Marshall.

'Has he been seen to yet?' he inquired.

'He 'aint been 'it, sir,' guffawed Pettigrew, 'though he's certainly lost 'is guts.'

' 'E'll be all right when we get him back, sir,' cut in Gadd. 'Perhaps you'd 'elp me.'

A few moments later Pettigrew and Taylor watched Gadd and the padre move off supporting Marshall.

'Well, well, well! Who'd 'ave bloody thought it?' muttered Taylor as he watched them go.

Later in the day the survivors of B Squadron were withdrawn. It had been decided to use the men as crew replacements for tanks that had hurriedly been repaired by the fitters who were now working day and night in their efforts to keep the tanks fighting.

Then in the afternoon Harvey and Allen were sent off to another regiment where they discovered that they were to fight as tank commanders, so desperate had the situation become in the last few hours.

At dawn on the following morning the two officers climbed into their vehicles manned by unfamiliar crews, then, in company with four other tanks, they moved out towards the enemy in an effort to wipe out the infantry and guns that were massing at one of the weaker points of Tobruk's outer defences.

As Captain Allen surveyed the enemy lines through his glasses a grim look spread over his weary features. He could see the anti-tank guns that would soon be opening fire on the approaching tanks, and he knew that this would be one of the toughest parties he had ever been on. His thoughts began to race madly as he suddenly realised all the unpleasant things which could happen to him in the very near future; then he tried desperately to rid himself of the paralysing tentacles of fear. He breathed deeply and filled his lungs with the fresh morning air. He drank in the beautiful colours of the eatern sky and remembered the people far off at home in England, sleeping peacefully in their beds. The world was not going to stop, the horrors would pass in a little while. One did not have to be an idealist to fight. He knew there was no question of God being on the side of the just, otherwise the tough enemy just a few hundred yards out in front of him would be terrified to stay and fight. No, it was just a question of obeying orders and fighting as a team so that one could hit the enemy as hard as possible all the time, and take bloody good care he wasn't going to win the war: otherwise it would be just too bad for those you had ever cared for when it was all over and the last shot fired. All a man needed was enough self-discipline to give the orders and pull the trigger while the chap on the other side was doing his best to make life short and unpleasant for you and get you first.

Major Harvey's tank was moving towards the enemy some twenty yards ahead on Allen's right flank. It was scarcely more than two hundred yards from the Germans. Suddenly Allen saw the brilliant flash of the anti-tank mine as it exploded beneath the track of Harvey's tank, blowing it off and immobilizing the vehicle. Immediately the anti-tank guns concentrated on the stationary target like a pack of voracious sharks heading towards a hunk of rotten meat.

Allen screamed at his driver over the inter-com to make for his friend's tank as he watched the red glow of the shells striking the thick armour. He saw the driver throw back his vizor and hatch, and climbing out, run for the safety of an unoccupied weapon pit. Harvey's tank began to belch out black smoke and a moment later it burst into flames. Allen shouted with joy as he saw Harvey come out of the smoking turret, like the devil emerging from hell, and then Allen's tank was hit, and he fell into the bottom of the tank screaming with the fear and the pain of his shattered legs. A second shell hit the tank as he lay on the oily floor, and the sky appeared through the hole it had made, then came another, scattering splinters about the turret and filling it with acrid fumes. Again Allen felt the fearful impact as a splinter hit him. He screamed again, horribly, in his pain and terror. There was a vicious thud as a third shell struck the hull, but failed to penetrate. The noise helped to pull Allen's scattered wits together. He tried to get to his feet to climb out of the turret, but his arms and legs seemed useless; then he crawled towards the driver's empty compartment and with the little strength that remained to him, he dragged himself over the empty seat, and there once again, was Harvey reaching in through the driver's hatch.

'You'll be all right now, Tony,' he said, when Allen had been lifted out and laid on the sand. 'I'll just hop on to your tank and get the first-aid box, then we can do you up a bit. Don't go away!' Then ignoring the bursting shells he climbed on to Allen's tank, and a German in a shiny, grey coal-scuttle helmet leaned both elbows on the side of his slit trench, and taking careful aim with his light sub-machine gun, fired a short burst into Harvey's back at a range of little more than fifty feet. For a second Harvey clung to the turret rim with both his hands, but the strength rapidly left his fingers, and falling backwards heavily into the sand, he rolled his head and grinning weakly at Allen with rapidly glazing eyes, he died.

6

Allen lay bleeding in the sand, much too weak and helpless to move, whilst the battle raged all about him. A few feet away sprawled the body of his friend, the flies already busy about the lifeless, staring eyes and open mouth. Allen, barely conscious from shock and loss of blood, gradually began to feel increasingly thirsty until the longing for a sip of cold water obsessed his very being. He remembered the cool streams on whose banks he had lain in the drowsy summer afternoons watching the sparkling water as it gurgled merrily over the stones. He thought of his friends at home sitting down to their afternoon tea and drinking from delicate porcelain cups.

'Oh, God,' he cried faintly. 'Water.' But there was no one to hear him. He rolled a little in the sand unknowingly causing it to clog his shattered veins from which the blood poured in streams.

He wondered what had become of his driver and wireless operator, for from where he lay he could not see their lifeless bodies spreadeagled where they had fallen after being riddled by machine-gun fire as they ran from the stricken tank.

He had a vague recollection of seeing his gunner lying dead in the bottom of the tank, but his mind was not very clear about what had happened in the vehicle after he had been wounded.

Allen had watched Harvey die but his own dreadful predicament robbed the moment of any grief.

The tanks still blazed and smoked around the wounded man, and the smell of the burning oil was stifling and choking, blackening those who had business in that cauldron of hell. The last tank burned and the squadron was no more; the firing ceased, and except for the noise of the ammunition exploding in the tanks, the din of battle gradually died away.

The German corporal who had shot Harvey, climbed out of the trench and followed by two soldiers ran the short distance to the tank.

'*Guck Mal, ob da noch jemand drin ist*[1]*!*' he ordered, and as the man climbed on to the tank the others looked at Harvey, but when they saw that he was dead they quickly turned their attention to Allen. The soldier called from the open turret.

'*Ja, ja da ist noch einer, der arme Teufel ist aber nicht mehr am Leben.*[2]'

The N.C.O. who was holding his water bottle to Allen's lips called to the man to leave the dead gunner and help carry the wounded officer to the medical-aid post. When the three men gently raised him, Allen saw for the first time the wreck of his shattered legs with the flesh hanging in sand-smeared curtains and the white bone glistening redly. The sickly sweet smell of the wounds reached his nostrils, nauseating him. The soldiers laid him down in the sand beside the trench that served as the first-aid post, and while he waited his turn in the short queue of broken bodies the corporal squatted beside him and lighting a cigarette placed it between Allen's pale lips. When, at last, the young doctor came to him he hurriedly bandaged the wounds, and giving an injection told the orderlies to take him away. They placed him on a stretcher and carrying him to an open truck they lifted him on to its wooden floor which was already occupied by a number of other wounded men. He saw Germans, Italians and British all lying there intermingled on the hard boards beneath the blazing African sun, and some were pale from the loss of blood and others were blackened by burns and all were in pain and rolling from side to side, and the

---

[1] 'See if there's anyone inside.'
[2] 'Yes, there is someone, but the poor devil's dead.'

sun drew the moisture from them and they cried for water, each in his own tongue, but the truck did not move until it was filled to capacity and there was no water for the thirsty tortured men.

Allen looked up into the blue sky, concentrating with all his failing faculties on anticipating the bumps that jerked his legs, transmitting to his brain searing waves of agony that forced him to moan in anguish. Sometimes his neighbour would be thrown violently against him, and then they would both cry out in unmusical chorus, hating each other yet powerless to move apart. The bandages that had seemed so clean and white when first he was lifted into the lorry were now all moistened and stained. The men cried for water. Allen no longer feared death, indeed throughout that dreadful journey he wooed it with his mind, knowing it to be the only relief from his suffering, but he did not die; neither did unconsciousness take him to her comforting bosom. It was only when he had completely exhausted himself by trying to hold his breath long enough to stop the heart that he knew was now beating but feebly from the loss of so much blood, that the truck was halted and the back lowered.

The wounded were carried into a large tent and placed on small camp beds. A German, bronzed and wearing only a pair of khaki shorts, rapidly went from bed to bed using the stethoscope that hung about his neck. From time to time he would pause a little longer beside a man, holding a wrist, lifting an eyelid; then he would signal to the orderlies to take away the body they had so recently carried in. When he had finished, the doctor left the tent and then, one by one, the wounded were lifted on to a stretcher and taken to his improvised theatre. An orderly came into the tent with a cup which he filled from an enamel jug, and when Allen saw and heard the colourless liquid flowing and splashing into the cup he could scarcely contain himself. Eventually the German came to him and lifting Allen's head held the cup to his parched lips while he swallowed the cool water in gulps, noisily like an animal. When the orderly took away the cup he tried to grasp it with his teeth but the soldier pushed him gently on to his back and smiling down at him went to the next bed where a German with a stomach wound lay gasping and writhing in pain. The orderly placed a finger in the cup and several times moistened the man's lips but would not allow him to drink.

Almost before the orderly had passed on from the next bed Allen felt the moisture break out over his body, cold and clammy, and then his thirst returned, the raging thirst that was, together with pain, to be his constant companion for many a long dreary day ahead.

The orderlies carefully lifted Allen on to a narrow table in the tiny tent that smelt strongly of disinfectant. Taking a pair of scissors they cut away what remained of his torn and bloody slacks, then they helped him out of his shirt and he lay naked.

The orderly was now unrolling the saturated bandage and Allen tensed himself and concentrated on vibrating his eardrums in an effort to ward off the pain that he knew must surely come. He felt the coolness as the dressings were removed; the doctor bent over him.

'It is not good,' he remarked. 'But we will do what we can. You will be better in a proper hospital I hope.'

Then he went to work. First he injected a drug into Allen's arm that soon made him feel pleasantly detached from his surroundings. It was as if he was an interested spectator of someone else's suffering. An orderly was made to hold a bottle of saline and a thin red rubber tube leading from the bottle was connected to an artery in the crook of

Allen's elbow. He felt the large needle as it entered his skin but was not conscious of any real pain. While the level of the colourless fluid slowly dropped, the doctor took a small instrument resembling a pair of pliers and commenced snipping off little pieces of jagged bone. Allen could hear sounds which resembled the noise of secateurs in the hands of a gardener pruning a rose bush, but there was no pain, and at last fresh bandages were wound about his legs and he was carried back to his bed, where overcome by weakness and the effect of the anaesthetic he fell into a fitful sleep.

Allen lay with closed eyes, dreaming of the piteous cries of his companions in the truck. The groans became more insistent and the breathing more stertorous. He opened his eyes and looked about him; for a moment he did not remember where he was and then it all came back and he knew that the sounds were coming from the man in the bed next to his. He looked across at its occupant and now, where the German with the stomach wound had been, lay a stained-bandaged head on a discoloured pillow, its owner drawing in breath in dreadful gasps while rolling his head from side to side. While Allen watched, powerless to aid, the man struggled frantically and raising his head and shoulders for an instant, fell back again on to the pillow. Once more he forced himself almost into a sitting position, and suddenly Allen saw the dark blood pour from the man's ear, splash on to his bronzed shoulder and stream down his arm on to the white sheets. The head fell back at last and Allen turned away sickened and horrified, but the dreadful moaning and gasping had now ceased, and in a little while the orderlies came and lifted the body on to a stretcher, and placing the soiled bedclothes at its feet, they carried their burden out of the tent.

Allen's thirst returned with his awakening and each

minute seemed an eternity before he was at last given a little water.

The sun was already climbing high into the cloudless blue of the sky, and Allen could feel its heat as the orderlies carried him to the ancient black ambulance marked with the large red cross. There was room for six stretchers, three on each side of the vehicle and they placed his on the lowest rack on the right-hand side. Allen, lying between the coarse, hairy blankets that irritated his naked body, looked about him. The bulge in the stretcher above told him it was occupied; the top one was hidden from his view. On the opposite side lay a fair-haired man, unconscious and breathing heavily, but a blanket covered him and Allen could see no bandages. Above the fair-haired one lay a large negro who had already disturbed his blanket. The whiteness of the dressings in which his lower chest and abdomen were swathed, contrasted vividly with his ebony skin. The gap between the tiers was so small that Allen could not see the person above the negro.

The doors were slammed, shutting out the sunlight; an orderly climbed on to the seat beside the driver leaving the six men alone on their stretchers, and the journey commenced, the journey which was to sear itself in Allen's mind as the epitome of torment and horror. The heavy ambulance bumped and lurched across the rough desert, each movement sending fiery darts of pain through his broken, roughly-set legs. He twisted from side to side as much as he could move himself, endeavouring to discover from which position he could wrest the slightest extra fraction of relief, and all the time he tossed and turned and writhed and groaned and cursed the God that made him, while the vehicle lurched and jerked its way across the desert. The negro soon began to twist on his stretcher, rolling his blood-flecked eyes and murmuring in deep, sonorous Arabic, called upon his Allah the Merciful. Once he caught Allen's eyes and looked imploringly at him and muttered a phrase in his tongue which Allen could not understand, then they each turned away seeking a new position that might give a momentary rest from pain. The next time Allen looked up at the negro he noticed that almost the whole of his dressings were stained with blood. A little later Allen's ears were filled with the wild, deep-throated screams of the tortured man, and still the ambulance bumped on and no one paid any attention to the wretched man. Allen looked away not bearing to catch the man's eyes. The day wore on, the sun's heat radiated mercilessly down through the roof, and the dust swirled about the dimly-lit interior, each tiny particle gaily illuminated as it passed through the slanting rays thrown by the tiny windows.

Allen longed for water. His desire for it became so obsessing that for a moment he forgot his pain. But soon pain became jealous of thirst, and so throughout that day they fought each other for supremacy in Allen's fevered brain.

The negro's cries grew feebler until finally they ceased altogether, and Allen, hoping that the poor fellow had become unconscious, looked again, but the man was limp and still, his mouth wide open, his eyes horribly upturned. The underside of his stretcher was soaked with blood, and in the places where it had already congealed the flies were busily feasting before the dust might settle, so robbing them of their repast. The man above Allen urinated, and the moisture dripped through the sagging canvas on to his blanket, and still they bumped onwards. Once they stopped for a brief respite as the driver and the orderly were forced to take shovels and dig the heavy vehicle free of the soft sand. No one came to look at them and soon the journey continued.

The sun was sinking when they halted for the night. The doors were opened and a villainous-looking Italian climbed in and glanced at each stretcher. He called to his companion and together they lifted out the body of the negro, staggering under its great weight. In a little while they returned, and lifting down the top stretcher on Allen's side they carried it away. The first man returned with a bottle of water and poured a little into the mouths of the remaining four occupants. As soon as Allen drank he sweated it out again and his thirst returned, but the orderly ignored his gestures for another sip and climbed out. He returned shortly afterwards with a hypodermic syringe. He suddenly seized Allen's bare arm and the wounded man, no longer capable of coherent thought and believing that the evil-looking Italian was about to give him a lethal injection, snatched it quickly away, whereupon the orderly struck him heavily in the mouth with his fist and taking the almost unconscious man's limp arm, he pressed home the needle. Soon the morphia began to take effect, and the awful motion of the vehicle having temporarily ceased, Allen at length fell asleep.

Shortly after dawn the Italian who had struck Allen awoke him and gave him another drink from the bottle. When he was properly awake he noticed that the fair-haired occupant of the stretcher opposite to his was no longer there. Allen looked up, and was relieved to see the bulge above his head which told him that there was someone else still alive in the dreadful vehicle. For a moment the idea came to him that the two Italians were driving them around the desert until they were all dead. He had no idea where they were supposed to be going or how long the journey might take; he was certain, however, he would not be able to endure another day such as the previous one.

After a while the Italians returned with the three empty stretchers and replaced them in the racks, sand and dried blood still adhering to the underside of the canvas. There was no one with whom Allen might talk; in fact he had only heard groans and the negro's agonized screams since the Germans had lifted him into the ambulance.

He lay waiting for the journey to recommence, thirsty but as yet not suffering the excruciating pain that he knew must return with the vehicle's first jolt. He longed to be home in England, in some clean, comfortable hospital among friends who instead of flowers would bring to his bedside a sparkling glass of fresh, ice-cold water, and he would drain each glass as it was handed to him. He thought of the men who had stayed at home, excusing themselves because their employers, not wishing to lose them, had glibly proclaimed them indispensable. He imagined them travelling home in their crowded evening trains from the offices they had quitted so sharply on the stroke of five-thirty. He could see them studying their evening papers and reading about the battles, hoping and praying that someone would finish it for them before the awful day should dawn when even they might be enmeshed in the toils of war – the fit young men with cold feet who left it to their neighbours to die and suffer for them the men who tried to believe they were also in the front line when the bombs began to fall at home.

'Christ, the bastards!' he cursed aloud. 'The lousy, gutless bastards!'

He remembered Peter Harvey and his steadfastness, his loyalty and sense of duty, and he vowed that if he should survive he would endeavour to maintain those high standards of his friend.

The noise of the engine being revved interrupted his

chain of thought, and the sweat poured from him as he anticipated with straining nerves and senses the ambulance's first jolt. Suddenly it came and the day's torment had begun. He tossed and turned, chafing beneath the coarse blanket until it fell to the floor beyond his reach and the flies feasted from the sodden bandages about his legs, and, gorged, they crawled about his naked chest and belly until their ceaseless irritation made him light-headed and he roared with hysterical laughter as his brain kept repeating the phrase – 'the patter of tiny feet!'

Several times that day the soft sand held them and the two Italians had to dig out the heavy wheels, working and blaspheming beneath the scorching, blistering sun.

In the late afternoon Allen gradually became aware that several minutes had elapsed since they had hit a bump, and he held his breath making a mental bet that if he could count up to fifty without a jolt then they would at last be on the hard flat sand which would mean that they were on a track. He began to count, but there was no bump. He counted faster, holding his breath and reached fifty, then to make absolutely certain he took a deep breath and counted up to fifty again. Just as he finished his ears caught the purr of the tyres as they caressed the tarred flat surface of a road.

'Oh, God, thank you!' he murmured, and after a while, when he was satisfied that there could be no more jerks, he relaxed, a smile about his lips, for now he had only his thirst and the flies to grapple with.

The sun was still brilliant in the western sky when they lifted out his stretcher, and carrying him into a white-washed courtyard they laid him down in the shelter of a high stone wall. He looked about him and saw other ambulances and a number of other wounded lying on stretchers.

He noticed several Italians sitting in the shade on some

stone steps that led up from the courtyard into the buildings, and one of these, a handsome, fair-haired sergeant wearing an Alpini uniform and carrying his left arm in a sling, was watching him. Allen looked away searching for someone with water, but he was disappointed. He moistened his dry lips with his parched and swollen tongue, and closing his eyes tried to imagine the ecstasy of swallowing a cold drink. He opened them again as a shadow fell across him, and there was the Alpini squatting down beside his stretcher and looking at him out of clear blue eyes. He smiled at Allen, and took a packet of cigarettes from his pocket, extracted one, lit it and placed it between Allen's lips.

'*Inglese?*' inquired the Alpini.

'*Si,*' replied Allen and there, his vocabulary almost exhausted, the conversation ended.

Allen licked his lips, '*Aqua?*' he inquired hopefully.

'*Ah, si si,*' grinned the Italian and lifting up the edge of the blanket to discover if Allen had been wounded in the stomach, he got up and disappeared through a doorway that led into the building. Allen kept his eyes fixed upon the door like a dog that waits outside a room for his master to reappear. At last, when Allen had almost given up all hope of ever seeing the Alpini again, he saw him come from the shadow of the doorway carrying a bottle with a tumbler over its neck, and as he walked towards him Allen tried to imagine the liquid flowing into his dried-out mouth. The Italian squatted down again and commenced pouring the orange juice into the glass, and all the while Allen's eyes were on it, hypnotized by the beauty of it, and the saliva began to flow into his mouth again. Then the glass was in his hands and he was filling his mouth with nectar. He felt certain that the moment was the most wonderful one of his life, and the Italian smiled, finding pleasure in giving happiness.

'*Amico*,' he said, patting Allen's shoulder, and getting to his feet he took the glass and bottle to the other stretchers. Thinking about it, Allen realized that never at any time during his twenty-two years had he desired anything so much as that drink, and it had been given to him by the enemy, not in the coldly formal manner as he would eventually be given his correct ration, but in the spontaneous gesture of true humanitarianism. It made him very content, for he knew he was beginning to understand a little of life. He wished Harvey had been with him. Two days' suffering was perhaps a cheap price to pay for such an experience.

It was becoming dark when two medical orderlies at last raised his stretcher and carried him up the steps into the building.

Allen lay on a table in a large stone-floored room. Two severe-looking nuns in white robes were bending over him untying the filthy, hardened dressings about his legs. He caught the eye of one and smiled up at her, but she did not return it and her look was cold and completely impersonal.

'Oh, God, let them be gentle,' he prayed in his helplessness, but the women were tired, they had been working over the table all day and there were still many more lying outside awaiting their turn, so they hurried at their task, ripping away the soiled dressings that stuck to the suppurating wounds, and Allen screamed once at the intensity of his agony, and then unconsciousness took pity upon him.

It was a quaint little harbour with white single-storey bungalows nestling close together on the side of the hill, green from the many palm trees that all sloped inland, bent by the breeze that blew in from the calm, azure sea. Alongside the stone jetty lay a shallow craft that was to ferry the wounded out to the large white ship, marked with red crosses, that lay a mile or so off shore.

Allen, lying on his stretcher, felt the heat strike upwards from the rusty iron deck of the ferry. The midday sun beat down on him, draining the moisture from his pain-racked body, and all the time the wounded around him cried for water. Water – *aqua* – *Wasser*, were the only words he could distinguish in the continuous murmur of his comrades in suffering. He gazed at the calm blue surface of the harbour and longed to let himself sink down through its coolness to the sombre depths below where pain would be forever banished, for now the agony of his legs had become almost unendurable. The sun in its violence bored into his brain as he gathered his strength for the effort that would break the fetters of his misery. He judged the distance, and decided that it could scarcely be more than a few feet and there was nothing between him and rail. He took a deep breath, and gripping the edges of the stretcher, with a sudden movement he rolled himself off the canvas and fell heavily the few inches to the burning deck. The broken bones of his leg stabbed into the flesh, and he lay tortured and screaming, the sound echoing up the little hillside. A German doctor hurriedly picked his way over the stretchers and bending down grasped him as he fought and struggled for the rail. The doctor shouted to an orderly and they brought a syringe which the doctor used on Allen's arm, and the orderly stayed beside his stretcher until he lost consciousness.

For a while he imagined he was dreaming. The haunting sadness of music played on a violin came to him. There was a gentle motion as if someone was rocking him in a cradle, then he opened his eyes.

He lay in a white cot, swung against the motion of the vessel. The room was large, stretching right athwart the ship, with wide glass windows on each side through which he could see the sky. The music came from a loudspeaker. He noticed that there were a dozen or so similar cots, all occupied. He moved his head and a Red Cross sister, noticing that he was awake, walked over to his cot and stood looking down at him.

The girl was fair and blue eyed. She could scarcely have been more than twenty, thought Allen, and she was very pretty in her uniform with the red cross on her breast.

'*Buon giorno,*' she said as she smiled at him, and then in Italian she inquired if he was feeling better.

Not understanding he shook his head.

'*Parlez-vous français?*' she asked.

He nodded, and she continued in French.

'Would you like something to eat?'

'Thank you, no, but I would like something to drink!'

She went away and returned with a glass of ice-cold orange juice. Then she fetched a bowl of warm water and sponged his face and chest and all the time the pleasant, sentimental music was being softly relayed throughout the ward.

A swarthy Italian was sitting up in a nearby cot, bandages about his back and chest. He was rocking slowly backwards and forwards and every now and then he would murmur:

'*Momma mia, oh momma mia!*'

The sister went across and spoke softly to him and persuaded him to lie down on his side. Then she gave him an injection of morphia and soon he became silent and still.

In the evening another sister, a dark-haired girl with gold-filled teeth, brought Allen a tray on which were several appetizing dishes. He tried to sit up, but he was now too weak, and the girl fed him a lightly-boiled egg from a spoon, and because he appeared to enjoy it she went away and returned with another. Allen found it difficult to believe that he was a prisoner of war.

He tried to sleep, but his legs began to pain him and he pulled his hair and turned his head from side to side to keep from crying out.

The dark sister came to him and felt his pulse and wiped the perspiration from his forehead. In a little while two orderlies came with a stretcher, and lowering the side of the cot they lifted Allen on to it and carried him to the operating theatre.

There were two doctors; one large and distinguished-looking who might easily have passed for an Englishman, the other smaller and of a distinctly Latin appearance. They both smiled at Allen and the tall one spoke in halting English:

'We shall soon have you feeling better. We can't send you home like this, can we?' And all the time they were undoing the bandages about his legs.

'Please don't hurt me,' implored Allen.

'This won't hurt at all, I promise you,' soothed the tall doctor.

When the dressings were removed, there was no pain, but Allen noticed a foul, decaying smell.

'Is it all right?' he asked not bearing to look at his shattered legs.

'Well, it might be much worse, but it will very soon be better.'

The doctors worked on his legs with forceps while at the same time saline was injected into his arm. He was quite conscious but felt no pain. He was almost enjoying himself, intoxicated by the anaesthetic.

'Where do you come from?' the tall doctor asked.

'I'm not allowed to say.'

'Oh, never mind, it is not important. I only inquired because many times I have been to England.'

'I come from London. My home is in Chelsea, in a little street just off the King's Road, if you know it.'

'Yes, I know Chelsea a little. It is your artists' quarters, I believe?'

'That's what they say.'

'Ah, you want to see Montmartre. Now that is the place to be inspired, but your London fog by the Chelsea embankment – what inspirations an artist can have there I do not know.'

And all the time they worked quickly and expertly on his legs.

'Am I allowed to ask where I'm going?'

'Of course – Napoli. You will be there tomorrow afternoon.'

'See Naples and die!' remarked Allen grimly.

'Everyone who sees Naples will one day die,' laughed the doctor.

'I believe it is very beautiful,' suggested Allen.

'Very beautiful indeed, and much more beautiful from the sea. Capri we shall pass, and you will see Vesuvio smoking above the harbour. Ah, it is most beautiful.'

He spoke rapidly in Italian to his dark companion, and after a short conversation he addressed himself to Allen once more.

'If you are a little better tomorrow we may be able to carry you out on deck as we enter the bay. I should like you to see it. You will remember it always.'

The following morning Allen felt stronger and was able to eat a little breakfast. In the next cot was a large, intelligent and pleasant-looking German who had been wounded in the arm. He had finished his meal and was sitting on the side of his cot swinging himself gently backwards and forwards with his foot on the deck watching Allen, and after a while he got up and walked over to him.

'How is the cruel enemy today?' he asked in fairly good English. 'I thought you were finished when they took you out last night, but you look fine now.'

'I feel better, thank you.'

'Then have a cigarette. They are only Italian, I'm afraid.'

He gave Allen a cigarette and lit it for him. Then he continued:

'Before the war I spend three months in Manchester in a cotton mill learning your methods and your English. Dreadful town!' And he shook his head reminiscently and went on:

'This ridiculous war. Three days ago I am *hauptmann* then they say tomorrow when the major returns to Germany on leave you will take over from him and be promoted, and in the afternoon one of you wretched Englanders comes in a tank and hits me in the arm.'

He was laughing at the irony of it.

'Now I shall never be a major. Still, perhaps the Führer will give me a cross, who knows?' And he winked at Allen.

The fair-haired sister came and drove him back to his cot and he spoke to her, teasing her in German and then laughed at her because she did not understand what he was saying.

Allen, for a while free from pain, felt happy and content amidst his comfortable and congenial surroundings. He was more than surprised by the kind and indiscriminate treatment he was receiving from the enemy. He lay in his cot surrounded by Germans and Italians and yet he was treated as an equal, while sympathy and kindness permeated throughout the pleasant ward. Allen began to wonder if perhaps it was the effect of his wounds together with the sweetness of the music that flowed unceasingly from the loudspeaker that was responsible for the overwhelming sensation of happiness and gratitude which seemed to fill his heart until he thought it might burst. He realized that never before had he been so aware of little acts of gentleness and kindness, and he knew that it was only with the advent of pain and suffering that these things had been revealed to him, and even then he felt grateful for it. Life suddenly assumed a new importance and meaning; it was as if he had lived all his life up to now without reason. He had missed the implications of deed and actions in his relations with others, he had waded through the shallows of life without ever plumbing the depths of sadness or climbing to the crests of joy. His soul was only just emerging after two decades of gestation. He felt his life was about to begin; he had achieved the age of reasoning.

Early in the afternoon the tall doctor appeared in the ward and commenced examining the occupants of the cots. At last he was bending over Allen and after feeling his pulse he said:

'You are stronger now, yes? I think that perhaps we can take you on deck as I promised.'

He turned to the sister and spoke in Italian. A little later two orderlies arrived and, placing Allen on a stretcher, they carried him out on to the deck followed by the sister. They rested the stretcher on a life-belt locker and the sister put pillows beneath Allen's head and shoulders and he was able to see about him. She covered him with an extra blanket to protect him from the wind's freshness, and as she bent over him a wisp of her straw-coloured hair touched the sick man's cheek, and he smelt its perfume – and then it was gone. When she had finished straightening the blanket she sat down at his side on the locker, and speaking in French she inquired:

'Is it not nice out here?'

'Very pleasant,' he replied.

The blue sea was calm and the sunlight sparkled on its surface. Allen was filled with pleasure by the beauty of the day and the kindness shown him by the doctor in having his stretcher carried out of the ward.

'There is Capri,' pointed the sister and Allen saw the green island rising steeply from the sea.

'Have you read *The Story of San Michele?*' she asked.

'By Axel Munthe?'

'Yes, that is the one. Well, those houses that you see, that is Annacapri, where he used to live. It is very beautiful, do you not think so?'

'I should like to have a holiday there one day.'

'Perhaps you will when the war is over. Your Gracie Fields has a villa over there.'

Allen could now see Vesuvius dominating Naples harbour, a thin column of dark smoke ascending into the blue sky from its seething crater.

'I hope you soon get well and then they will send you home. Your family will be very worried about you I expect. Are you married?'

'No,' he answered.

'Ah, you will soon find someone when you return to England,' she teased.

Presently the ship slowed down as it began to enter the crowded harbour, and the orderlies reappeared and carried Allen back to his cot. At last the engines ceased, and Allen felt the slight thud as the ship came alongside the dock, and a little later he heard the gangways being lowered.

Several well-dressed women entered the ward followed by some army officers, among whom, Allen noticed, was an elderly, bearded general. The women went to the cots distributing fruit, sweets and cigarettes. When the party reached Allen the fair-haired sister explained that he was an Englishman who had been taken prisoner. One of the women smiled at him and speaking in English she said:

'You will be well taken care of in Italy and the time will soon pass. Why, before you know it, you will be back again in England.'

The bearded general stared down at him.

'I 'ope you will be 'appy,' he said, and gave Allen his hand.

'Thank you, sir.'

The party moved on, leaving Allen lying there and wondering if the same reception was given to the enemy when they arrived as prisoners in England.

The orderlies had come to carry him ashore. The sister lowered the side of the cot.

'Hurry up and get well. If I am ever near your hospital I will visit you,' she promised.

They had lifted him on to the stretcher.

'Good-bye, sister, and thank you for all you have done for me.'

'*Arrivederci!*' She smiled and shook hands with him and the orderlies carried him away.

They placed his stretcher on the dock with many others to await the coming of the ambulances that were to take them to the station. He lay there looking up at Vesuvius and soon his legs began to complain and his thirst returned, but now there was no fair-haired sister to comfort him, and just when he thought that if he had to lie there any longer he would begin to scream in his pain, the ambulance arrived and he was lifted in. They drove over cobbled stones jolting the wounded on their stretchers and Allen cursed and blasphemed and vomited into the bowl that an attendant held for him.

On the hospital train an Italian doctor gave him an injection of morphia which kept him in a pleasant and detached coma until they eventually came to the hospital.

7

Doctor Michael Donovan stood in the entrance hall watching the wounded being carried into the prison hospital. He was short and had been inclined to tubbiness before the meagre rations and long hours of arduous work had removed all traces of fat from his body. He looked about forty-five and his hair was greying a little at the temples.

He spoke to the young doctor standing at his side.

'And where the hell do they expect us to put all those poor devils? Why, we're overcrowded as it is and short of staff as usual. Ah, well, it's no good hanging about here, we'd better go and see what they've brought us this time.'

The orderlies lifted Allen off the stretcher and laid him on the bed. The effects of the drug were beginning to wear off and the pain was returning. He opened his eyes and saw that he was lying in a tiny room with three beds on either side. He noticed that only one bed was occupied, but he closed his eyes pretending to be sleeping for he was so exhausted that he did not want to make the effort to speak. When the orderlies had gone Allen heard a cheerful voice from the occupied bed inquire:

'You all right, old man?'

Allen forced himself to reply.

'Yes, thank you, just a bit exhausted, that's all.'

'I'm Dennis Watson,' continued the voice. 'Got bagged six months ago. Shot through the pelvis as clean as a whistle. What's wrong with you?'

'Hit in the legs when they knocked out my tank. God, I could do with a drink. Is there any way of getting one around here?'

'There's a glass over here, but I'm afraid I can't get it for you. Never mind, someone will be along in a minute. You know, if you're badly shot up you've come just at the right time. There's a Red Cross Commission due here any day now to examine us, and, if we are ill enough, to recommend us for repatriation.'

'Christ, I hope I'm that bad!' exclaimed Allen with some fervour.

At that moment Doctor Donovan entered the room.

'Well, Dennis,' he exclaimed, 'I see they've brought you company. Who are you?' he inquired looking down at Allen.

Allen saw the cheerful face and the keen, smiling blue eyes, and was comforted.

'I'm Tony Allen, and I'd give my soul for a drink of water.'

'Here you are, Doc,' said Dennis Watson, 'I've got some over here if you would pass it across to him.'

Allen drank greedily, and the doctor took the empty glass from him. Then he held Allen's wrist and felt his pulse and after that he listened to his heart beats with his stethoscope.

'When were you wounded?'

'About a week ago I suppose, although I seem to have lost count of some of the days.'

'When were you last dressed?'

'Two days ago, I think.'

'I know you must be all in after the journey, old man, but I want to have a look at you. I'll send the orderlies to fetch you in a few minutes.'

'If you really think it's necessary then you must I suppose,' said Allen, dreading the coming ordeal.

'Yes, I think we ought to have a look. Why for all I know there may be nothing at all the matter with you.'

'I wish to God you were right!' said Allen.

Allen lay naked on the table in the little *sala di medicazione* while Donovan removed the saturated dressings.

The injured man began to roll his head from side to side in anticipation of the pain he knew must come.

'Take it easy, son. I'll tell you when I'm going to hurt you. They looked after you pretty well in the ship, didn't they?'

'Yes, they were very kind – very kind indeed,' said Allen reminiscently.

'Well, I'm afraid you won't find things quite so good here, but we seem to manage in spite of everything. Here we go.'

He lifted the dressing from Allen's knee and dropped it into an enamel bucket. Allen was sickened by the smell from the exposed wound.

'Scarcely compares with Chanel 5 does it?' remarked the doctor making a wry grimace. 'Never mind, it will all heal up in time just as soon as I can get rid of the infection. It looks as if most of your tank is still in your leg. Be able to sell yourself for scrap one of these days if you're ever hard up.'

The doctor was examining Allen's other leg.

'They certainly made a mess of you, didn't they?'

'Will it be all right?' inquired Allen apprehensively.

'In time. If I had you in an English hospital it wouldn't take so very long; I'm afraid you can't expect the same results here, but in a little while we'll fix you up just like new.'

He took a steel probe from the sterilizer.

'This will hurt a bit, but it won't last long.'

Allen bit into the pillow to stop himself from screaming out as the probe was driven into his shattered flesh to seek out the splinters of metal.

'I think that will do for now. We'll leave you in peace for a few days and that will give you a chance to regain your strength.'

'For what? So that I can go through this performance all over again?'

'Take your fences as you come to them, old man. The others do.'

Later that evening as Allen lay in an exhausted stupor Donovan came quietly into the room and stood gazing down at him. After a little while he crossed over and sat down on the edge of Watson's bed.

'How is he, Doc?' inquired Watson.

'Pretty bad. All nice and septic just like you were. Still, time will tell. He's going to smell a bit, that's why I put him in here. After all, you're a bit ripe yourself. I thought we'd put all the bad and smelly ones in here then you won't notice each other.'

'That's mighty kind of you, Doc.'

'Don't mention it.'

Allen grew weaker. The pain, when the effects of the drug which the doctor let him have began to wear off, was excruciating, and he rolled backwards and forwards exhausting himself until he fell into a fitful sleep. He refused to eat anything except a little fruit, but he drank large quantities of water. He was depressed by the action of the sulphonamide and was frequently sick.

Donovan, anxious to let him build up his strength, left the dressings as long as he dared, but they quickly became saturated with the foul-smelling, thick brown pus that oozed from the wounds.

Once Allen dreamed he was back in England. It was a sunny afternoon in early spring, and he was walking hand-in-hand with Mary along Queen's Gate on their way to Kensington Gardens. He was so happy, and the sun shone and the world was perfect. Then he awoke, remembering his dream. His legs were full of pain again, and he knew that he was a prisoner banished from England until the war was over and that Mary was no longer there, while no one had yet assured him that he would recover the use of his legs. He thought that if ever a man had good reasons for giving up the struggle for life, he had. Before he could hope to get well there would be months of pain and discomfort and probably years to be spent as a prisoner. It simply was not worth it, and so he made up his mind to do nothing further to help himself get well.

Dennis Watson, who was suffering considerably from his own wounds, did all that he could to encourage Allen towards recovery, but his kindly efforts were invariably rewarded with monosyllabic replies, and Allen said little to invite conversation.

At the end of a month he was as weak as he had ever been. His weight had dropped by several stones and when he lay naked on the operating table it seemed to him that the bones of his hips must soon break through the tightly-stretched skin.

Donovan was working on his knee.

'When shall I croak, Doc?' asked Allen in a weak voice.

The doctor stopped what he was doing and crossing his arms looked down at Allen. After a few moments silence he replied:

'That's entirely up to you. If you carry on like this you could easily make it by tomorrow night. What the hell's wrong with you? Don't you want to get better? Haven't you got folks at home worrying their heads off about you? After all, this bloody war won't last for ever. You'll get home one day and your legs will be practically as good as new by then. You hurt my professional pride, my boy. I don't take kindly to failure, and I've spent bloody hours working on you and worrying about you all times of the day and night, and you, you ungrateful blighter, you don't even try!'

The doctor was smiling, a challenging glint in his kindly eyes as he waited for Allen to reply.

'I don't care very much. It's no fun being like this. Miles from home in a bloody wop hospital, half starved and full of aches and pains! It's not quite so bad for you. You are at least busy and then the time passes quickly, and after all, you are on the right end of the probe, so to speak.'

'Your attitude is quite wrong, Tony. Once you start to get well obviously the pain will get less. There's plenty for you to do here when you can get about, and if you've got the guts to last the course, this experience, unpleasant as it is, will do more to develop your character and teach you more about human nature than a whole lifetime spent at home, and what's more, the course is free, gratis and for nothing! Take Dennis Watson, for instance. He's got it just as badly as you if not worse, and never once during all the time he's been here have I heard him complain. All he wants is to get fit and be as little trouble as possible to us poor, overworked doctors.'

'I haven't complained, Doc.'

'Well, perhaps you haven't, but you don't make things easy for us as young Dennis does.'

'What do you want me to do then?'

'Just make up your mind to get well as quickly as you can and take on a more optimistic view of life. I'll do the rest.'

'All right. I'll try, Doc. You make me feel ashamed.'

'Splendid. That's what I wanted to do.'

The Doc returned to examining Allen's knee. At last he said:

'If I opened this up on the other side it would drain properly, and then we'd go ahead like wildfire, I'm sure.'

'Oh, Christ! We're off again!'

'If you'd rather not, say so, and we'll leave it.'

Allen thought for a moment or two.

'Very well, Doc, you win. Do I get an anaesthetic this time?'

'Of course. I'll go and get George Parker.' He went out of the room.

In a short while both doctors returned and while Donovan busied himself about the sterilizer, Parker took some cellophane and wrapped it around a piece of cotton wool. Then he poured some transparent liquid from a phial on to the wool, and came towards Allen.

'Just breathe deeply and keep your eyes closed. There's nothing to it, you'll be in dreamland in a jiffy.'

Allen emptied his lungs and Parker placed the pad over his mouth and nose and Allen inhaled as he was instructed. As soon as he did so he began to choke. He struggled to get free of the suffocating pad, but Parker pressed firmly down and Allen could not escape from it. He became terrified and still holding his breath he fought with all his strength, but an orderly held his arms and another his feet. He had never been so fear stricken, he was certain he was about to die and then, with his lungs almost bursting he was forced to inhale deeply. Suddenly he became relaxed and breathed normally just before he lost consciousness.

The operation was successful, and after he had recovered from the shock Allen began to feel a little stronger. Soon he became more interested in his surroundings. So far he and Dennis Watson were the only occupants of the small room, and now they began to talk and each told the other of his experiences in the desert, and then they talked of their homes and families.

One morning, a few days after Allen's operation, Donovan came into the room.

'Got some good news for you chaps; we're getting a Red Cross sister to help. I understand she's a good looker too, so she ought to brighten things up a bit around here.'

'When is she starting?' asked Watson.

'In a day or so, I believe.'

For a while they discussed this interesting piece of news and then Donovan looked at Allen and inquired:

'By the way Tony, have you done anything yet about writing home?'

'Come to think of it, Doc, I don't believe I have.'

'Well, isn't it time that you did, or are you just sulking?'

'Nobody loves the poor boy!' remarked Watson.

'And I shouldn't bloody well wonder, if that's how he goes on,' added Donovan. 'You've got some parents, I believe? They must be very worried about you. You get on and write a letter or I'll amputate a leg just to teach you a lesson, my boy.'

Allen did as he was told and sent off a cheerful letter to his parents.

The days passed slowly for Watson and Allen, since they were unable to leave their beds. They had little to look forward to – only the weekly distribution of Red Cross parcels and the coming of the mail, and so far Allen had received no letters.

Donovan possessed a portable gramophone, and on one occasion when he had finished in the theatre for a while, he brought it into the room where Allen and Watson were lying. Resting it on a vacant bed he began playing some classical records.

Allen listened to the plaintive sadness of the Intermezzo from *Cavalleria Rusticana*, and all at once he recaptured the feelings he had experienced in the hospital ship. Once again life and its meaning became apparent to him, and he was disappointed with himself for having failed to remember this during the weeks of suffering since he had left the ship. The music strengthened him, and he saw beauty again; he remembered all that Donovan had done for him and was grateful.

Donovan looking at him lying there, believed he knew what thoughts were passing through Allen's mind, and once, for an instant, their eyes met and their glances held, and then Donovan was certain, and he was content.

More wounded arrived, and the little room filled up. Patients from the other rooms who could walk came in to see the new arrivals and question them about the fighting. The news from the front was depressing.

An officer lying in the next bed to Allen had lost a leg. The other had been broken by a shell splinter and was badly infected. The wounded man lay in his bed staring at the ceiling and made no effort to recover. Donovan talked to him just as he had spoken to Allen, and Allen hearing him felt ashamed for the wounded man. He and Watson did what they could to encourage the poor fellow, but he just lay there and scarcely spoke, becoming weaker and weaker with each day that passed.

Allen had been sleeping for some time when he was awakened by what he thought was Watson snoring. He was just about to call out to him to keep quiet when he realized that the light was on and Donovan and an orderly were at the bedside of the officer who had lost a leg. He was struggling for breath in quick and dreadful gasps so that Allen wanted to shut out the sound of it. He began to count each laboured gasp: one, two, three ... sixty-seven, sixty-eight, sixty ... and then he realized that the noise had suddenly ceased.

He watched as Donovan closed the dead man's eyes. They brought a stretcher and carried the body out into the corridor where they left it until the morning, because the Italian guards refused to open the doors and allow the corpse to be taken down to the mortuary.

The sister entered the room.

'*Buon giorno*,' she said smiling pleasantly, and when she had gone each man was comforted and warmed by her femininity and cheerfulness. It was as if a breath of former happy days had penetrated the prison, giving promise of happier ones to come.

The Italian officer in charge of the censoring of the prisoners' mail had, through laziness, allowed the letters to accumulate until the pile became so formidable that he ordered his corporal to burn it. Somehow this news came to the ears of the Senior British Officer, who sought an interview with the camp commandant. The Italian officer was duly reprimanded and the corporal punished by being confined to camp for a week. During the week of the corporal's confinement to barracks the guard marched up and down the stone corridor that gave entrance to the little rooms, stamping their hobnailed boots and banging their rifle butts throughout the twenty-four hours of their duty.

The sister bent over Allen, doing something to his bedside table. She spoke softly in French:

'Quick, take these before the others see,' and she took from the breast of her apron a paper bag containing two eggs.

Down in the other ranks' ward Ghulam Khan lay dreaming of his village in a far-off frontier province. He was weakened by dysentry and terribly emaciated after several months in the unforgettable Tirana camp, but today he felt a little stronger and for the first time since he had arrived at the hospital a week ago he climbed out of bed. He found he could still stand unaided. He let go of the bedpost and stood there, wearing only an old khaki shirt. He thought he would try to find the latrine. He tottered slowly and cautiously forward, supporting himself as he went, until he came to the sentry standing outside the door. Ghulam Khan grinned down from his bearded six foot three at the small Italian, and tottered on. The sentry watched him take a few more steps then raising his short carbine took careful aim and shot the tall Pathan through the heart.

The camp commandant was very distressed and apologetic, but even so he endeavoured to have the last word in his interview with the angry S.B.O.

'Poor man,' he said. 'He was so sick. What a happy release for him!'

Donovan was dressing Allen's legs.

'They're coming along splendidly, my boy. We'll have you walking in next to no time. I think I'll put you in plaster now and let you alone for a few weeks. You should thank me – it will save you having to be dressed every two or three days.'

'Whatever you say, Doc.'

'That's the spirit. Now you really seem to be co-operating. I can tell you, when you first came here I never thought you'd make it. That lecture I gave you was positively my last trick. If you hadn't taken any notice of me that time, this very minute you'd be pushing up the daisies or whatever it is that grows in this ruddy country.'

The padre had been kind and encouraging, and one

Sunday, when he was feeling better and Donovan was in the room, Allen asked:

'Do you think I might be carted along to the service tonight, if it's not too much trouble?'

'I expect it could be arranged. Yes, I'll fix it up for you, Tony.'

Two orderlies carried Allen to the little room where the padre held his Sunday services and laid him down on the stone floor. The padre gabbled through the prayers and psalms, and Allen, when it was all over and he had been taken back to bed, realized that the only outcome of the whole episode was a certain amount of extra and quite unnecessary work for two hard-worked and willing orderlies. He never asked to attend again.

The prisoners in the hospital lived on rumours.

'The Red Cross parcels have been stopped!'

'The repatriation commission arrive tomorrow!'

'All Jews are to be sent to Germany!'

'The walking wounded are to go to the camps!'

'The Pope is coming to visit us!'

'Mussolini has been assassinated!'

More wounded arrived to take the place of those who had recovered and been sent on to the camps, and of the less fortunate who had died.

Dennis Watson received a parcel from his wife and immediately shared out its welcome contents with Allen. The sister frequently smuggled in eggs, fruit and potatoes, and all these little gestures of kindness and generosity helped to make life more tolerable for the two men.

Allen's legs had been encased in plaster for nearly six weeks. The discharge had soaked through and stained the plaster and the smell coming from it became worse as the days passed. Maggots formed, and feeding on the putrescence, fell bloated and gorged from the plaster to share Allen's bed. He endured it as long as he could, but when at last a colony of bed-bugs decided to make the plaster their home as well and kept him awake day and night with their constant biting and irritation, he implored Donovan to remove the filthy things.

It was several days before the Italians were willing to allow Donovan the use of the only pair of plaster shears that the hospital possessed, and when eventually the plaster was cut through and lifted from the wound, the stench that rose from the crawling, living mess was appalling.

Allen retched as the plaster came away and Donovan quickly dropped it into the bin.

'Wonderful, my boy. It's done the world of good. One more should finish the job.'

'Oh, God, no! Anything but that, Doc!' exclaimed Allen.

The doctor thought for a moment before replying.

'Well, perhaps we'll leave it for a few days, but I warn you, if there's no improvement – on with the plaster.'

The hospital had accumulated a good library from the books that had been supplied by the Red Cross. The Italians, in their suspicion, had contrived to ruin most of these by ripping off the covers in search of hidden messages from England. This search frequently extended to parcels of cigarettes when the Italians would tear the paper from the tobacco. Now that Allen was regaining his strength he spent much time in reading. He studied the lives of famous philosophers, and was much interested in Nietzsche and his approach to life through suffering. He read Huxley and Jeans, and thought about the universe, and had interesting discussions with Watson and the other officers who visited their room. The religious leaders fascinated him with their assumption that God had made man in His own image, prophets who had lived thousands of years ago when man had scarcely learned to walk upright. Yet people still followed their teachings believing that man, unlike the other animals, was immortal and that God, who created the universe in all its unbelievable and incomprehensible vastness, was moulded in human form, and that the choice of good or evil was man's passport to a crown or everlasting torment. The conceit of man! The folly of those who endured a lifetime of economic slavery because they believed their reward was waiting for them in heaven! With what skill could the politician manipulate the words of Christ to suit his party's need! Allen knew that those days were quickly passing and that free and compulsory education would enable all but the moron to think these things out for himself. Wars had been fought between Moslem and Christian, Catholics attacked Protestants and everybody persecuted the Jews.

Humility, charity and tolerance, the very things for which the gentle, inspired and romantic revolutionary gave his life were forgotten when religions clashed. Everybody must believe in something. The primitive savage worships the sun because he fears it. It evaporates the water, dries the soil, and causes fire and famine. The simple person, not given much to thought, believes in the next life as the gambler puts his hopes on the next spin of the wheel; the strong man believes in himself, and if he is intelligent, in his own insignificance when he contemplates the works of his unknown creator.

Allen spent many hours pondering over the meaning of life, and he felt that he was beginning to understand it. Wars were necessary to preserve individuality. If people believe in different things then they must clash; if all believe in the same mode of life they become sheep. In war it is not only brutality and beastliness that exist, but compassion, generosity, kindness, self-sacrifice and courage. It is necessary to journey through the dark forests of suffering before attaining the sunlit plains of happiness. Never before had Allen spent so much time in thought.

Watson and Allen had the little room entirely to themselves once again, and now they occupied adjoining beds so that they could play chess on the small table placed between them. Allen was setting up the pieces one evening when Donovan came into the room carrying a bottle.

'Look, boys,' he said flourishing it. 'Enough for two filthy hangovers and a drop to spare for me.'

Allen had not touched alcohol since he had been wounded; for the time being he had lost all desire for it.

'What is is, Doc?' inquired Watson.

'Vermouth. I prescribe it medicinally for both of you so you'll have to swallow it, and then if Tony's a good boy he shall have a lump of sugar to take away the taste.'

Donovan took their tumblers from the bedside tables and filled them almost to the top with the golden fluid, then he found another and poured in a little for himself.

'Cheers!' he said, and they all drank.

'I'll leave the bottle with you and if you finish it I might be able to find another where that one came from, so go to it boys and have yourselves a party!' And Donovan went away.

The two men drained their glasses and Watson shared out what was left in the bottle.

'Not so bad, is it Tony?'

'No. I'm beginning to feel a little high already.'

Watson poured the liquid into his mouth and lying back tried to gargle with it, but the Vermouth was too strong and he choked, spluttering it out over the pillow.

Allen laughed while Watson coughed, and then they were both laughing. When Watson had regained his breath he began to sing *Swanee River* in a strong but unmusical voice and Allen joined in. Afterwards they sang Loch Lomond, and Allen noticed that there were tears on Watson's cheeks.

'Let's escape, Dennis.'

'How?'

'Climb out of the window.'

'But we're on the sixth floor.'

'Doesn't matter, we've got sheets – hundreds of 'em – knot 'em together and away we go.'

Watson entered into the spirit of the game and they pulled and tugged the sheets from underneath them and tied them together.

'There are more on those beds over there if only we could get at them, Tony.'

'Just you leave it to me,' and Allen, who had scarcely moved without assistance, sat up and slowly swung one leg, stiff and straight, over the side of the bed. Then he stopped for a moment to gather his breath and began to move the other leg. He felt little stabs of pain, but he took no notice.

'You off somewhere?' asked Donovan poking his head into the room.

'Tony's escaping, Doc,' announced Watson.

'Sure I'm escaping. I'm going home. Had all I want of this bloody place and its ham-handed abortionists.'

'What about your trousers? You'll have all the girls after you if you don't put some on,' said Donovan.

'That's right – I'm going to have a woman.'

'Now you're talking; make a new man of you,' said the doctor.

Allen gritted his teeth, determined to get out of bed. He

was hurting himself, and the pain killed the effects of the vermouth and little beads of sweat formed on his brow.

Donovan strode across the room and gently put his arms about him and laid him flat in the centre of the bed. Then he commenced to untie the knotted sheets.

A little later he said to the two drowsy and exhausted men:

'Good night, boys, don't wet the beds!' and switching out the light he went away.

The much-rumoured repatriation commission at last arrived, and each officer who had been seriously wounded or was suffering from illness was carefully examined. One morning Donovan came into the ward where Watson and Allen lay.

'See this list,' he said. 'It contains the names of all those lucky ones who are to be repatriated. Now, who wants to have a look?'

Watson stretched out his hand and snatched the list from Donovan. He searched through the names.

'Oh, boy, we're both on it!' he shouted a few seconds later. Then he began to read out the names of the other officers who were to be sent home.

'Captain Donovan!' he yelled, then, 'How the hell did you make it, Doc? We didn't even know the board had seen you!'

'It's me heart!' laughed the doctor.

That was the first either of them knew of Donovan's bad heart.

'Got any idea as to when we shall be going?' Allen asked.

'God knows. The commandant says in a few weeks. More like a few months I should think, judging by the speed with which things move in this country.'

'Yippee!' yelled Allen at the very top of his voice.

Sergeant Hawkins had been shot through the right lung. Donovan had worked upon him with skill, and Hawkins had survived and was each day gaining in strength. The commission had examined him, and that morning Donovan had the task of informing him that he would not be going home because it was felt he would make a complete recovery in a few months.

Throughout that day, after receiving the news, Hawkins lay on his bed not speaking to anyone, overwhelmed by his disappointment. He had been so certain of repatriation; it was the one hope that had kept him alive during the long months of suffering – and now he was to remain a prisoner after all.

That evening, when the Italians switched off the lights in his ward, he thought of his pretty young wife and of how near he had been to having her once again in his arms, and he wept in the bitterness of his disappointment. Just before dawn he reached out to his bedside table and feeling for his tin of jam he picked it up and tearing off the already opened and bent-back lid he slashed his wrists and cut his throat in the darkness, and bled silently to death with his comrades sleeping about him.

A week or so after the names of those to be repatriated had been published, Donovan said to Watson:

'It's time our Tony took to walking. Don't you think so, Dennis?'

'Oh, God, here we go!' exclaimed Allen. 'Just one damn thing after another!'

'Yes, my boy, we'll make a start, or do you fancy yourself in a nice comfortable bath chair for the rest of your life?'

'But I haven't any clothes.'

'I can stand it, if Dennis can. Now I'll get an orderly while you prepare to walk. Would you like a glass of vermouth?'

'Yes, please. I reckon I could fly on that rot-gut!'

Allen carefully and slowly manoeuvred his legs over the edge of the bed and sat there, his legs stretching out stiffly in front of him encased in their bandages.

'That's fine as far as it goes, but let's have a little action, a little mobility, so to speak,' coaxed Donovan.

Allen commenced lowering his legs to the ground and felt the heaviness on his knees. Donovan leaned back against the wall, arms crossed, watching. The orderly stood beside Allen who now had both feet on the ground and, holding on to the rail at the foot of the bed, was straightening himself. With a smile of success on his face he stood erect and let go of the bed rail.

'Well done, Tony!' cheered Dennis.

'Come on, Tony, come to me,' said Donovan, fixing his eyes upon Allen and stretching out his arms towards him, and Allen drawing strength from Donovan as he stared back at him was instantly reminded of one saying 'Take up thy bed and walk,' and he winked at Donovan and took a slow and unsteady step forward, sliding his bare foot along the cold stone floor. He started to move the other foot up to it and shrieked as the sharp metal in his knee bit into the newly-healed flesh. Donovan saw the blood staining the bandage.

'Get him to the theatre! Now, at once!' he snapped at the orderly who was supporting the fainting man. Then he hurried from the room and Watson could never remember having seen him look so angry or upset.

One Sunday afternoon when Allen was recovering from his first effort to walk, Dennis Watson asked:

'Why don't you go to the padre's services any more?'

'It's not worth bothering the orderlies. In any case I don't get anything out of it.'

'But surely that's hardly the right attitude. You go to give thanks.'

'I'm afraid I don't believe in this business of praying. During the short time we're here we have to rely on ourselves or other human beings. We're far, far too insignificant for our Creator to bother with once we've been formed.'

'I disagree with you entirely.'

'You mean you believe prayers are answered?'

'Of course, if you have sufficient faith.'

'Sufficient faith is no more than a desire or will to do something, and a person who sets his mind upon a certain thing frequently attains it.'

'Don't you believe we should give thanks for the mercies we receive?'

'If you achieve your desire or if something pleasant happens to you, then you are happy and your happiness radiates to others. If you do someone a kindness their joy gives you pleasure. What more should there be?'

'And what happens when you die?'

'You die, that's all. The fact that we happen to be the most advanced form of animal life on this world may be sufficient justification to call ourselves human beings, but to assume that since we have promoted ourselves to the rank of human being we are therefore important enough to be entitled to another life and that our Creator is interested in us as individuals is, to my mind, the most incredible conceit.'

'Very few religions accept your belief there, and after all, you've not had much experience of life yet, have you, old man?'

'Perhaps not, Dennis, but that's what I feel. I had a friend in the desert, and this chap, as soon as he got loose in a town, filled himself up with booze and then made for the women. To every right-minded Christian he was a sinner, an absolute outsider, and yet he was the kindest and most unselfish man I ever knew, and if the world had a few more like him it would be a much better place to live in. You know, Dennis, what I keep feeling lately? I feel that if Christ could have met him they would have walked away arm in arm.'

'Perhaps this friend of yours will grow out of his bad habits in time.'

'I doubt it. You see, he's dead. He was killed trying to patch me up after he had pulled me out of my tank.'

An officer came into the room to ask if any library books required changing, and there the discussion ended.

The day came when Allen walked the three yards from his bed to the window. He stood looking down into the courtyard many feet below and after a while, having gathered his strength, he journeyed the three yards back to his bed and lay down exhausted, his heart bursting with the pride of achievement.

'Christ, I made it! Christ, I made it!' he kept repeating, feeling as if he had just won the final of the men's singles at Wimbledon.

Donovan found him a battle-dress, shirt and a pair of slippers, and one morning they helped him to dress. He remembered that it was the first time he had worn clothes since the day Peter Harvey had died.

The sister entered the room and suddenly stopped, staring at Allen.

'Ah, Tony,' she exclaimed in French and went to him and kissed him on the cheek while Watson cheered.

'Tell her I'll be walking next week, Tony,' and Allen translated this information.

The next morning the sister produced from inside her apron a blue scarf which she knotted about Allen's neck. He noticed the pleasant perfume that still clung to it.

'There, now if your mother could see you she would be very happy again, for she would see that you are now almost recovered.'

'Speak a little more slowly please, Sister. My French is not all that good.'

'Have you no girl friend at home waiting for you?' she asked.

'I don't need one with you here, do I?'

'Don't be stupid. I shall be thirty next year, and you are only a baby. Besides, you know very well I'm married.'

The sun sent its rays slanting into the little room, spreading warmth and gaiety.

Happiness is everywhere, thought Allen, if one's nature is sufficiently sensitive to absorb it. Flesh and the Devil, sin and evil, rivers of blood, the wrath of God, and he laughed, for the world was beautiful and there was no evil and God smiled.

The days sped by, and Allen grew stronger as he exercised his legs and discovered that he could still use them. He became confident of the future and looked forward to it. He was able to make little journeys to the other rooms leading off the long corridor, and he talked to bed patients whom he had never seen before but had only heard about from Donovan, and those other officers who had visited him from time to time.

There came the afternoon when Donovan had him carried down the six flights of stairs so that he could go for a walk in the hospital grounds escorted by armed Italian guards. Allen was unable to walk very fast, but the other officers went slowly so that he should not be left behind. It was an odd group as it leisurely made its way down the avenue of blossoming orange trees – men legless and on crutches, men without arms, others leading the sightless.

Dennis Watson made his first, faltering steps, and soon both officers took their exercise together, limping painfully up and down the long stone-floored corridor, for it was only on rare occasions that the Italians would allow them to go down to the sunny garden.

Watson and Allen were gazing from their window into the courtyard far below. A large staff car entered through the tall wooden gates, and the duty bugler sounded the general's salute. The men came to attention and remained standing there while the general stepped out of his car. Suddenly he noticed a minute Neapolitan who had forgotten to remove the cigarette from his mouth. The general left the camp commandant who was greeting him, and running up to the soldier pulled the cigarette from his lips and smacked his unshaven face, and all the time he was screaming abuse at the unfortunate man. Both Watson and Allen roared with laughter at this undignified spectacle, but they took good care that their mirth went unnoticed from below.

The mournful wail of the air-raid siren awoke the officers. They listened to the scampering of heavy boots as the Italians ran sleepily to their posts; N.C.O.s blew their whistles, and men were shouting, and above it all could be heard the noise of the approaching planes.

'They're after the town', announced Watson. 'Now we'll see some fun.'

'Hope they don't try for us by mistake,' remarked Allen.

The sound of the engines increased as the planes passed overhead and the building throbbed with their noise. The anti-aircraft guns were firing and the little room was illuminated by their flashes. The two officers climbed from their beds and stood in the darkness by the window gazing towards the town, which they knew to be only a few miles distant. Vivid flashes at short regular intervals lit up the night sky, and seconds later they heard the explosions of the bursting bombs. As they looked they saw the fires start, and soon the sky was brilliant with reflected flames from the town, and the bombers roared overhead on their journey home.

'Wish I was up there, Tony; they'll be landing on some lush green aerodrome in Blighty before dawn breaks.'

Allen, once more in bed, let his thoughts fly with the homing planes.

The camp commandant sat at his desk in the office just off the courtyard. His new dove-grey uniform fitted him perfectly, and his black field boots were a credit to his batman, as he elegantly crossed his legs. He was a swarthy, handsome man, and the waves in his glossy hair were kept strictly in place by the net he always wore in bed and when in his office. He contemplated the S.B.O. standing before him. Then exhaling a cloud of blue smoke, he said in English:

'My dear Colonel, but this bombing, it is not good, no! my men they are naturally very upset; you see some have their families living in the town. They do not like having to leave them alone while they are forced to remain here and guard you.'

'That is not my concern, *Colonello*.'

'But in a way, my Colonel, I am afraid that it is so. We have no proper blackout in this hospital. It was never thought to be necessary, but now, alas, circumstances have greatly altered, and much against my own personal inclinations we must impose restrictions. All for your own good, of course. You would not like to be bombed by your own countrymen, would you, my Colonel?'

'That is quite unlikely, *Colonello*. This hospital is illuminated with a cross so that it can be distinguished at night from the air. You know as well as I do that the light is a landmark. I suppose you now intend to extinguish it at night?'

'You are quite wrong in your assumption. I repeat, it is for your own good. And now to continue. All electric light bulbs, except in your operating theatre, will be painted dark blue. This is to be done immediately. All lights will be switched off as soon as it becomes dark. If there is a raid, or even a warning of one, your men must not be seen at the windows, for, as I have already explained to you, my men are most upset and it would be quite understandable, although most regrettable, if they should begin firing up at the faces they saw looking down at them.'

The Italian stopped speaking to blow more smoke rings.

'Is that all, *Colonello*?'

'That is all, my Colonel.'

The S.B.O. saluted and withdrew. He was escorted back to his quarters by the armed guard.

In the afternoon the bombers returned heralded by bugle, whistle and siren. The men stood back from the windows, unseen from the courtyard as they looked towards the town from which the smoke was still rising after the night's visitation.

Watson was the first to see the vapour trails high up in the cold afternoon sky.

'There they are boys, see 'em!' he cried.

Mailer, an American, began counting aloud in his pleasant Western drawl.

'Twenty-six it is; Fortresses all. Give it to them, Yanks!' he yelled.

'Christ!' exclaimed Allen, 'If they're American they'll drop them anywhere. Look out, boys!'

'I say, you chaps, these frightful Americans,' said Mailer, in a fairly good imitation of Allen's voice, and everyone laughed.

They saw the flashes as the bombs burst on the town, and later they tried to count the explosions, but they became a continuous roar and it was impossible to distinguish each burst. Smoke climbed into the sky and they saw the distant glow of the fires.

The Fortresses passed high over the hospital on their way home. The men were counting.

'They're all there,' cried Watson.

'Up the Yanks!' said Allen embracing Mailer, and then the sister came into the room and the officers suddenly became silent and shamefaced.

In French she said to Allen:

'Tonight I have a surprise for you. I shall come here just before eight o'clock, and I want you to be dressed and looking very smart. Do you understand? You must not go to bed.'

'What's it all about, Sister?'

'Never mind, wait and see. It is a surprise.'

When she had gone Allen lay on the bed and tried to imagine what it could be.

'She's taking you to the opera, that's what it is,' suggested Watson. 'I wonder if she knows you haven't got evening dress with you.'

Allen could not overcome the feeling of excitement, for so little that was really pleasantly surprising had happened to him since the war began. The time passed slowly, and then the guards came to fix the blue light. It was almost impossible to see.

Sister entered the room.

'Let me look at you, Tony.' She straightened the scarf she had given him and smoothed his hair.

'Now come with me,' she said.

'Don't be late home, and don't do anything I wouldn't do,' admonished Watson.

Sister led the way down the corridor until she came to a room that had been vacant for several days. The blue bulb gave a poor light, but Allen saw the figure standing by the window looking down into the darkened courtyard. It was a woman with straw-coloured hair. He could not see her face. He noticed that she was wearing a black Persian lamb coat and black glacé kid shoes.

Sister asked in Italian:

'This is the one, is it not?'

The woman by the window turned on hearing the sister's voice, and Allen recognized the fair-haired sister from the hospital ship.

The pretty girl came towards him, and offering her hand spoke in French:

'There, you see, I kept my promise.'

'I will come back in an hour,' said Sister, and went out of the room leaving them together.

'Are you still working in the hospital ship?' asked Allen.

'No, not any more. You see, a few weeks ago it was sunk, but fortunately it was near Sicily and so they were able to find some of us. Still, let us not speak of that. I want to hear how you are getting on. It is quite wonderful that you walk again so soon.'

The fair-haired girl never saw Allen after that night, for although she was now working in another part of the hospital, the camp commandant, having heard of her visit to the officers' wards, forbade her ever to do so again.

Donovan came into the room just after lunch and stood

looking at Watson and Allen. Then after a few seconds he said:

'All right, boys, start packing!'

'Where are we going?' Watson asked hoping his guess was correct.

'Where would you like to go?' inquired Donovan.

'Home!' they shouted in unison.

'That's it, that's where we're going,' announced Donovan, and cheering was already breaking out from the rooms along the corridor.

The officers who were to be repatriated packed what little kit they had into their Red Cross boxes and waited for the ambulances that were to take them to the station.

Two Italians carried Watson down the six flights of stairs.

'Do you think you can manage all those stairs, Tony?' asked Sister.

'I think you ought to go on a stretcher,' advised Donovan.

'I was carried up, and I'll walk down, even if it kills me,' laughed Allen.

'All right, if that's how you feel about it. Stay here until I'm ready and I'll help you down,' said Donovan.

When he had gone out of the room Allen spoke to the sister.

'I don't know how to thank you for all you've done for me, Sister. I shall always remember your kindnesses.'

'That's nice of you, Tony. Now hurry up and get really fit again, and then when the war is over perhaps you'll come here for a holiday and we may meet again.'

'I should like that very much.'

They exchanged their addresses.

'I shall write just as soon as the war is over,' said Allen.

'Please, I would like to hear how you get on. You must

find some nice girl. I'm sure you'll soon be very happy. I do hope so, Tony.'

'Come along, me boy!' called Donovan, 'or do you wish to prolong your stay in sunny Italy?'

'Good-bye, Sister, and thank you again.'

'Good-bye, Tony, and good luck,' and she kissed him on the cheek and softly whispered:

'And I shall pray that you will very soon forget your more unpleasant impressions of Italy.'

'You have already helped me to do that,' he replied.

Donovan came into the room, and shaking hands with Sister he wished her good luck.

Allen was almost exhausted when he eventually reached the waiting ambulance. He climbed up the step at the back of the vehicle and Donovan pushed him gently from behind.

'Get a move on, I want to get home before I'm too old to enjoy myself,' he said.

At Rome the party changed trains, and as they were walking to the platform, a woman, recognizing that the men were British, put out her tongue at Donovan.

'She didn't like you very much, Doc, did she?' remarked Allen.

'Silly bitch!' snorted Donovan.

'It's that lecherous look you have about you, Doc; I can't blame her, really I can't,' commented an officer who was walking with the group.

Then came the day that Allen had dreamed about and longed for – the day that he had thought would never come: the day he dragged himself up the gangway of the British ship, waiting in the neutral port to take them home.

Allen shared a small cabin with Watson, and while the two officers were unpacking their few belongings, Donovan came in.

'Got some bad news for you,' he said.

'What is it now? Don't tell us we've got to go all the way back to Italy again,' remarked Watson.

'No, something nearly as bad. The bloody ship's dry.'

The three men discussed this item of news, and then Allen said:

'I have an idea. Come on, let's go up on deck.'

'Not me, Tony. I feel a little weary. I think I'll lie down for a while,' said Watson.

Donovan took his pulse.

'You're all right, just worn out I expect; anyhow you'll have good doctors to look after you from now on, so I think I'll just fade out of the picture and take things easy for a bit.'

They left Watson and went out on deck and stood by the rail watching the last of the stretcher cases being carried aboard. A few yards from them was the ship's chief officer. Allen studied the large man with the tough, rugged features. Leaving Donovan, he limped up to him and stood leaning beside him.

'What time does the bar open?' he inquired casually.

'There's no bar, I'm afraid, in this ship, it's a dry one.'

Allen said nothing, and after a short pause the chief officer turned to look at him.

'It's a bit hard, but it's not our fault. The ship's medical officer makes the rules. I expect you chaps could do with a drink too. Don't suppose you got much in Italy.'

'Not a drop,' lied Allen.

'Well, let's go and have a look in my cabin. I believe I could lay my hands on a bottle of gin. Come along.'

'That's very kind of you, but do you mind if my friend comes? His need is almost greater than mine.'

'Not at all, bring him along!'

Allen signalled to Donovan who was pretending to be deeply interested in the scene below.

'Come here, Doc!' he shouted.

The chief officer poured out three liberal helpings of gin and offered his guests water or lime juice.

Allen sitting back on the seat felt very content as he swallowed his drink. He had recovered from his wounds, and now he was on his way home. He realized he was one of the lucky ones.

The chief officer refilled the glasses.

'It's a pleasure to drink with you fellows. You must have had a hell of a time.'

'You people do a good job at sea. It can't be all honey,' conceded Donovan.

There was a knock on the door, and one of the ship's officers stepped over the sill.

'Hullo, Maitland, come and join the party.' The chief officer introduced Donovan and Allen to the second engineer.

They all had another gin and then their host said:

'Take our friends along to the engineer's quarters and look after them. I'd better go on deck, we'll be sailing shortly.'

The two officers followed Maitland to the after part of the ship. He led the way into a fairly large cabin in which two men were already sitting drinking canned beer.

'Chief, this is Donovan and Allen, two thirsty travellers on their way home.'

'Well, give 'em a drink,' said the chief as he shook hands. Portway, the electrical engineer, poured out three beers.

Donovan drank some beer, then he said:

'It's very kind of you, very kind indeed. It's a damn shame this ship is dry, but we've waited so long so I suppose we can wait a little longer until we get home.'

'You don't want to worry any more about that,' laughed the chief engineer. 'You can have as much beer as you like, and we can manage the odd bottle of gin or Scotch. You can pay us, but that won't break you because it's all duty free. You'll have to drink it down here, I'm afraid, for if your medical people find out that you're getting drinks there'll be a fuss, and also your pals will probably get jealous. You come along down here whenever you feel like it – make this place your home.'

When the two officers left the engineer's quarters it was dark, and the ship was well out to sea, all her lights blazing and displaying the illuminated red cross that proclaimed her to be a hospital ship.

'I think I've had about enough, Doc,' remarked Allen outside his cabin, 'I'm afraid I'm sadly out of practice.'

'Me too, me boy. I don't know whether it's me or the ship's that rolling. Good night. Don't disturb our Dennis.'

Inside the cabin Watson said sleepily from his bunk:

'And where the devil have you been all this time? I thought you'd fallen overboard. They've been searching half the ship for you. The chief medical officer himself has been here looking for you.'

'I couldn't care less. I've been otherwise engaged,' said Allen climbing laboriously into his bunk.

'What about the light?' asked Watson.

'Oh, yes, the light,' and he got up and switched it off.

Allen awoke from his slumber and stared up at the face of the R.A.M.C. major who had been gently shaking him.

'Where have you been?' inquired the doctor. 'We've been searching all over the ship for you.'

'Up on deck,' Allen replied.

'Everyone else has been examined.'

Allen was beginning to feel a little angry at being disturbed.

'I promise I'll keep alive until the morning if you'll leave it that long.'

'That's not the point.'

'Look, I'm very tired and I've had a most strenuous day. Couldn't I be left alone for my first night on British soil?'

'Oh, very well. Good night.'

'Good night!'

The major switched off the light and went away.

'You're getting touchy in your old age,' remarked Watson from the top bunk.

'That's right. Good night, Dennis.'

It was a warm sunny day and Allen was limping along at Donovan's side as they promenaded up and down the deck.

'What will you do when you get back, Tony?'

'Stay on, I suppose, until it's over anyway.'

'I should get a job if I were you. If you remain in the service you'll only get a staff job; as far as you're concerned regimental soldiering is out for all time.'

'That, coming from my medical adviser, is cheering news, I must say.'

'Well, let's face facts. You were all shot to hell. You're jolly lucky to have any legs left at all, although I say it meself. You can't expect to play scrum-half for the army after that lot.'

'Why this advice about settling down? To hear you talk anyone would think I was an old man.'

'Be sensible. You could probably get a good job if you left now and took the trouble to look around. You want to find yourself a nice little girl and lead a pleasant home life; after all, you've certainly earned it.'

'At the moment I'm letting the future take care of itself.

I'm going to enjoy myself for a bit and try to beat off the effects of the last few years. You know exactly how I feel about you without me making you a speech of thanks. You've saved my life, Doc. Were it not for you I wouldn't be on my way to England, home and beauty. I just want you to know I'm grateful.'

'That's okay, Tony. Glad to have been of service, and if I can ever help you in the future just let me know.

Portway stepped out on deck and joined the two officers.

'We'll go and have a couple of quickies before lunch. I expect you're about ready for one now, aren't you?' he inquired.

'That's a very hospitable suggestion and one not to be lightly turned down,' laughed Donovan.

Donovan leaned over the rail and gazed down at the water swirling along the ship's side and sparkling and shimmering with the reflection of the coloured lights. A chill wind blew about him and he pulled his greatcoat closer. He was pleased to be going back to England, but was neither confident nor very enthusiastic about the future. He had been glad of the opportunity of going out to Egypt for it offered a means of escape from the awful loneliness he had experienced when his wife had died in the accident just before the war. For a few months he had tried living on in the large house and keeping up his practice, but the place was too full of poignant memories; memories that only whisky could dispel. So he had sold his practice and taken a job in a hospital, and then the war had come and he had joined the R.A.M.C. He had been kept very busy and there had been cheerful companions and plenty to drink and now he was going home again: a homecoming, only with no one to welcome him. He knew his heart was in a pretty poor condition and that he would be invalided out of the army. He knew quite well that he had only got a year or so at the most, and if he did not live quietly it might only be a few months, but the knowledge did not disturb him. He wondered vaguely about the future and decided it could wait.

That night there was a party in the engineer's quarters. Maitland had invited four of the nurses, and there was dancing to the music of a portable gramophone. The record was finished and Moira, who had been dancing with Portway, came and sat down beside Allen on the leather seat.

'You ought to try, Tony,' she said. 'I'm sure you like dancing.'

'My legs aren't that good, so I don't think I'd better risk it yet.'

'Don't be silly. Come along, at least try.'

'That's right, you make him,' said Donovan who was listening to the girl as she endeavoured to persuade Allen.

He danced, and found it was easier than he had imagined. He felt very pleased with himself. One more milestone reached, he thought.

'Well done, Tony, you're doing fine,' Moira remarked smiling into his eyes.

Allen held her closer as he attempted a few more adventurous steps, and discovered that his legs could manage them.

The party continued. Donovan sat on a bunk and threw empty beer cans through the open porthole. One of the nurses was sitting on Portway's knee.

Maitland looked at his watch.

'I shall have to be going below,' he announced. 'Anyone care to come and have a look at the engines?'

'I would,' replied Allen.

'What about the steps; can he manage them?' asked Donovan.

''Course I can manage 'em,' argued Allen, for the drinks had given him confidence.

'I'll go with him,' said the doctor.

'That's right, I'll take my medical adviser with me,' remarked Allen.

'And I'll come too,' announced Moira.

The party eventually reached the engine room, and Maitland pointed out various things and explained their working. Allen stood by the shaft as it turned, shining in its bearings.

'That's nearly a hundred yards long,' said Maitland. 'And there's another one over there on the port side.'

They began to climb the steep ladders that led out of the engine room. Before he had reached half way, Allen's legs began to ache, and for a while he rested on one of the tiny platforms.

'All right, Tony?' inquired Donovan. 'Take it easy, there's no hurry.'

'Yes, I'm okay, Doc. Give me time and I'll make it.' After a few minutes they continued. Once happening to glance upwards he caught a fleeting glimpse of white thighs, black stockings and knickers, as Moira climbed above him; then he looked away, feeling that he had taken an unfair advantage of the pretty girl.

The early morning wind blew chill as Allen and Donovan stood muffled in their greatcoats leaning over the rail, gazing towards the distant coast that was becoming increasingly distinct as the hospital ship speeded homewards.

'There it is, me boy, and you never thought you'd see it again, did you? No, and I didn't think you would either at one time.'

'If it hadn't been for you I wouldn't have, Doc.'

The ship was manoeuvred silently into the dock by the little tugs that fussed about her. A few dockers stood watching.

'At least the natives aren't openly hostile,' remarked Donovan as he studied the sullen expressions on the men's faces.

A man with a microphone had climbed on to a crane that overlooked the foredeck on which a number of the repatriates had gathered.

'Come on, chaps, let's have a song. Your folks at home will be listening in,' shouted the man on the crane.

Someone began to sing *Roll out the Barrel*, and the men joined in, and when they had finished the man on the crane shouted.

'Jolly good. Now let's have three cheers – hip, hip . . .'

'Makes me sick,' said Donovan to Allen. 'Why don't they get cracking and get us ashore, or are they trying to turn us into a bloody E.N.S.A. show?'

'Probably we're not expected.'

The two officers went down to the engineers' quarters. The chief engineer entered the cabin.

'Engines finished with at last, so now we can really get down to some farewell drinking without having to worry about going on duty again.'

The cardboard box beneath the seat was full of empty beer cans.

'Perhaps I'd better see what's happening,' suggested Donovan. 'There'll be an awful stink if we get left behind.'

In a little while he returned.

'Would you believe it? Some bloody brass hat from the War Box is supposed to make a speech of welcome, and he hasn't turned up, and until he does – here we stay!'

'Hooray! I hope the blighter never comes. This party

is too good to break up now,' said Maitland attacking another can and absent-mindedly throwing the empty container through the open port. They listened to it bouncing noisily on the dockside below. They drank on.

The chief engineer placed a chair in the centre of the floor.

'Everybody's got to sing a song. Come on, Doc. You start, up on the chair with you. Up she goes.'

Donovan climbed on to the chair helped by the chief amidst cheers and shouts.

'Christ, this ship's rolling like hell!' he said and began to sing the *Mountains of Mourne*, and they all joined in. The chief climbed on to the chair and nearly toppled off, and Portway sang *The Bladen Races*. The door opened and Moira stepped over the sill and quickly closed the door behind her to shut out the noise of the singing.

'Come along, you two soldiers, or you'll be left behind. All the others have gone ashore; the train will be off any minute now.'

'I don't want to go, I'd much rather stay here,' said Allen who stood isolated on the chair in the centre of the room.

'Don't be silly, Tony, come along. You're holding up the hospital train.'

The engineers followed the two officers, and the chief insisted upon carrying Allen's Red Cross box for him and taking his arm, as together they staggered down the narrow gangway, bouncing from rail to rail.

Down on the dock the O.C. train tried to hustle the two officers aboard while the repatriates leaned from the carriage windows cheering the party.

'Now *Auld Lang Syne*,' shouted the chief, and pushing Allen's Red Cross box into the O.C. train's arms he ordered:

'Here, you hold this a minute.'

And on the dockside Allen and Donovan joined hands with the engineers and moving in a circle they sang *Auld Lang Syne*, and the men crowding the carriage windows joined in. The Press photographers clicked their cameras, and then at last the harassed guard blew his whistle and the train moved off, leaving the port behind.

8

Allen walked through the park in the early morning. It was spring again, and the crocuses and daffodils were flowering and all was green and fresh and bursting with life. He came to the wooden seat on the edge of the water, close by the Peter Pan statue, and there he sat down to watch the mallard and the divers as they waited expectantly to be fed. A moorhen called unmusically, and he heard the staccato tapping of a woodpecker. From the distance came the continuous muffled roar of London's traffic.

It was his second day at home and he was not feeling particularly happy. In Italy he had looked forward so much to this homecoming, but somehow the reality had become an anticlimax. His parents had welcomed him and done all that was possible to show their delight at having him back again, but he found it difficult to talk to them. It was as if they had become strangers, and he soon began to long for the company of men who would understand him. Sitting there in the morning sun he thought wryly of last evening. After dinner he had announced his intention of going out, and his mother had suggested he should take his father with him. He knew that both his parents had been a little hurt when he had gone alone, but he had felt stifled, and the urge to get out of the house and walk about the streets and talk to other people had so obsessed him that he had been forced to go, and he was disappointed that neither his mother nor father had understood this desire. Once he was out of the house he began to feel free again. He could do as he pleased, go where he liked; there were no armed guards, he was no longer a prisoner. From now on he could obey his own will.

He walked to his favourite pub which he had not visited for over three years. The smoke-filled room was crowded with men and women and it took some time to get served. He sipped his drink and gazed about him, and then he saw, standing at the far end of the bar, three men whom he had known for many years. Looking at them he thought it might have been only yesterday since he was last here. The men were standing where Allen had invariably noticed them in former times. He studied their faces trying to deduce how they had been spending the war, and as he looked at them one of the men caught his eye and beckoned to him to join them.

'Hullo, old man, how are you? We knew you were back. You've had a pretty tough time, haven't you?' 'said one.

'Oh, it might have been a lot worse. Anyway I'm going to enjoy myself for a bit now. How's the war been treating you?'

'We've had our ups and downs you know, but on the whole I suppose we can't grumble.'

'What are you in?' inquired Allen tactlessly during a pause in the conversation.

'Well, old man, we're in the Fire Service. Can't all be like you. Much as we'd like to see a spot of action, someone's got to stay at home, and you may not realize it but we've had some pretty bloody raids here since you've been away.' The man looked at his companions who nodded modestly in confirmation.

'I'm sure you have,' said Allen, but looking at the three fit young men he found it difficult to understand their attitude. He remembered that they had been well known as local sportsmen and he had admired them and looked up to them, and often during the years he had been away he used to wonder what they were doing. And now here they were drinking beer and in the Fire Service. He felt very disillusioned.

He heard the barman say rudely to the sergeant in battledress:

'I've just told you, soldier, there's no more draught Bass, there's only bitter. There's a war on, you know, and we're rationed.'

One of the men spoke to the barman.

'Four pints, Steve, please.' And when Allen tasted his drink he exclaimed:

'This is Bass!'

'Of course it is, old man, but don't tell everyone – after all, we are regular customers.' And Allen could not deny the logic of his statement.

'How did the Italians treat you?' asked one of the men, seeking to change the conversation.

Allen knew it was useless trying to explain to them what he had experienced. Their minds would not grasp his sensations. Describing agony to someone who had only felt pain in its milder form would be about as impossible as trying to describe an orgasm to a person who has only been slightly sexually stimulated. In any case, he sensed that they were not really interested in what he had been doing.

Sitting by the Serpentine that morning in the park he allowed the beauty of the scene to dispel some of his gloom. Gradually he became very lonely and longed more than anything for the company of someone from the squadron or from the camp, and then he remembered that Donovan was spending his leave at a London hotel. Allen got up from the seat and limped out of the park on to the Bayswater Road where he found a telephone box. He waited a moment or two and then he heard Donovan's welcome voice.

'Can't you ever let a chap sleep?'

'Not on a morning like this. I'm coming round for you straight away so hurry up and get breakfasted.'

'Don't you dare to mention breakfast to me. I've got

the wickedest hangover I've had in years and you wake me up, tell me it's a lovely day and then talk of food. Why I ever saved your miserable life is more than I can understand; it must be the perversity of human nature. Still, I suppose you'd better come along.'

Allen sensed that Donovan was looking forward to seeing him and his loneliness left him as he hurried towards Marble Arch.

Donovan climbed out of bed and turned on the bath. He felt dreadful, and his head ached with the whisky he had been steadily drinking ever since he had arrived in London. He had wandered from bar to bar hoping to find someone he knew or someone with whom he could talk, but he had met no one but strangers, and now Allen was coming to see him. He tried to whistle a few notes of *The Rose of Tralee* but quickly gave it up, for the noise and effort made his head ache even more. Lying in the bath he turned on the cold tap until the chill of the water almost took his breath away; he knew it could not be doing him any good but he did not care. The whisky had given him indigestion, making his heart flutter until he thought it would stop beating altogether, but he no longer worried about dying. There was nothing to live for; there was no more enjoyment to be had from life. He had had enough; the loneliness suffocated him.

'I should have thought you would have had your fill of P.O.W.s,' remarked Donovan as he finished dressing.

'Trouble is I'm bored already, Doc. I feel completely out of things. I don't seem to have anything in common with the friends I knew before the war, no point of contact, and I'm sure my parents are finding me quite a trial.'

'Your poor parents must have found you trying from the moment you were born. However, we won't go into that for the moment. You can make yourself useful and pour me out a large Scotch – the bottle's on the cupboard.'

Donovan walked across to the window with a tumbler almost a quarter full of neat whisky in his hand, and gazed down at the busy, sunlit street, and after a few moments he turned around and spoke to Allen.

'Here we are, with time on our hands, in lovely weather like this, and wasting it in London. We ought to be on the coast, not hanging about here.'

Allen nodded in agreement, then thought for a moment.

'Can you sail, Doc?' he inquired.

'Tony, me boy, I'm with you. I can think of nothing I'd like to do more. Now, where?'

Allen rested his forearm on the tiller, keeping the lively sixteen-footer close hauled as he beat to windward to pick up the moorings, while Donovan lay stretched on a thwart holding the jib sheets and balancing himself with his feet against the centre board, for the breeze was stiff and the mainstay was awash. He gazed towards the whitewashed cottages of the little Cornish harbour and sighed with contentment.

'This is the life, Tony, just lazing about all day and not a thing to do.'

'Coming about!' warned Allen.

'Here we go, never a moment's peace,' grumbled Donovan as he quickly clambered to the opposite thwart, and hauled in the flapping sail.

'Let's have it a bit smarter next time or we'll miss stays,' said Allen grinning at Donovan.

'I'll give you bloody stays, me boy,' was Donovan's terse reply.

One evening as the two men sat in the bar parlour

of the little harbour's only inn, Allen looked across at Donovan.

'I feel alive again down here. You know, Doc, the people are different. They're kinder and more understanding, more friendly.'

'That's because they live by the sea. They don't rush madly about like the people in the big towns, fighting for their very existence. These people depend on nature for their livelihood. If it's blowing a gale they just wait patiently until it blows itself out. They know there's nothing they can do about it. It's their fatalistic attitude and outlook that gives them their calmness – serenity you might almost call it. This was a good idea of yours, Tony. Like you, a few more days in London and I would have gone mad. It was worse than the camp, worse than solitary confinement. This is the place where one can adjust oneself and prepare for the time when one has to take up the threads again.'

The days passed quickly. The weather held and the sun shone, and the two men sailed in the daytime and drank beer with the fishermen at night. Both Donovan and Allen were contented and relaxed as they enjoyed each moment to the full.

At the end of their month's leave, as they were sitting in the train speeding towards Paddington, Allen said:

'Thanks for continuing the cure, Doc.'

'What do you mean?'

'Well, looking after me on my leave like this.'

'Don't be silly, Tony. You would soon have got into the swing of things again. Anyhow, I should be thanking you for the idea. Perhaps one day we'll go back.'

'It's a funny thing, but since I've come home I don't like people as much as I used to. Once I could be pleasant and friendly to anyone I met, but now I find myself analysing their characters and laying bare the weaknesses that they try so ineffectively to hide. I feel ashamed for them.'

'Not one of us is perfect, me boy.'

'No, of course not, Doc, but if only people didn't try to pretend they were something quite different. I just can't help it, but I always know what they're thinking, and I feel embarrassed when they begin to act a part.'

'You'll get used to that sort of thing as you go through life. A sensitive nature's all very well among sunsets and mountains and flowers and what have you, but it's a bloody handicap when you're dealing with the realities of life, of that I can assure you.'

Just before the train drew into Paddington Donovan squeezed Allen's arm and said:

'You'll be all right, me boy, but get out of the army just as quickly as you can and take a decent job. You come and see your uncle Mike if you're ever in trouble, and don't wait until then. I want to know how you're getting on, so let's see you now and again.'

Before Allen had made up his mind about leaving the army he received orders from the War Office to proceed to a training establishment, where, after a short refresher course he was to take up his duties as an instructor.

Transport was waiting at the station to drive him to the unit. He reported to the adjutant, who after shaking hands with him, said:

'If you'll come with me I'll show you to your quarters. They're not so bad – we manage to do ourselves pretty well here. I expect you're about ready for a little quiet soldiering after all you've been through. By the way, we've got a pal of yours here, old George Amery. He knows you're coming. You'll see him in the mess before dinner.'

'What's he doing here?' inquired Allen who was looking forward to meeting Amery again. He remembered the last time he had seen him, on the occasion when he had delivered the tank to brigade headquarters months ago in the desert.

'He's an instructor – does gunnery. He's got a gong now. Did you know?'

'No, I didn't; I'm afraid I've been a bit out of touch for the last year or so.'

'Oh, well, you'll soon catch up with things again. Now here's your room. We'll get your batman to cart up your things and then we'll go and have a gin.'

When dinner was over Amery suggested to Allen that he might care to stroll to the local for a pint or so before going to bed, and on the way Allen asked:

'How do you like it here, George? Must be a bit different to the Regiment, I should imagine.'

'Oh, it's certainly different to the Regiment,' laughed Amery. 'You know, you would never believe it, but some of the chaps have been here throughout the war. They've become a part of the place. Dynamite won't move 'em, although when people like you and I come along they get a bit anxious. I don't expect you'll care a great deal for it here, but you'll find plenty of good men about the place. I'll tell you the sort of attitude that prevails. A few months ago I wanted to get my wife down, so I let it be known I was after a flat. Eventually one of the instructors came along and asked me if I'd care to take over a place he was occupying. I went round and had a look at it and agreed to take it. As I was leaving after a couple of drinks, the chap shook me rigid by saying: "I shall be damn sorry to leave this house. We've been in it for two years, and now, just when my wife is going to have an infant they post me overseas. It's just too damn silly, really. I'm far more use here than with a regiment, just as a regimental bloke is wasted here until he's properly trained as an instructor." '

'I don't think I shall take very kindly to this place somehow,' said Allen.

'Oh, it's not so bad. They're not all like that. You'll meet a few genuine cases who have been trying unsuccessfully to escape for months.'

Allen leaned against the wall of the lecture hut while Captain Frampton rested his weight on the long wooden pointer and addressed the cadets gathered round the sand table. Captain Derek Frampton had so far managed to have a very good war. He had been a territorial officer before the outbreak of hostilities so he had suffered none of the unpleasantness of having to pass through an O.C.T.U. When his regiment had been ordered to the desert he had quickly reported sick on account of his left eye, which, as he explained to the medical board, occasionally pained him. He knew, of course, that no one doubted his courage, for was he not a keen sportsman and something of an amateur boxer too? Captain Frampton was speaking to the cadets, impressing them with the authority and command that rang in his cultured voice.

'You've got to get in and kill 'em, men. Knock out their tanks and kill 'em. Remember, every Boche who gets away lives to fight another day!'

As they were leaving the hut Allen overheard a young officer say to his companion:

'Jolly good the way he puts it across. I bet he knows what he's talking about. I hope we get someone like that for a squadron leader when the time comes.'

There was a considerable amount of work to be done, and Allen had little spare time. The training was interesting and the cadets were naturally very keen to succeed.

They were carefully weeded out as the course progressed and many who were unable to keep up to the high standard required by the staff suffered the disappointment and humiliation of being returned to their units.

From time to time friends of Allen from the Regiment would arrive as instructors, and then they would hold little reunions in the local, which had been placed out of bounds to the cadets.

It was a glorious summer; it seemed to Allen that the sun shone every day, and whenever he had any time for leisure he used to go along to the swimming-pool which lay in a small clearing surrounded by woods. One sweltering afternoon he was lying there half asleep in the sun at Amery's side. A man on the top step of the diving platform was shouting to someone in the water and Allen, catching something familiar in the voice, glanced upwards.

'Good heavens, that's Harry Morgan. Haven't seen him since Egypt!' exclaimed Allen.

'What's that, old man?' asked Amery sleepily. 'Morgan, did you say? Yes, that's him: went up to the desert and cricked his back climbing out of a tank so they say, and got sent all the way home again. Shame, isn't it? Such a long, beastly journey all for nothing. There, just watch that dive. Almost up to Olympic standards, wasn't it?'

'Marvellous, Harry!' shouted Amery as Morgan surfaced after a perfect double somersault and dive into the pool. Amery winked his left eye at Allen and rolling over on to his back he fell asleep again.

Allen learned a good deal about conditions in England, and some of the things he heard came as a shock to him. He was told of the dock strikes, the go-slow movements in the vital armament factories, the strikes for higher wages, the wastage of petrol that seamen paid for with their lives to bring to England's shores, the black market and all the innumerable and popular little fiddles that were a part of the nation's everyday life. Once he had felt that England could not fail to win the war if only because of her citizens' patriotism and integrity. Now he was not quite so certain. He began to suffer from periods of depression, and he felt that he no longer possessed the capacity for enjoying himself as he had done in the past. He became critical of people and suspicious of their motives.

One Sunday morning, when he was at home on a week-end's leave, he reluctantly allowed his mother to persuade him to accompany her to church. He studied the unprepossessing features of the young curate, noting the characterless chin and prominent teeth. There was no power, no inspiration in the affected voice as it led the congregation in prayer.

'Almighty and most merciful Father, spare these Thy servants from the cruel and wicked enemy as he besets our shores and skies.'

Allen smiled softly to himself as he imagined the same prayer being uttered probably even at that moment in churches a few hundred miles away to the very same God, only this time they would be spoken in German. He doubted if they could be heard amidst the bedlam of screams and falling masonry as the block-busters fell whistling from the skies. Then a feeling of restlessness overcame him, and his legs commenced to ache so that he fidgeted in his pew. On a sudden impulse he gently squeezed his mother's hand as it lay on her lap and getting up, he slipped quietly out of the church, the curate's voice following him down the aisle as he went, gradually becoming fainter until at last he heard it no more.

'Thank God for that!' exclaimed Allen piously.

He received several letters from Donovan, and then one Saturday they met by arrangement in London.

'You're looking fine, Tony. I've certainly never seen you fitter.'

'Oh, I'm well enough, I suppose, but this place is beginning to get me down. I'm too much out of things. I don't know what the hell to do, either. Anyhow, enough about me, how are you getting on, Doc?'

They talked for a while and then Donovan said:

'I've been thinking. What you need is to get out of England for a while. You obviously can't stay on in the army. I've told you all that before, so why not get a job abroad? Somewhere out East where the climate will be kind to your legs?'

'You know, Doc, I've thought about that more than once. I've often toyed with the idea of having a look at India. Their troops are impressive enough.'

'Well, I don't promise anything, but your Uncle Mike might be able to help you there, me boy. I've got a brother-in-law in a business house out there and he's over here at their London office for a few months – if he hasn't already gone back.'

'My Irish horse doctor!'

'Well, like me to try?'

'Yes, I think I would.'

They visited several bars, and each was crowded with men in uniform with their women. There were Americans, Poles, Free French and Dutch all struggling together as they elbowed their way to and from the bar in the smoke-clouded atmosphere.

Donovan was getting a little drunk. He had disappeared in the crush at the bar, and as Allen waited for him to return with the drinks, he took out his cigarette case; while he was searching his pockets for the matches an American held a lighter to his cigarette.

'Thanks, pal,' said Allen.

'Thank you,' replied the American.

For a moment or so they chatted airily together; then the American major said:

'Care for a drink?'

Allen explained that someone was in the process of getting him one. At last Donovan reappeared with three large whiskies.

'I saw your friend,' explained Donovan.

Allen introduced Donovan.

'Just call me Tex,' said the American, then he looked at Donovan and asked:

'What crowd you in?'

'Me, I'm neutral, I'm an Irishman.'

The American laughed.

'Didn't know there were any Irishmen outside of the United States.'

'He was our doctor in the prison-of-war camp, and a bloody good one too,' explained Allen who was really beginning to feel the effects of the whisky.

'Were you guys in a prisoner-of-war camp?' the surprised American asked.

'We certainly were, and Tony here, now he was shot to hell, weren't you, Tony?'

'That's right,' said Allen trying to appear a little modest.

'Well, what do you know!' exclaimed the American. 'How did you get back? Did you escape?'

'Show him your legs, Tony,' said Donovan.

'Don't be silly, Doc, not here.'

'Go on. Show him.'

'Not here.'

'Then I will; after all, I put the bloody things together for you,' said Donovan, and bending down he began to pull up Allen's trouser leg. Then they were all struggling and laughing together and the American insisted on taking them back to his mess, and that was the last Allen remembered until he woke up in his Chelsea home late on the Sunday morning with an aching and throbbing head.

Donovan was as good as his word, and a few days after their week-end together in London Allen received a letter from a Mr Goodge, the London manager of Templeton & Co, inviting him to attend for an interview.

Mr Goodge explained to Allen that if he was given an appointment with the company he would be expected to spend three months at their London office learning a little about the organization before being sent out to India to the Bombay branch. At the end of the interview Goodge looked at his watch.

'Nearly lunch time. Come and have a bite with me if you're not doing anything?'

'Thank you very much, sir, I'd like to.'

During the meal in the crowded grill-room Goodge chatted about the company's work, then he said:

'You'll no doubt find things a little frustrating in India. I spent nearly twenty years out there, enjoyed myself quite a bit too, but one never really gets used to the deadly effect the Indian Civil Service has on business life. I don't care who you are, at some time or another you are simply bound to lose your temper – not that it does the slightest good; in fact it only increases your blood pressure. I believe things are pretty gay out there at the moment with the army using it as a jumping-off ground for Burma. If you go you'll probably meet a lot of your old friends, that is, if you can persuade them to discharge you.'

'That won't be difficult. I have a friend, a doctor who tells me they won't hesitate to release me if I want to go.'

'Is that Donovan?'

'Yes. He's a great chap. Did wonders in our camp. Almost worked himself to death saving lives and patching us up.'

'You'll like his brother-in-law, if you haven't met him already.'

'No, I haven't yet.'

'Nigel Dermott. He's down in Madras most of the time. Went back two days ago. You'll meet him one of these days. You'll be travelling around a fair amount of the time.'

When Allen received the official letter signed by Goodge offering him an appointment with Templeton & Co, he immediately sat down and wrote a reply accepting the terms. Then he set about obtaining his discharge from the service, but this presented little difficulty since such were the nature of his wounds that he could never again be fit enough for active service. The unit medical officer arranged for him to attend a medical board, and after appearing before it Allen was sent on leave pending confirmation of its findings. This, the president informed him, was a mere formality since he would automatically be discharged; it was just a question of his disability rating for pension purposes.

Once he was back in Chelsea with only his thoughts to occupy him, Allen wondered if he had after all done the right thing. He was a little sad to leave the army and tried to imagine what the future might have in store for him as a business man. He wrote to Donovan thanking him for his help in getting him the job, and suggested a meeting for the coming week-end if Donovan was not on duty at his hospital.

One evening Allen was having a drink by himself in the same bar in which he and Donovan had been celebrating on their last night out together. A drawling voice said:

'Well, hullo there, Tony. Going to have a Scotch?' and Allen recognized Tex, the American major.

'What a night that was, the last time I saw you,' remarked Allen. 'I haven't quite recovered from it yet.'

'Yeah, you gotten home all right anyhow.'

'Yes, but I don't remember much about it.'

'Oh, you were fine. Just went quietly to sleep in a corner, and then Doc woke you up and took you home in a taxi. Don't you remember?'

'No, I'm damned if I do.'

'Quite a man, that Doc guy of yours,' said Tex reflectively after a little pause in the conversation.

'I couldn't agree with you more. I think the world of that man,' replied Allen with a depth of feeling.

'He seems to think quite a lot of you, too.'

'I wouldn't know about that,' said Allen.

'I'd like to see him again. He does me good. Sort of an uplifting guy,' laughed Tex.

'Well, he'll be in London this week-end, I hope, so we might arrange it if you're free.'

'Yeah, I guess I am at that. I'll give you my number. I gave it to you last time but I suppose you don't remember that. Now, what about it, shall we go some place else?'

In a tiny little drinking club in Knightsbridge Tex got into conversation with three American nursing sisters who were drinking with an R.A.F. officer. Introductions followed and the squadron leader ordered six drinks and the party was under way.

Bill, whose fair moustache resembled the wings he wore above the ribbons of the D.S.O. and D.F.C., rattled some coins on the glass-topped bar of a dancing club just off Holland Park and exclaimed:

'Well, girls and boys, it must be my round again. Scotch, everybody? This is the life!'

Allen was dancing with the red-haired sister, whose name was Mildred. Their cheeks were touching as they circled the tiny floor.

'I say,' said Bill, 'I've got an idea. Let's all troop back to my place. I've got a flat near here and the folks are away in the country so we can make as much noise as we like. What about it? All those in favour say aye!'

Tex and Allen each bought a bottle of gin, and then they found a taxi and drove to Bill's flat.

They danced to the music of a radiogram that stood in the corner of a spacious and tastefully furnished lounge. One gin bottle was already standing empty beside its half-filled companion on the little lacquer table.

Phyllis, the pretty dark sister, who had been quiet for some time suddenly sat up in her armchair:

'Yippee, let's go to town! Who plays strip poker?' she cried.

'Now we're talking, honey,' said Bill as he began to search for the playing cards. The others sat down on the floor.

Tex was winning; he was fully dressed. Allen sat bare-footed in his shirt and trousers. Bill was stripped to the waist, bronzed and muscular, but he still wore his shoes and socks. Mildred had taken off her jacket, shoes and stockings, and Phyllis was wearing most of her clothes. It was Frances, the little fair, blue-eyed sister who was losing. She had quite a pile of garments at her side, and as she lost again she swung her legs around so that she had her back to the party, and fumbled beneath her skirt.

'Here go my panties!' she exclaimed, dropping them on to the little pile.

The night wore on. Tex and Frances had disappeared

although the girl's clothes still lay on the floor. Bill was sitting at the piano playing sentimental music, while Allen danced with the half-naked redhead.

Phyllis was studying Allen as he danced.

'God, you sure must have suffered hell with those legs, Tony darling!' she said.

Working in an office in war-time was something of an experience for Allen after his period in the army. Punctually at 5.30 all activity ceased and the staff hurried away to their homes in the suburbs. Some of the men did fire-watching, others were in the home guard, and all talked incessantly of their experiences. Allen found it difficult to adjust himself to his colleagues, but he did not try very hard since he knew he would only be at the London office for a short while. He was looking forward to the day when he would leave for India.

Donovan and Allen were having dinner in a Soho restaurant. It was a Saturday and the West End was crowded, but the two men were enjoying themselves and the food and the wine were good. Allen was sailing for India on the following Wednesday, so it was a farewell party.

'I wish you were coming along, Doc,' said Allen.

'I can't be holding your hand for ever, you know,' replied Donovan.

'The trouble is, I've lost the capacity for enjoying myself. I feel I'm completely useless and just killing time until I pass on. It's not a very satisfying feeling, fulfilling no useful purpose.'

'Well, you've got a decent job now. That's something for a start.'

'I suppose so. But I can't kid myself I'm really doing any

good. Perhaps it's England in war-time. I had a hell of a party with Tex the other night – we met some American nurses and we all went back to some chap's flat. While it lasted I imagined I was having a whale of a time, now, whenever I think about it, I go all hot with shame and remorse.'

'Oh, come off it, Tony. That's being a little immature. You haven't done anyone any harm and it all makes for experience. Anyhow, don't worry, it's bound to happen again.'

'I envy you. Look at the good you do in your profession. It must give you tremendous satisfaction to know that all the time you are helping others.'

'My dear Tony, the sooner you finish that brandy and drink some more, and the sooner this pointless conversation ends, the sooner we shall begin to enjoy ourselves, which, you may remember, was the prime object of this meeting.'

'Sorry, Doc, I'm with you.'

It was shortly after midnight that it happened. They were drinking whisky in a night club just off Piccadilly, and leaning with their backs against the bar watching the cabaret through the thick blue haze of tobacco smoke that rose into the beams cast by the spotlights.

'I don't feel so good. Think I'll get a spot of fresh air,' said Donovan, and when Allen looked he saw the beads of perspiration standing out on his friend's pale forehead.

'Okay Doc, let's go.' And he stood close to Donovan to assist him if necessary.

Outside in the cool night air Donovan recovered a little as they walked along the south side of Piccadilly towards Green Park.

'How do you feel now? Shall we get a taxi?' asked Allen.

'Just don't talk, Tony. I'll feel better soon,' replied Donovan.

They came to Green Park. Donovan's steps began to falter and then he stopped altogether for a few seconds, and a groan escaped his lips. Allen took his arm.

'Come on, Doc, just keep walking, you'll feel better in a minute. It was the awful atmosphere in that place.'

Donovan disengaged himself from Allen's arm and took hold of the railings with both his hands.

'Oh, God, I've had it, Tony!' he said faintly, and loosening his grip he slowly sank to the pavement.

In a few minutes the ambulance arrived and they lifted Donovan on to a stretcher.

'Stay with me, Tony. Don't leave me all alone,' he pleaded, and Allen took hold of his friend's hand and held it tightly until they came to the hospital.

'Please wait in here,' said a sister. 'We'll look after him.'

'He wants me to stay with him,' argued Allen.

'Please stay here. We will examine him first and then you can see him.'

When she had gone Allen sat down on the long bench that stretched down one side of the room, but after a little while he got to his feet and commenced walking up and down, thinking about Donovan. After an hour or so, the sister reappeared.

'Was he a friend of yours?' she inquired.

9

Allen limped slowly along Knightsbridge. The streets were empty and silent. He came at last to the Park, and then to Exhibition Road where he turned off until eventually he reached his home in Chelsea. He had been crying, and never in his life had he felt lonelier or more deserted. It was just getting light as he entered the house and his mother heard him as he climbed wearily upstairs.

'Is that you, Tony?' she called from the other side of the closed door.

'Yes, Mother. Good night,' he answered.

'I don't know where you've been. You should be more considerate. We can't help worrying about you, dear.'

'I'm sorry, Mother. Good night.'

In the late afternoon the ship sailed down the Clyde towards the golden sunset. The wind blew cold about Allen as he leaned on the rail watching the mountains slowly disappearing astern. His tight mouth turned up at the corners as he wryly remembered the last time he had left British shores. Inexperienced, happy and in love with Mary, he was ready to conquer the world; the sun shone in his heart and life's every second was to be enjoyed. Now, scarcely three years older, he was crippled, toughened by brutality, bloodshed and physical suffering, cynical and disillusioned, and as he looked down at the broken, white-crested grey water he knew that if only he possessed sufficient courage, he had it within his power to save himself further misery by slipping quietly into its healing depths. He turned from the rail and went to his cabin conscious of his cowardice and despising himself. He poured out a large measure of gin into a tumbler and splashed some water into it from the tap in his wash-basin. Afterwards he climbed into his bunk to await the future, a future in which he had little confidence. He often thought of Harvey and Donovan, the two men he most admired and respected, and now they were dead, and he envied them and longed for their company. Occasionally he remembered the kindness shown to him when he had been wounded, and how he had looked upon that period of suffering as his soul's awakening. Now, looking back, he sadly realized that nothing further had ever resulted from it, and so he attributed it all to delirium and the shock caused by his wounds.

The convoy zigzagged its way westwards leaving Ireland to port as it headed into the heavy grey seas of a North-Atlantic gale. Allen kept to his cabin, appearing irregularly for meals and boat-drill. The ship was a dry one, but being forewarned he had included in his cabin luggage sufficient gin to last him for the month's wearisome voyage. He ate his food usually without speaking, hating the strangers with their boring conversation who sat at his table; then, having finished, he would hurry back to his cabin and climb into his bunk and in the solitude he would drink his gin and think of the past, while the ship ploughed into the gale, the seas crashing over the bows and sweeping and frothing their way aft until at last, free of their weight, the vessel rode buoyant again. All the time the wind howled and screamed eerily about the rigging and deck-houses, and Allen, on the verge of drunken sleep, would court the desire that a U-boat might claim yet another victim before he regained an unwelcome consciousness.

The long days passed, and the ship turned south, taking the seas to starboard and then, gradually, the gale blew itself out and the ocean grew flat and grey. Darkness now set the stage for the phosphorescent display as the vessel glided rustlingly through the waters of the night.

Again the course was altered, and the ship passed

through the straits of Gibraltar and into the warm, blue waters of the placid Mediterranean. The passengers took new courage and the long-deserted decks echoed to their laughter and footsteps, and at night passion had its play in the secret places of the boat-deck. In the morning a ship's officer announced over the loudspeaker system that the boat-deck would be placed out of bounds after darkness. And all the time Allen kept his own company and drank his way Eastwards, the envy of the thirsty planters who had set sail unprepared.

The ship rolled at anchor in the broken, muddy water off the barren rocks of Aden, and dark and glistening the dorsal fins of sharks broke the surface, leaving a widening wake as they speeded and threshed their way to the refuse floating alongside. The heat was oppressive and the sky heavy and overcast through which the sun broke redly. The passengers were bathed in sweat and every movement was an effort. Allen kept to his cabin and cursed each time he was forced to climb from his bunk to refill his toothglass. Once, through an alcoholic haze, he remembered the voyage home with Donovan and the engineers, and he wept in his self-pity and loneliness, while above his head on the wooden deck, passengers ensnared by the sensuous beauty of the tropical night, made love with reckless and noisy abandon.

Through the monsoon the ship beat its way east across the rolling, white-capped, leaden seas, and overhead the sky was always overcast, and the sun never shone, nor at night did the stars appear.

It was shortly after midnight that the two Japanese torpedoes struck the ship. The first one hit well below the water-line forward of the bridge blowing a huge hole in the ship's side through which the sea poured into the hold. The second burst in the engine-room turning it instantly into an inferno hideous with the screams of scalded and drowning men.

Allen was thrown out of his bunk by the force of the first explosion. He was still lying on the deck of the cabin when the second torpedo struck the ship. He heard a woman screaming. Her high-pitched shrieks of hysterical terror had a sudden sobering effect on the man, and struggling to his feet, he staggered towards the door of the cabin and tried to open it, but the hinges had been partly sprung by the explosion, and he could only open it an inch or so. He called out, but no one came to help him. Now the woman had ceased screaming. He experienced no feeling of panic or fear, and he grinned wryly to himself as he realized that this was what he had several times almost hoped might happen. Then he climbed back on to his bunk.

In a little while he began to think of his friends from the squadron who had already made the journey that he was now commencing. He wondered if in a little while he would be meeting them again. He thought of Peter Harvey, whose toughness and courage had so often inspired him during the darker moments: Doc Donovan, who had saved his life, and then had tried so hard to help him back to a normal existence again: dear old Walters, who had clung so desperately to the squadron, shepherding it along until the bitter end, and Desmond Skeffington, the man who, born without courage, had fought every cruel inch of the way to overcome his fear and remain with the squadron. These were the real men, the unsung heroes. Suddenly it occurred to Allen that he owed them something. They were the people who had influenced him, the men who had helped to mould his character, and he realized then that each one had left a bit of himself in his personality. If he went down with the ship, there would be nothing left of them any more. He knew then that there was something he had to do for these people. What it was he had no idea, but that was not so important at the moment. In time it would come to him. The immediate task was to get away from the ship and keep alive.

He swung himself off the bed, flung on his life-jacket, and scrambled across the sloping deck. Bracing himself with one foot against the bulkhead, he grasped the door and began to pull with all his strength.